the flirt alert

AN ENEMIES TO LOVERS ROMANCE

KAYLENE WINTER

Dear Readers,

While this book is a work of fiction, it contains story-lines that may be triggering for some of you.

My goal is to handle these topics with care, but I want to make sure you have all of the information before diving into this book.

In this book one of the main characters has epilepsy.

Please consider your own triggers when deciding whether to read this book.

Love,

Shay

Prologue

Tonight's the night. I know it. I *feel* it.

Devon left early for practice this morning. When I woke up I found a beautiful card with a note to "wear something nice" and the address of a Hollywood hotspot.

My heart melted.

The time has come. *At long last.*

I had to scramble to be prepared, but I've pulled out every trick. My entire body is waxed, polished and lotioned. My eyebrows have the perfect microblade. My hairstylist fit me in for a balayage and blowout a couple of hours ago. I dug out my Louboutins to wear with the little black Prada dress I bought for this profoundly special occasion.

By the end of tonight, Devon and I will be engaged. The thought makes my stomach flutter with excitement. Or hunger. No carbs have passed my lips for nearly eight weeks. God, maybe I'll splurge tonight and have some potato purée...

God, Shay. Keep it together.

I put the finishing touches on my makeup. Subtle but sultry. I'm going to knock Devon's socks off. Maybe I'll even give him a blowjob tonight if the diamond is big enough.

Kidding.

I've adored Devon from the day I met him my freshman year at UCLA. We hit it off immediately at a frat party and have been inseparable ever since. He and I share a complementary sense of humor, work ethic, and ambition. After college, at his request, I put my own aspirations on hold to support him in his athletic career. After all, he has a limited window of opportunity and I can figure out what I want to do...whenever.

He and I have been through numerous ups and downs. Devon had tremendous success in college followed by a surprisingly low NFL draft pick that, at least, kept us in Los Angeles for his rookie season.

Unfortunately, he suffered a terrible knee injury during preseason, which took six months to heal. The next year, his contract wasn't renewed. I found the best trainers and athletic mental health coaches and we got to work. Day in and day out, he visualized. Got strong. Prepared himself.

Then it happened. He got a break. We moved across country to Cincinnati when he was offered a one-year contract as a backup quarterback. Two games in and his coach promoted him to starter and he led the Bengals to the playoffs with record-shattering statistics.

By the Super Bowl, every team that originally passed him over suddenly came calling. We're west-coasters, though, and two days ago my man signed a multiyear, multimillion-dollar contract with the Las Vegas Raiders. Training camp starts next week. While he's there, my plan is to pack up our West Hollywood condo, put it on the market and fly to Sin City to locate the perfect house in the perfect gated community.

We're leveling up.

I twirl in front of the full-length mirror. I look pretty epic. Definitely suitable to be the wife of an NFL starting quarterback. Thank God all the sacrifice has been worth it. We've hit the jackpot. I can't wait to start planning the wedding. I'm going to make every single one of my Pinterest dreams come true.

Shoot. I'm getting ahead of myself.

My phone pings with a text from the driver I hired to take me to the restaurant. It's not too far away, but Devon is meeting me there so there's no need for us to have two cars. Within ten minutes, I push through the door to BOA Steakhouse, ignoring a flurry of paparazzi who are fawning over some actress.

The hostess leads me through the busy restaurant to a corner table where Devon is already seated. When he sees me coming, ever the gentleman, he stands and helps me into my chair. My God, he's gorgeous in a tailored black suit that makes him look every inch the NFL star he's become.

"You look stunning, Shay." Devon's smile is dazzling and confident when he reaches across the table to take my hand.

I blush, thrilled that he's noticed the effort I made to look nice for him. It's not always the case. "Thank you. You look incredible yourself."

We toast with champagne, and the evening unfolds in a magical haze. We talk about his contract, a staggering $86 million deal over the next four years making him the highest-paid quarterback in the league. He's excited and animated when he tells me about his new coach and teammates.

As I listen, pride swells in my chest when he talks about his goals and his determination to be the best. He's worked so hard for this, and I've been there every step of the way, supporting and believing in him. Our future has never seemed so bright, so full of promise.

We're nearing dessert when the conversation unexpectedly turns to me, which is rare. "What about you, Shay? What would you like to do with your life?"

"Um..." I hesitate, because I'm so confused by his question. I can't find the appropriate words, so I opt for the truth. "Well...obviously, I want to be with you. I like supporting your career. I'm excited to raise a family and build a life together."

"That's it? Your ambition is to be a housewife?" His smile fades. His eyes go cold. He pulls his hand away, leaving me feeling suddenly adrift.

I blink, taken aback by his tone. "Well, yeah. I want to keep up my charity work, of course. But, I'm totally fine supporting you and our family in whatever way possible. It worked for my mom. Isn't that what we talked about? Isn't that what we planned?"

"I don't remember ever having that specific conversation." He leans back in his chair, his face hard.

I stare at him as my mind struggles to make sense of what he's saying. "What do you mean?"

"Why wouldn't you have your own life outside of mine, Shay? Your mom and dad are from a different era and sorry, no offense, but I don't want to be with someone who's content riding my coattails. I want a partner who has her own life. Her own ambitions. Someone who can be a real partner to me, not just a pretty face to stand by my side." Devon's voice is softer now but no less hurtful.

The words are like a slap. Have I not been a partner to him in the truest sense of the word? He wouldn't be in the position he's in without me. I feel tears sting my eyes as I try to comprehend how my perfect fairytale is turning into a nightmare.

"Devon...I still don't get what you're saying. After years of sacrifice, it sounds like you want to break up with me now that we've finally made it." The words taste like ashes as they come out of my mouth.

"You seem to have a different recollection of the past few years." He looks away, his face set. "But, yes. Since you haven't taken the copious amounts of free time you've had on my dime to figure out your own future plan, I think it's time for us to go our separate ways."

I'm stunned stupid as my world crumbles around me. The future I'd dreamed of. The life I'd imagined. All shattered in an instant.

"You can't be serious," I choke out the words as tears spill down my cheeks. "We've been inseparable for more than *eight* years. Baby, you don't want to *do* this. Not after everything we've been through, everything we've built together. I'm the one who *knows* you. I'm the one who has your *back.*"

When he looks into my eyes I don't see any love or compassion whatsoever. The man I thought I knew doesn't seem to be there. "I have to do what's best for me. This is my time, my moment. I can't let anything—or anyone—hold me back."

"No. This can't be happening." I shake my head. Disbelief wars with the agony that's ripping through my body. "How can you throw everything we built away?"

He reaches for his water glass and takes a swig. Motions for the server to bring us the check. "This has been coming for a long time. You're great, Shay but you've never loved me for me. You adore the idea of a life you like to imagine we'd have together, but I could be anyone. As my agent advised me, I need to find a life partner who's my equal. Who has her own things going. I know you're hurting, and for that I'm truly sorry. Breaking things off now is the best thing for both of us, even if you can't see it."

I sit like a statue. Shocked and broken. Unable to find the words to fight for our relationship. To argue he's wrong. I want to make him understand he's making a terrible mistake. All I can do is cry. Tears are pouring out of my eyes in hot, angry waves as the reality of what transpired sinks in.

Tonight was supposed to be the start of our forever. The beginning of the next phase of our lives. Instead, it's a cruel, brutal end that leaves me shattered and alone with nothing to fall back on.

I'm not enough.

Devon won't even look at me as we wait for his payment to process. His face is set and determined. Literally how he looks on the field before he throws a hail-Mary touchdown on fourth down.

I wonder if what he said is true. Do I genuinely love him? Maybe I don't know him at all.

I thought we were building something real, but clearly I'm wrong.

As I follow Devon through the restaurant, not knowing what's coming next, I have an even gloomier thought.

What if my entire life has been a lie?

Chapter One

Six Months Later

What the actual fuck?

It's scarcely November and it's snowing in Seattle. From my corner office, I watch thousands of fluffy flakes drift in lazy spirals to the pavement fifteen stories below. We rarely get winter weather in the city. Never this early in the year.

Though it's nearing eight a.m., the sidewalks and streets are practically empty. The city shuts down at the slightest hint of snow and today is no different, leaving downtown almost quiet and peaceful. Unfortunately, the turmoil in my mind churns like the froth on my extra-hot, double tall vanilla latte, which is cooling on my desk.

I'm about to get my day started when I notice a woman wearing a bright-pink coat and matching beanie with ridiculously high heels stop at the entrance to the building. She looks up at the sky, sticks out her tongue and whirls around in a circle with her arms outstretched like a little kid.

God, to be so carefree. Too bad she's going to break an ankle in this weather.

"Austin, bro, you're gonna love this!" Miles Stojanović, aka Stodge, my best friend and business partner in our multimillion-dollar casual gaming company, Hungry Llama, barrels into my office like a tornado. He holds a snowboard in one hand and shoves a brochure at me with the other. "Executive retreat booked at Crystal Mountain. Look at this place. There are rooms to hold meetings and team building exercises. Lodging is onsite. Good food. Solitude so we can focus. I've even reserved the Summit House at the top of the mountain for a send-off dinner. Plus, if people want to ski or snowboard, it will be perfect."

Stodge's enthusiasm always puts me in a fantastic mood. It's infectious; exactly like his passion for the business we started in college. He's a creative genius, friend to all and the heart of Hungry Llama. I'm the numbers and operations guy who largely stays behind the scenes. Our opposite strengths have made us unstoppable in the gaming world. The past eight years have been an incredible ride.

"Yeah, it checks all the basic boxes." I lean against my desk and study the brochure. The thought of being trapped on a mountain isn't appealing at all. "How much is it going to cost? We're there for business, not to have fun."

Miles drops the snowboard and makes himself at home in my DXRacer Master gaming chair. "Dude. You've got to lighten up. We're gonna gross close to a billion dollars this year. Puzzle Pet Paradise is crushing." He leans forward. "The team is exhausted. Showing them how much we appreciate them is equally as important as the day-to-day shit."

"Day to day *shit*, eh?" I flip through the glossy pictures of the resort's proposed schedule and menu while my business partner spins around in my chair, full of childlike joy that always seems to bubble up no matter what the situation. It kinda reminds me of pink-coat girl on the street from earlier.

He shakes his head slowly like I'm killing his vibe. "Dude, seriously. Loosen the fuck up. We all need a little AFK time."

"I'm not saying no. I'm reminding you we have bigger issues to solve." The truth is, Miles and I have a key role to fill at the company. "We need to hire a Marketing and Events executive like...yesterday."

"Already done." Stodge comes to a full stop and drums his knuckles on the armrest. Looks me in the eye, then averts his gaze.

Jesus. His impulsiveness. "What. Did. You. Do?"

"You can't get mad." He holds up his hands defensively. "Let me explain..."

I bridge my fingers across my nose. "*Stodge...*"

"Fine. I'll rip off the bandage. I...I offered the job to Shay." Miles cowers like I'm about to lob my keyboard at him.

The room grows as cold as the winter storm outside my window. *Shay Stojanović.* His twin sister. A she-devil. My chest tightens as memories from my past bubble up like acid. The mere mention of her name gives me hives. Being around her every day? *Fuck* no.

"Your sister?" I choke out, my voice rising. "VP of Marketing and Events? Has she ever held a *job*, Stodge?"

Miles shifts uncomfortably, still avoiding my eyes. "She's got the appropriate experience and gave me the idea for the retreat. More importantly, she's my family and needs a break."

"Not at the company you and I have built together. No way. Not a fucking chance," I snap. This is the ultimate betrayal. "You *know* how I feel about her, Miles."

"I do. But I don't quite understand why something that happened nearly a decade ago needs to define you." He's quiet now as he rubs his chin thoughtfully. "I mean, it was high school. Can't you let it go?"

Easy for him to say. I get up and stare out the window again. The snowstorm is all but over, save one or two straggler flakes. Thinking about that fateful day makes it hard for me to breathe. What Shay did still haunts me.

I don't see any reason to let it go. "You weren't there."

"Thank fucking God I wasn't or I'd have killed you both. I told you she was going through some, eh...stuff. We were *kids*. Do you truly *still* hate her?" Miles doesn't understand. He doesn't have a mean bone in his body.

He's a live-and-let-live kind of guy. Things roll off his back.

For me? Not so much.

I squeeze my eyes shut and try to push the memories away. "Yeah, I do. I can't explain it except to say, with all due respect, she's the complete opposite of you and there's no way I'm entrusting her with such a big role at my company."

"Uh...*our* company. And sorry, that's not good enough." There's a note of stubborn determination in his voice that I recognize. He rarely plays the card, but when he does...yeah. Stodge isn't letting this go.

I try another tactic. "Marketing isn't a remote job. We need someone who's in Seattle—who can come into the office every day."

"I'm well aware." He leans so far back in the chair I'm afraid it's going to fall over. "Trust me on this. I know Shay is my twin but after things ended with Devon, she was forced to move back to Seattle. I promise you, she's a great fit for the company. She needs this job and I'm asking you to get on board. If it doesn't work out, I'll take full responsibility."

The raw sincerity in his eyes makes me feel trapped. Hires of this magnitude are ordinarily unanimous decisions. We've worked too hard to build Hungry Llama into a gaming juggernaut to fuck things up for a favor to his sister. It sucks balls that I don't have a choice but to see how this plays out.

"Look. Since you already offered her the job without even mentioning it to me, my condition is simple. I can't—won't—work with her directly. She'll report to you." I cross my arms defiantly.

He runs his fingers through his hair. "Austin, *no*. I supervise hundreds of remote employees on the development and creative teams. You manage the entire executive team. Besides, having my twin sister report to me? That's *weird*."

"Do you seriously think Shay's going to respect my position? She's a spoiled princess. The ultimate mean girl. Someone who chases status not substance. If she weren't your twin, there's an excellent chance I'd fire her before she logs into her computer." I stand and pound my fist on the desk.

Miles leaps from the chair and squares up to me. "For fuck's sake. We're grown-ass adults. Shay has never said a bad word about you. Do you think you may have blown things out of proportion? We've all changed dramatically since high school. Can't you give her a chance?"

I shake my head, a cold certainty settles in my stomach. I never told Miles the whole story. "*No.*"

There's a long silence where Stodge and I stare at each other with eyes narrowed. Even at our most competitive, the two of us don't fight. Ever. If he pushes this any further I'm afraid our record won't remain intact.

Eventually he speaks, his voice heavy with resignation. "Fuck it. If you run into issues, I promise you won't have to interact with her."

"Thanks." I feel a hollow ache in my chest, knowing that I may have won this battle but in all likelihood, I'll lose the war.

Stodge is deflated. "Uh...yeah. Sure." He picks up his snowboard and stands at the door, presumably waiting for me to say something else.

When I remain stoic and silent, he slips out without waving. The door clicks shut behind him, leaving me alone to stew about the situation at hand. I was a kid with a load of brains, a shitty home life, and zero social skills.

I was also hopelessly smitten with my best friend's sister, who happened to be the most popular girl at school.

She ruthlessly chewed me up and spit me out without a second thought. Miles wasn't there to witness it because he was otherwise...occupied. The aftermath could have ended our friendship, but Shay moved away so... Anyway, seeing Shay again is going to suck but I can't let the situation fuck things up with Miles. I'm smart enough to know if it comes down to it, he'll always choose his twin sister.

You can't change who your family is. I live with this sad truth every fucking day.

Goddammit.

Oh, I know it's been years and I should forgive and forget and all that.

Revenge sounds better, though.

Yeah. Much better.

I should be a bigger person. I'm no longer a scrawny, insecure geek. I've built Hungry Llama into one of the hottest companies in the world. I'm not hurting for cash. I own several properties. I have no problem getting laid. I'd like to think I'm a decent boss. I support a ton of philanthropic causes.

So why can't I let it go?

Because I want to bring her down a notch.

Yep. That's it. I want to give her a taste of her own medicine.

I'll let Miles know I've changed my mind and Shay can report to me. Then I'll be an asshole. Not any asshole, a *subtle* asshole. Take great pleasure in making her life miserable until she quits on her own accord. That way I'll get rid of her and keep my friendship with Miles intact.

I stand at the window.

It's snowing again. Everything is quiet.

The world might look peaceful from up here, but I know better.

A storm is beginning, and I'm standing directly in its path.

Chapter Two

One Hour Later

Today's my inaugural day at Hungry Llama. I can't believe my good luck. It's *snowing*, a rare occurrence this early in the year. On my way into the office building, I even caught a few snowflakes on my tongue.

It didn't help. My nervous system is a tangle of live wires.

Too much change. So much disappointment. Never-ending anxiety.

When Devon broke up with me, I had no choice but to move back to Seattle into my parents' house. *Everything* was in Devon's name. Our condo. The cars. Furniture. Dishes. Electronics. The few things that I kept were clothes, shoes, handbags, and some personal items. I had to *beg* Devon for cash to fund my trip home—which was ultra humiliating by the way.

My long-term relationship has been reduced to my personal belongings and the ten grand he begrudgingly deposited into my bank account. In return, I blocked his number and unfriended him on all social media accounts. He might have broken things off, but I'm the one who officially ghosted him.

When I returned to Seattle, I thought my parents would be empathetic. That I'd have a soft landing. I figured it would take a few months to heal. Regroup. Figure out my next steps. Stuff like that.

I had a rude awakening. My parents loved Devon, apparently, and seem to blame me for the demise of our relationship. Mom goes on and on about why I stayed so long without a commitment. Dad grumbles about how I essentially abandoned my career to follow him around the NFL. They're giving me a serious dose of tough love...and a six-month deadline to get a job and figure out my life's plan.

Everything is just...hard. I'm heartbroken. Devastated. My life's in shambles. I could use a little nurturing. Would that be too much to ask?

Besides, nothing is the same here in Seattle. Connecting with girlfriends I'd lost touch with was a disaster. Mindy is married with children. Bianca lives in Florida now. None of us kept in touch after high school, so I'm not surprised we're not friends anymore. More casualties of my relationship with Devon, I guess.

All in all, my homecoming has been harsh.

So fucking harsh.

I'm lonely. Scared. Broke. At rock-fucking-bottom. All the things I promised myself I'd never be. That was the purpose of pouring my heart and soul into Devon, after all.

Look where that got me.

My job search has been excruciating. For some reason, companies aren't terribly enthusiastic about hiring a woman whose primary profession was being the supportive girlfriend of a rising NFL player. Every rejection is one additional reminder that I'm an idiot. It's my own damn fault for putting his career to the forefront and neglecting my own.

Last week, I was about to sell off my designer clothes on The RealReal when my twin brother Miles saved the day.

We were having dinner and, after a little twin bonding, he quizzed me about all the things I'd done to support Devon's career. Miles helped me remember everything. How I built his social media following by making engaging content. Managed his day-to-day schedule. Networked like a madwoman to ensure we were invited to VIP events where he could make NFL connections. Threw elaborate parties which became the most coveted invite in town. Volunteered at high-profile nonprofits to position him for photo-ops.

It *was* a full-time job. More than.

Miles assured me my experience would easily translate to positions within the corporate world.

Over the past few months he's asked for my advice on some marketing initiatives. He was shocked at how much I know about data-driven marketing. I showed him some tricks on how to grow Hungry Llama's followers and he implemented them—they grew their engaged audience by nearly ten percent. He wants to do a corporate retreat with his top executives, so I researched and found a unique but cool venue.

I knew they had an opening at his company for Vice President of Marketing and Events, but it never occurred to me I was remotely qualified. It took a few weeks but eventually he convinced me to accept the position.

My wonder twin made me feel like a worthwhile human being for the first time since my breakup.

The idea of working with Miles is a dream come true, though having such an important title is intimidating. I mean, I'm all for faking it until I make it, but this is well...a whole new level. Nepotism aside, I have a lot to prove.

Reporting to Austin Andrews, my brother's best friend and business partner, is...terrifying. He's a big deal now. I read up on him over the past few days. He's come a long way from the nerd who had a huge crush on me in high school. Now he and Miles are among the most successful entrepreneurs in the Pacific Northwest.

Hopefully he'll remember me fondly. I'm going to need all the help I can get in my new role. Because if I don't pull this off, I'm back to square one.

And thank God I didn't end up selling my designer clothes. I'll be able to get by for a couple of months without repeating an outfit at work. Today, I picked the perfect ensemble for my Hungry Llama debut. Underneath my limited-edition, bright-pink Dior wool coat,

I'm wearing a vintage Alexander McQueen asymmetrical black suit and ankle boots.

During my pageant years, my coach always drilled it into me—a girl's got to look great for her grand entrance, first impressions and all that.

Looking sharp and ready to conquer the world, I feel amazeballs until I enter the lobby of the corporate headquarters. That's when I realize I've made a grave miscalculation by not visiting the offices before my start date.

A gargantuan statue of Bert, Hungry Llama's mascot, looms in the forefront. A glass security wall separates the entry from reception. I peer inside. The entire place is buzzing and it's not even nine in the morning. The thing is, no one's dressed up. Not by a long shot.

Several women wear warm sweaters and leggings. The dudes sport jeans and hoodies. All around there's an inordinate amount of athleisurewear. Good God, someone runs by wearing pajama bottoms and *slippers*.

Holy shit, I'm going to stick out like a sore thumb.

My heart starts pounding when the reality hits me. I don't *belong* here. This is going to be a *disaster*.

I'm about to turn around and go home when I see Miles and an incredibly handsome man walking toward me, deep in conversation. As they near, they both notice me gawking at them through the glass partition.

Miles's face lights up when he sees me and swipes a card to unlock the door. "Shay! Welcome! Come on in. You remember Austin Andrews, my business partner?"

Austin Andrews? Holy crap. I'd never have recognized him. He's devastatingly handsome. Dark-brown hair shaved on the side and long on top. Square jaw with a smattering of stubble. Brown eyes with bright flecks of gold. He's so *tall*. Built. God, he looks like a professional athlete.

I flash him my warmest smile. "Of course. Hi, Austin. It's so wonderful to see you again."

"Shay." I see a flicker of undisguised displeasure pass over his face. He doesn't look at me, he looks *through* me.

Huh. That stings. We'd always been cool, hadn't we? Shouldn't that count for something?

Maybe not. He is a *man* after all.

Ignoring Austin, I focus my attention back on Miles, whose enthusiasm puts me back at ease. "Everything's ready to go. You'll report directly to Austin, but will be working with both of us."

"There's no time to waste. Let's go over the upcoming launch schedule." Austin looks around at everything but me. "With two games releasing in Q1, we're woefully behind on the marketing plan. You'll need to jump in immediately."

I follow the two of them to a conference room where designs and concepts for both games are laid out. "These look fun. Can I get access to the builds so I can start working on ideas?"

Austin cocks an eyebrow, clearly skeptical. "I don't want ideas, Shay. That'll waste our time. You need to work with your team to devise the *best* worldwide launch strategy by the retreat. Then execute. *Period*. These games are crucial to our financial targets."

"Don't worry, Austin. I'll get up to speed quickly. Trust me." I bite back the snarky retort on the tip of my tongue in order to reassure him. I mean, he has a decent reason to be concerned about my capabilities, obviously. His condescending tone makes me mad, though.

Determined.

And why the attitude? What a dick.

Miles puts his arm around me protectively. "Shay, I've left a ton of this information in your office. Why don't I help you get settled and then I'll introduce you to your team."

"Don't babysit her, Stodge." Austin glares at the two of us. "You vouched for her, now let her do her job."

Miles furrows his brow and opens up his mouth to say something but I grab his arm. "Don't worry about me. I've *got* this."

Austin rolls his eyes and turns back to the game designs. I'm thrown in at the deep end as the three of us spend the next couple hours going over game release schedules. As the meeting drags into hour three, I do my best to show enthusiasm. But, it's hard when I'm overwhelmed with information and Austin's shitty attitude feels like a weight pressing down on my chest.

I didn't expect today to go this way. Is he testing me to see if I'll survive in this fast-paced environment? I'm seemingly going to fail if Austin's judgmental death glare is to be believed.

For the millionth time today I ask myself, *did I make a mistake?*

Mercifully, Miles wraps things up on a positive note. "I'm so glad you're here, Shay. You're going to do great things for us."

"Thanks, Miles. I won't let you—either of you—down." I hug him and hold on a little too long, soaking up the comfort and the reassurance only my twin can provide.

I walk out the door followed by Austin, then Miles. Without a doubt, I can feel Austin's eyes burning a hole through me but I resist the urge to look back. I won't give him the satisfaction of knowing his weird attitude bugs me.

I know what's up. Underneath his handsome face and rockin' body, he's conceivably the same geeky kid he was growing up. Intense. Focused. Nerdy. I don't need to understand what goes on in that head of his. I'm not going to let him kill my buzz. I'm happy to be here and grateful to work with my brother.

If I have to tolerate Austin, I will.

I have no choice.

Chapter Three

Three Hours Later

The view from Miles's office is similar to mine, though on clear days he can also see a slight glimpse of Mt. Rainier.

When we set up Hungry Llama HQ, we chose this building for a reason. Watching the ferries glide back and forth between the downtown waterfront and Bainbridge Island is soothing. Meditative. A welcome respite from the daily pressures of running a thriving gaming company.

I'm definitely not feeling meditative and Zen today, though. The snow has predictably been replaced with seasonally appropriate rain. The entire sky is gray and foreboding, which mirrors my feelings about having Shay Stojanović working at my company.

I thought I had her figured out.

Then she smiled at me like we were old friends.

I couldn't stop staring at her golden-blonde hair cascading around her shoulders. Deep-blue eyes. Peaches-and-cream complexion. Full lips. Smokin' hot bod—narrow waist, big tits. The prototype of my video game fantasy girl. My cock nearly burst through my jeans at the sight of her dressed like she belongs on a New York runway, not a tech office in Seattle.

From that moment a few hours ago, I've been untethered by her mere presence in the building. All I can think about is calling her into my office then bending her over my desk and fucking her.

Thoughts of which make it hard to pay attention to Miles, who's delving into the fine details of the UI development schedule for our upcoming game releases. He's in the middle of explaining the tweaks they're making to Bistro Bonanza's level designs when the door opens, and *she* walks in.

You'd think she'd feel out of place, but no. Shay is still effortlessly cool with an edgy vibe. She's fucking stunning. She's *always* been stunning.

Too bad she has a cold, black, calculating heart.

Shay hugs her brother and smiles like she doesn't have a care in the world but as our eyes lock, I see it—a shadow. A flicker of something that belies her bravado. Like she's trying to put on a brave face.

Though I've steeled my heart to callous women like Shay, I feel a strange tug. A sensation that's both un-comfortable and familiar, and it fucking irks me. From the time Miles and I became best friends, though I tried to hide it, I always noticed his sister.

Noticed. Hell. More like obsessed over her. After what happened, I even convinced myself I was *in love* with her for a hot minute.

Shay played me for a fool. Drew me in and made me feel like I was cool. Convinced me I was good-looking and desirable. Gave me confidence...

Possibly the most profound moment of my life was a fucking joke to her. Oh, I learned the hard way that someone as beautiful as Shay could be so, so cruel.

"Shay, did you and Austin get a chance to connect after lunch?" Miles glances between the two of us, his brow furrowed.

I can hardly even muster up an excuse. "Nope. My meeting with Brad went long."

"Brad Pitchel, our Chief Revenue Officer." Miles directs his comment at Shay before looking back at me. "Well, I'm late for a meeting with Mona White, our *Chief Technology Officer*. Austin, if your schedule is still clear, maybe you and Shay can chat about the budget and expectations for the launch campaign." He stops at the door with parting words, "Can you please be a good leader and explain to Shay who's who on the executive team? We don't have a full sit down until the retreat and there's no point in hiding the eight ball when she's got to plan the schedule."

I could kill him. *Literally* kill him.

"Austin, I hope we haven't gotten off on the wrong foot." Shay's voice is shaky. "I do want to thank you for this opportunity. I'm looking forward to contributing—"

"Save it." I interrupt. "Let's get real. VP of Marketing? A big leap from 'girlfriend of NFL big-shot quarterback.' I'm not going to lob softballs at you so you can feel good about yourself. This is a demanding, relentless job. A *critical* job. No offense, but I don't have the time to make niceties and pretend I'm happy Miles brought you here when you aren't qualified for this role. I mainly hope you don't fuck up everything your brother and I have built."

Shay's face flushes, but she maintains her composure. "I don't need you to coddle me. I'm going to give everything I have to the team..."

"Oh, *undoubtedly*." My voice drips with sarcasm. "Word of advice? Try not to distract the *team* with cheerleading routines. Or drunken orgies."

Shay nearly chokes and her eyes grow wide. I feel a pang of guilt. I've cut her to the quick and can't deny that part of me enjoyed it. But another part of me—the part that's never stopped desiring her—feels horrible.

I push those thoughts away. Hungry Llama is my life. My passion. I won't let anything—or anyone—stand in the way of its success. Most of all, not Shay.

"Let's talk marketing budget." I motion for her to sit at the small table adjacent to Miles's desk.

Shay stoically sits across from me and we dive back into our discussion. I try to throw her off her game, but she holds her own, surprisingly, and her ideas are insightful and fresh. She's crammed in a wealth of knowledge of the company and our products in a few short hours.

When we're done, she gets up to leave but turns back toward me. "Austin, Miles did me a big favor by hiring me, but I understand why you're not on board."

"Do you?" I try to reconcile the snarky girl I knew in high school with the reticent woman standing before me now. I've seen glimpses of vulnerability. Hints of something deeper. Could she have changed?

She shrugs. "Of course. I've never had a real job before. Now I have a big title with even bigger responsibilities. It stands to reason you'd be worried."

Jesus. She's so far off the mark it's not even funny.

"What the hell *have* you been doing all these years?" I can't stop myself from asking. "It's pretty selfish to drag Miles into whatever drama you're involved in. Not after you essentially ditched him when you left for college."

Shay shuts her eyes. Bites her lip. "You're correct about one thing. I got so wrapped up in an idea of what my life was supposed to be and lost track of everything else. Including Miles."

"Why would you do that?" My lingering disdain gives way to slight curiosity.

Her eyes blink open. "It's complicated. Look, I'll do my best to change your mind about me if you'll give me a chance."

Before I can answer, Shay disappears into the hall.

Huh. She *seems* different from the arrogant, take-no-prisoners girl I once knew. Still, I can't shake the feeling that she's truly lost. Struggling to find her way.

It doesn't matter though. I won't allow myself to get lured into feeling sorry for her. Whatever happened to make her this way, I bet she deserved. A big slice of humble pie never hurt anyone, least of all someone like Shay.

Anyway, there's work to be done. Games to be created. A company to run. Like it or not, Shay's a part of Hungry Llama until she quits or Miles says otherwise. He's my ride or die so I'll have to find a way to work with her, even if I can't trust her.

Even if I can't forget the way she annihilated me.

Miles returns a few minutes later. "I wanted to give you two some time alone. Did you try to be nice at least?"

"Dude, I'm profoundly unhappy with how you sprung this on me." I rake my fingers through my hair. "There's a million reasons why her being here is a bad idea."

Miles sinks into his gaming chair. "And a million reasons why it's an *amazing* idea." He thunks his legs up on his desk. "Many people underestimate my sister. They always have. She's an admirable person when you get to know her. Will you do me a favor and give her a *real* chance? Please? She needs a win."

I don't want my relationship with my best friend and business partner to be affected by tension between me and his sister. He and I have too much history. I'll do my best to move past my negative feelings toward Shay. Not to mention the complicated feelings of lust she stirs up in me merely by existing.

"I'll try, Stodge. I will." I glance at my phone and notice I have about a hundred unopened emails. "I'm not going to go easy on her though. Everyone who works here has to contribute like a boss."

"That's fair. Wanna grab a beer later?" Miles grins as he reclines so far back it looks like he'll topple over.

I walk over to him so we can bump fists before I head back to my own office. "Sure. It's going to be real late though. Someone saddled me with something unexpected today and my day got totally fucked."

The image of Shay is a constant distraction during the rest of my day's tasks. Visions of her permeate my mind as I put out various fires ranging from a disgruntled vendor to reviewing business insurance bids. As the day bleeds into evening and it's time to meet Miles, I have no choice but to take matters into my own hand.

Ducking into my private bathroom, I pull out my cock and grip it tightly. Move my hand up and down in short, quick strokes. Needing more, I reach down between my legs and tug and twist my ball sac. Picture Shay's plump tits spilling out of her black suit, taut nipples begging for me to suck on them. Imagine myself bending her over, ripping off her panties and sliding into her tight, wet heat. Smell her arousal as she creams around my dick. Hear her moan my name and tell me to fuck her harder. Feel her clench around my shaft as I pound into her like a madman.

White-hot heat shoots up my spine and I spurt all over the sink and floor. I slump back against the wall and slide down to sit and catch my breath.

Jesus. Shay's still my every fantasy.

Can I fully put my feelings aside and objectively give her a shot?

Only time will tell.

Chapter Four

One Week Later

I've been at Hungry Llama for a week now. Everyone here is awesome and has been nothing but supportive.

With one exception. Austin Andrews. Working with him is stressful. I never know what to expect.

Eh...scratch that. I *do* know what to expect. Snarky. Mean. Icy. Aloof. Condescending. Dismissive. *All of the above*. Always quick with a dig about cheerleading or my designer clothes or whatever comes to his mind. It seems like every interaction I have with Austin is a stark reminder of my apparent high school sin: being popular.

I don't get it. I'm not clear when his feelings about me turned so nasty. Back then, he never stopped staring at me. Even after...

I mean, what was I supposed to do? My brother and I had considerably different interests, so we weren't actually hanging out. Austin and Miles were shy and I was a full-blown social butterfly. While they played video games, I was always with my girlfriends. Going to dances. Partying. Fooling around with hot guys.

Anything to fill the void after my pageant life ended.

For years, it was all I knew. From the time I was a little girl until I turned fifteen, Mom and I traveled all over the country so I could compete. From the Washington State Cinderella Pageant to the Universal Royalty Pageants in Austin, Texas, I was on track to level up to feeder pageants into Miss Teen USA. Then...I had to quit.

I learned a lot during those years. How to speak in the presence of a crowd. How to take criticism like a champ. Organization. Confidence. Poise. Skills that came in handy for a relatively pain-free high school experience. Also, excellent training to deal with assholes like Austin, a.k.a. Mr. Judgypants.

I swear, if he and Miles weren't business partners, I'd give him a piece of my mind. How he treats me is so out of line but I'm not going break. Or tattle to my brother. Miles went out of his way to help me get through this tough, scary time. My salary is excellent and the experience I gain here will help my career in the long run.

I'll simply have to deal with an emotionally stunted jerkwad who despises me for no reason. No matter how nice I am to him, he seems to have made up his mind that I suck, which is annoying, but *whatever*.

As much as I'd like to avoid him, unfortunately, I've got to put up with his cranky ass for a bit. I'm in charge of Hungry Llama's three-day corporate retreat at Crystal Mountain—which is precisely five days from now. I plan on knocking it of the park because no one can throw together an event better than me. But it's no small feat to pull this off. I hope he appreciates the amount of effort it's taking.

Who am I kidding. He's going to give me all kinds of grief about the budget, which I need his sign-off on. Might as well get the unpleasantries over with.

As I approach his glass-walled office, I can see him talking to his computer monitor, which means he's on a call. With a noon deadline looming to provide proof of payment to the venue, I have no choice but to wait. Oh well, it's an outstanding opportunity to covertly observe him for a few uninterrupted minutes while he's busy.

I mean, checking out grown-up Austin is no hardship. He's incredibly easy on the eyes. No, that's underselling him. He's devastatingly handsome and takes excellent care of himself. It's definitely hard *not* to stare. The transformation from awkward teenager to gorgeous, confident man is quite something to behold.

His edgy drop-fade haircut is hot, hot, hot, I love how he leaves it long and textured on top. If he weren't such a dick, he'd check off every physical characteristic category on my list. Good hair—check. Square jaw with ever-present stubble—check. Solid, buff physique—check. Strong, capable hands with tidy, clean nails—check. Manly cologne used sparingly—check, check, check.

Austin dresses well too. Casual, of course, but upgraded. He wears his shirts a *tad* too tight, which shows off his muscles. His jeans are designer and he has a thing for cool, funky boots that look custom made. I'll give him credit where credit is due; the former geek has leveled up.

He'd be a five-star flirt alert if I were to use my old high school rating system.

Mainly because he's successful too. Austin and Miles are the youngest billionaires in the region. They're both well-respected and wickedly smart, but have entirely different leadership styles. Austin is serious where Miles is relaxed. Austin is all about numbers, data, and implementing corporate processes. Miles is passionate about creating and innovating. It's a great partnership. It definitely is.

Oooh. Austin's furrowing his brow at the caller. It's a look I'm used to having directed at me. Is it weird that I'm beginning to find it kind of...sexy?

Oh. My. God. I wrench my gaze away.

No. No. No. No. *No*.

What am I doing? I am *not* getting a crush on Austin Andrews, a man who hates me and who I'm beginning to hate too.

My heart beats wildly. Not out of fear. It's pure anticipation.

Crappity crap crap crap.

Why-oh—*why* does he have to be so *infuriatingly* attractive?

I furtively sneak a glance back over at Austin to find him staring at me like I'm the most exasperating person on the planet. He motions for me to come in so I push his door open and slip inside his office. Our eyes lock as I approach his desk. An unexpected burst of electricity ignites me to my core and almost makes me take a step backward.

Whoa.

Austin shudders like he feels it too then flicks his eyes to his monitor and snarks, "What do you need, Shay?"

Huh.

Maybe I was wrong about the zing. Probably for the best. It's not like I'm going to hook up with my brother's best friend. My *boss*. That would be a terrible idea.

Rolling my shoulders back, I stride closer, take a deep breath and try not to let his coldness derail me. "I need your sign off for the corporate retreat budget. I've mapped out a three-day schedule for you to review and approve."

"Christ." He barely glances up. "I don't have time for this so let's get it over with now. I can spare ten minutes, tops."

Trying to exude confidence in his presence is challenging, but I give it my best effort. "I sent you the agenda in Slack, but I've also printed it out." I hand him the schedule. "Miles told me it should be a mix of teambuilding, corporate planning, and fun. If you have any input, I'll be happy to make adjustments."

"Let me see." He picks up the schedule and studies it while I chew nervously on my thumbnail.

DAY 1:

- **6:00 AM:** MEET AT OFFICE TO BOARD BUSES.

- **8:00 AM:** ARRIVAL, CHECK IN & WELCOME BREAKFAST (TRADITIONAL BUFFET AND COFFEE BAR)

- **10:00 AM:** WELCOME, STATE OF THE UNION AND OUTLINE OF THE RETREAT (MILES, AUSTIN)

- **11:00 AM:** TEAM ICEBREAKER ACTIVITIES (SHAY)

- **12:30 PM:** LUNCH BREAK (TACO BAR)

- **2:00 PM**: OVERVIEW OF UPCOMING RELEASES AND STRATEGIES (EACH DEPARTMENT)

- **4:00 PM**: RECREATIONAL ACTIVITIES (SKIING, SNOWBOARDING, SNOWSHOEING) OR FREE TIME

- **7:00 PM**: GROUP DINNER & OPTIONAL KARAOKE (SALMON BAKE)

DAY 2:

- **7:00 AM**: OPTIONAL MORNING YOGA & MEDITATION (SHAY)

- **9:00 AM**: BREAKFAST (DINER STYLE OMELETS, HASH BROWNS, COFFEE BAR)

- **10:00 AM**: WORK ON BIG PICTURE STRATEGIC PLAN (LED BY MILES, AUSTIN)

- **12:00 PM**: LUNCH (DELI SANDWICH BAR)

- **1:00 PM**: STRATEGIC PLAN BREAK OUT SESSIONS (BY DEPARTMENT)

- **3:00 PM**: BREAK

- **3:15 PM**: PRESENT STRATEGIC PLAN TO ENTIRE TEAM (ALL DEPARTMENTS — 15 MINUTE INCREMENTS)

- **5:30 PM**: BREAK

- **6:30 PM**: 8-COURSE NORTHWEST FARM-TO-TABLE DINNER ON THE SUMMIT. (DRESSY CASUAL, LAST GONDOLA DEPARTS 11 PM)

DAY 3:

- **7:00 AM** OPTIONAL MORNING YOGA & MEDITATION (SHAY)

- **8:00 AM**: BREAKFAST (CONTINENTAL BUFFET AND COFFEE BAR)

- **9:00 AM**: WRAP-UP AND FEEDBACK SESSION (ALL DEPARTMENTS)

- **11:30 AM**: APPRECIATION AWARDS (MILES, AUSTIN)

- **12:30 PM**: FAREWELL LUNCH (SUSHI, POKE BAR)

- **2:00 PM**: CHECKOUT & 1ST BUS DEPARTURE OR RECREATIONAL ACTIVITIES (OPTIONS: SKIING, SNOW-

BOARDING, SNOWSHOEING)

- **7:00 PM**: LAST BUS DEPARTURE.

He looks up at me quizzically, but doesn't say anything.

"Usually these things take months to plan out and I didn't have a bundle of time so…" I shift the weight between my aching feet and lament my decision to wear five-inch Louboutin's to work.

He flicks his eyes up and down the schedule. "It looks comprehensive. My concern is the dinner on the summit. It sounds a little bougie. An eight-course meal for thirty people?"

"It's regional farm-to-table. The cost is approximately twenty thousand dollars including wine and beer." I brace myself for Austin's reaction and find myself word-vomiting. "The thing is, Hungry Llama is extraordinarily profitable due to the hard work of your executive team, who have been with you for years now. Some of them are traveling from overseas to be here. I think giving them a unique experience will be well worth the cost. The company can afford it and it will create lasting memories and loyalty."

He nods, though his face remains impassive. "Agreed. So why aren't we doing this for the entire company?"

"Uh..." It's all I can do not to roll my eyes all the way back in my head. "I started a few days ago, if you want an entire company retreat or even a holiday party, I can make it happen, but I'll need longer than a week."

Austin hesitates and his gaze lingers on me before he answers, "Look, Shay, I may not be thrilled about working with you for obvious reasons, but I want this event to succeed and I always take care of my staff. Never question that."

My mind ratholes on the "obvious reasons" comment for, well, obvious reasons.

"May I ask why you have a problem with me?" I cross my arms in front of my chest. "Until last week, I haven't seen you in, what...nearly a decade? Did I miss something?"

His eyes narrow and he shoos me with his hand. "Ten minutes are over. Budget approved. Time for you to go."

I'm so shocked by Austin's abrupt dismissal, I can't think up a decent retort.

Which pisses me off to no end.

Hot or not, I retract my assessment. The guy hasn't leveled up. Not one bit. He's a condescending asshole.

As I trudge back to my office, I can't help but feel defeated. When Miles brought me onboard, I was so excited to work with my brother and his best friend.

It seemed like an opportunity of a lifetime.

Now, I'm beginning to think this job is my worst nightmare.

Chapter Five

Ever since Shay joined Hungry Llama I haven't been myself.

I spent the better part of the past decade despising her and everything she stands for. Now I'm supposed to supervise her and maintain some level of professionalism, though I've jerked off every fucking day—sometimes twice—since she joined the company.

It's tough.

So *fucking* tough.

She's so goddamn beautiful and has this way about her...

Argh! *No!*

I didn't realize how much my hatred for her crept into my life until I've had to see her every day. It's pervasive and, quite frankly, a little unhealthy. From the women I date to the type of people I surround myself with, I've made a conscious effort to avoid anyone who is any way superficial—like Shay. Anyone who puts too much effort into their physical appearance is out. Status chasers—out. Money flaunters—also out.

It was today o'clock when I realized I'm a fucking hypocrite.

A few days ago, Shay admired my designer jeans and commented about how much she loves my haircut. It made me cringe not because she was being complimentary to me about my looks—trigger alert—but I realized I've somehow become the very embodiment of the type of person I loathe.

I'm fucking shallow. It started when I began earning stupid money. For fuck's sake, Hungry Llama's valuation is currently over a billion dollars. Miles and I are *billionaires*.

I live in a five-million-dollar condo. I strictly wear certain brands of clothes. My grooming routine is meticulous bordering on obsessive. I work out, without fail, seven days a week so I look pleasing without a shirt.

Who the fuck am I and what happened to the Austin Andrews who couldn't stand people like me?

Who the fuck am I trying to impress?

"Dude?" Stodge waves his hand in front of my face. "Eyes on the road."

I shake my head to clear it of self-loathing. "Yeah, sorry."

It's the crack of dawn. Miles and I are driving to Crystal Mountain together instead of riding on the buses Shay arranged. I suggested it under the guise we could prepare for our presentations without interruption and get there before our executive team arrives.

In actuality, I need a reality check. Badly. I'm slowly going insane.

When I see Shay sashaying around the office in her sexy business outfits, I want to scream because I fucking hate her so much. I also hate that I want to fuck her until she's the one who screams—with pleasure.

The fantasies I have of pulling her tight little skirt up over her ass, bending her over my desk and ramming into her from behind...it's what I beat off to every single night. Mornings too. Sometimes during the day.

Jesus. I'm obsessed with her. Like I always used to be.

Not that I can tell Miles any of this. Inappropriate. So *thoroughly* inappropriate.

"We have two hours." Miles switches the playlist to the ambient music he listens to nonstop. "Should we go over what we're going to say?"

I switch it back to classic rock. "I can't listen to that shit unless you want me to fall asleep and crash."

"I thought it was copilot's choice, my bad." Miles reclines in the passenger's seat. "So, you approved the agenda?"

I nod. "Yeah. It was pretty great honestly, given the short time frame she had to pull it together."

"I knew Shay would come through. All you had to do was give her a chance." Miles doesn't even hide his pride.

I roll my eyes. "It's an *agenda*, Miles."

Miles regards me seriously. "Look, it hadn't occurred to me when I gave her a job that you'd still be carrying so much animosity. Is there a way for us to talk through it before we get up there?"

"What's there to say, Stodge?" I can't help but wince. "I'm never going to like her. You weren't there. What she did was..." It gives me hives to talk about Shay with Miles. My loyalty is with my best friend, but he's put me in a shitty position. I never wanted to be in the middle of the twins, yet here I am.

He blows out a breath of frustration. "I know that night was weird. Is there any way you can give it all a rest? It was so long ago and there's a lot you don't know."

"Oh *really*," I drawl in utter contempt and sarcasm.

He recoils. "Fuck you."

"*Fine*. That was uncalled for. I'm being a dick." I motion for him to continue.

"If you want me to tell you." He pounds his palm with his fist. "But...I'll need your word that you won't use *anything* I tell you against her. I want to be honest with you, but what I'm about to say has got to be kept in the vault."

I'm absolutely taken aback. "Jeez. It must be pretty bad."

"I'll repeat. I'm Dead. Fucking. Serious." He holds out his hand. "We need to shake in sworn secrecy."

Miles is never unnecessarily dramatic. *Ever*. If he's breaking out our childhood oath, this is important to him. I grip his hand and we shake. "I promise."

"Fine. I'm trusting you because you're like family to me. If she finds out I've told you though, it'll be...bad. Profoundly. Fucking. Bad." He hangs his head and shakes it slowly, as if picturing a fate worse than death.

Just like that, I'm beyond the curiosity phase. I'm in the "tell me fucking now" phase. "Stodge. Seriously. I know I've been annoying about Shay, but anything you tell me stays between us. I don't fuck around like that."

"I know. Okay. So, do you remember when she was thoroughly into competing in those beauty pageants?" He pinches the bridge of his nose and glances at me.

I nod. "Yeah."

"Well, you might remember when she quit." Miles looks off into the distance. "She told everyone otherwise, but it was because she had a serious health scare. Her doctor put her on strong medication and it took a long time to get the correct dosage. The side effects were...rough."

I nod my head for him to continue. "Go on."

"The diagnosis devastated her. She was embarrassed." He keeps eye contact with me, which I'm guessing is to gauge my reaction in real-time. "The meds made her forgetful, erratic. Extremely reactive. Shay always tried to keep it together because she didn't want anyone to know about her condition. My family hid it from everyone. Even you."

"Well, you did a commendable job. I never had a clue." I don't even try to hide my surprise. I want to ask what this mystery illness is, but I know better than to interrupt Miles when he's in a sharing mood. His programming brain has its own train of thought.

He purses his lips. "Shay's *always* been excellent at putting on a brave face. She was trained by my mom at an early age. The toddlers and tierras shit taught her how to paste on a cheery smile and hide her true self at all cost."

I think back to that time. I was so infatuated with her and loved—and also hated—how free and unbothered she seemed to be. A relentless flirt, Shay chewed up the guys in my school and spit them out. She partied. Got into petty competitions with her friends. Ignored Miles then acted like he was the greatest brother in the world. Then there was the night she set her sights on me and…well.

I didn't want anything to do with her brand of chaos after that. It hurt too badly.

"Yeah, well it doesn't change anything. There's this thing called personal responsibility." Although Stodge's revelation helps the pieces fit together, I'm not ready to concede. "None of what you've told me excuses what she did."

Miles's voice is tinged with sadness. "Fine. Maybe it gives you some context, though. Shay totally struggled and she doesn't have a great recollection of her junior and senior year. She moved to LA for a fresh start. She needed to regain some of her equilibrium. Have stability."

We drive in silence for a while, giving me headspace to think about what Miles said. As we turn up the drive up the mountainside, the dense forest gives way to glimpses of snow-covered peaks. I think about what he's told me and find myself feeling irritated by the thread of empathy weaving its way through my body.

"There's something else," Miles mutters. "I might as well get it all out there."

"Might as well," I agree, though I dread hearing anything else about Shay that will tug at my heartstrings.

Miles furrows his brow. "As you know, the man she dated throughout college and hoped to marry dumped her in spectacular fashion a few months ago. She gave up everything to support his career and he threw her away like trash."

"Yeah, I saw the news." My jaw tightens. I'm unmoved but also strangely annoyed at the thought of her with that smug asshole.

Stodge takes off his Hungry Llama beanie and squeezes it tightly like he's choking it. "*Asshole*. He convinced her to postpone business school and focus on him and his career until he signed a major contract."

"*Puh*-lease." I raise an eyebrow. "You want me to break out the tiny violins? She got what she wanted. Lived the high life on the arm of a man with status who let her spend all his money. Then he got tired of her. It's not exactly the most tragic of tales. She had to know he was going to trade up when the real money came in."

"Trade up? Have some fucking respect, dude. She's my sister." Miles shoots me a glare.

I shake my head in shame. "I apologize. I can't seem to stop being a dick, that was completely out of line."

"Damn fucking straight." Miles slaps the dashboard. "Shay fucking loved him. Did everything for him. She *made* that guy's career. Who do you think researched the industry to make sure he was in the right place at the right time? She ran his social media. Found a way to make him known to all the top agents, business advisors, and lawyers. Assembled his entire wellness team. Shay also volunteered at some of the biggest charities in LA to elevate Devon's status and put him front and center. She never asked for accolades, she only wanted him to have the success he craved. Well, he got it. Signed the biggest contract in football and kicked her to the curb with nothing—when he should be kissing the ground she walks on."

I know zip about the world of professional sports, and this sounds a bit far-fetched, but I don't want to have a beef with Miles. "Look, she's your sister and you'll always have her back, as you should. I'm sorry if I've gone too far with my beef. I've been pissed that you hired her without discussing it with me. And seeing her again? Yeah, I've been pissed about the entire situation."

"That's fair." He visibly relaxes at my confession. "I'm sorry too. I should have come to you before offering her the job. I wanted her to have a chance to shine for a change."

I consider his words. The Shay I remember and the Shay I've recently encountered seem worlds apart. I have a lot to process. "I get it. You want the best for your sister."

Miles shrugs. "Facts. Maybe this retreat, away from everything, can be a fresh start for all of us."

"Hmmm." I look over at him and smile. "I'll try. How 'bout that?"

As we wind up the steep, windy road to the resort, the grandeur of the snow-packed mountain is revealed with every twist and turn. I pull into the parking space and with the next few days looming before us, I decide to try to keep an open mind.

For Miles's sake at least.

I'm grateful for the bond we share as friends and business partners.

If it means giving Shay a fair shot, so be it.

Chapter Six

A Few Minutes Later

It's nearly seven a.m. and I've been up all night ensuring everything is ready for the corporate retreat.

Well, me and my small-events team, Thad, Cecily, and Natalie. There's no way I could have done this on my own. The four of us arrived yesterday morning to get the place ready. It's been a ton of hard work, but everything's fallen into place. I'm going to make sure everything we have planned goes off without a hitch.

If for no other reason than to piss Austin off when I succeed.

I've had remarkably little sleep this week and I should be exhausted, but adrenaline courses through my veins. Nothing is more rewarding than pulling off the impossible—and anyone who's ever planned an event will tell you organizing a professional retreat for thirty executives takes longer than a week. Yet, I'm fairly certain we've nailed it. The next three days are going to slay.

When it's over I'll have time to rest. I haven't had any incidents in a while so as long as I take my meds and sneak in a nap or two, I should be fine. There's no time to worry about myself now though. Everyone will be here in about an hour. Barely enough time for me to walk the event and take care of any final details.

I run into Becky, the resort manager, in the lobby of the Silver Skis Chalet. "Morning, Shay. How was your room?"

"Bussin'. Amazingly comfortable. Are we ready for check-in?" I gaze outside at the winter wonderland. Crystal Mountain is absolutely spectacular. The entire resort is blanketed in a few feet of pure, untouched snow, which glistens in the early morning sun.

Becky looks at her clipboard. "Yes. All the condos have been freshened up. The gift baskets were delivered. We're good to go."

"Cool, thank you." I check the list on my tablet. "Oh, and when will the lifts start running?" Ski season won't start until day after the retreat, but I've arranged for my executive colleagues to enjoy the inaugural runs of the season.

She smiles. "Four on the dot."

"Shay?" Cecily approaches with Natalie following close behind. "Would you be able to give your approval on the welcome station?"

Becky waves and heads back to the office. I follow my staff through the side door outside to where the winter wonderland has been transformed into what looks like a Hungry Llama theme park. Bold blue and purple banners featuring Bert, our mascot, dance in the crisp mountain breeze. Strategically placed spotlights in the identical colors illuminate the halls and footpaths. The entire vibe is super fucking extra.

Down the path, Thad scurries around setting up the hot chocolate bar by the welcome desk. He's placed glass jars filled with snowman-shaped marshmallows, peppermint candy canes and cinnamon sticks next to the commemorative Hungry Llama mugs. As we approach, I feel an overwhelming sense of pride. "Wow. You guys. This looks incredible."

I go over my list and finish delegating tasks when I see Austin and Miles pull up to the front parking lot. My brother exits the SUV wearing a vintage ski jacket and maroon corduroy pants, followed by Austin. I can't help but stare. He looks like he's stepped out of a winter sports catalog wearing trim jeans, a black puffy coat, a beanie, and a thick scarf wrapped around his neck.

Miles spots me and waves, looking downright giddy. He tugs at Austin's coat and points to the Bert snow sculptures lining the walkway. I make an adjustment to the welcome banner and head over to greet my bosses. Austin's eyes are already on me, scrutinizing.

"Welcome to Crystal Mountain," I say with my brightest smile pasted on. "Should I walk you through the resort before the buses arrive?"

Miles grips my shoulders and pulls me into a hug. "Shay, this looks so fantastic. I can't wait to see the rest."

"This way." I motion toward the grand double doors, noting that Austin has yet to even say hello. *Jerk.*

Sexy jerk.

No. No. No. No.

Pushing all thoughts of sexy Austin out of my mind, I open the door and lead Miles and Austin through the lobby to the ballroom where most of our group meetings will be held. The chalet's high, vaulted ceilings are adorned with chandeliers made out of elk horns. Hungry Llama banners hang elegantly from the walls, alternating with large projection screens. At the front, a raised podium stands proud, ready for the speakers. Rows of plush chairs are neatly arranged behind small desks, each with a branded notepad and pen.

"Wow," Austin murmurs, visibly impressed. "This is...incredible."

"We managed to pull it all together." I try not to react to Austin's praise. "The podium's fully set up with our technology. Paul from IT will be here to guarantee we have a seamless transition between presentations. Someone on my events team will be on standby at all times to concierge any needs we might have over the next three days."

Miles nods appreciatively. "Shay, I agree with Austin. This looks dope."

"Well, there're other things for you to see." I gesture toward a door at the rear of the ballroom and lead them in that direction. We venture down a corridor lined with doors. "These are the breakout rooms," I explain. "Each is set up for smaller groups to brainstorm and strategize."

I open the doors for them to peek inside. It's a cozy space, with comfortable seating arranged in a circle. A smart board hangs on one wall, while another displays a beautiful mural of the ski runs on the mountain. Branded stationery packs are placed at each seat.

Austin examines the setup, then looks at me, eyebrows raised. "Every detail is perfection, Shay. This... This is rad."

I can't help the genuine grin that spreads across my face. "Thank you, but there's even more."

Our tour continues down the corridor that loops around and connects with the main entrance. The dining hall is a vast space with floor-to-ceiling windows offering panoramic views of the snowy landscape outside. Large, round tables, draped in deep-blue tablecloths, dot the room. Various iterations of Bert are the centerpieces.

Along the back wall, the hotel staff is setting up an elaborate buffet. The cold food is already out, a tantalizing display of smoked salmon, fruit, bagels and three different flavors of cream cheese.

Miles whistles appreciatively. "Holy shit. This is beyond what I even imagined. You've turned this retreat into an *experience*. I can hardly wait for everyone to get here."

"It's important for the executive team to feel appreciated." I nod enthusiastically. "If there's one thing I learned in fundraising, people are willing to give ten thousand percent if you treat them well."

Austin is subdued, but the admiration in his eyes is impossible to miss. "You've done an impeccable job."

"I want everything to be perfect." The compliment, notably coming from him, hits different. Makes my heart race.

Austin's gaze lingers on mine, the intensity and electricity between us is unmistakable this time. "Well," he eventually says, clearing his throat, "it's impressive."

The sincerity in his voice takes me by surprise after so many days of him being so, well, shitty. I can't help but blush. "I...I...um."

"I told you she rocked at this stuff." Miles slugs Austin in the arm. "Admit you were wrong."

Austin rolls his eyes. "Never. We still have to get through the next three days, Stodge."

Aannnnnd, jerk Austin is back in a flash.

Miles wraps an arm around me. "I knew you'd pull it off. But honestly, I didn't expect anything remotely this cool. It's fantastic! It's almost like we're a grown-up company now."

There's still a lot to do before the buses arrive, so it's time for me to extricate myself. "How about we get you checked in before everyone gets here?"

"Good idea." Miles and Austin follow me to the check-in desk.

I hand them each their keys and a welcome bag. "Here you go, gentlemen. Everything you need for the retreat, from room keys to schedules, is in there."

Austin's fingers graze my arm as he accepts his bag. His touch is light and fleeting, but it leaves a trail of warmth that lingers. For a moment, everything fades, and I imagine it's the two of us in a world of our own. The feeling is overwhelming, leaving me exhilarated and breathless.

"Alright, folks, we've got a long day ahead." Miles breaks the spell. "We'll go drop our bags in the rooms. Why don't you join us for breakfast? I'd like to get a jump on the marketing presentation, unless you're going to be tied up overseeing everything here."

I nod, grateful to be acknowledged as the VP of Marketing and not only a party planner. "The event team can handle most everything going forward so I can focus on what's important."

"Good, see you in, say, ten minutes?" Miles is already heading toward the car. Austin hesitates, then follows, turning briefly to give me one final lingering look.

I let out a sigh of relief only to be startled by Becky. "Girl, you are in trouble with a capital T."

"What?" I whirl around. "Why?"

"That fine-lookin' boy has it bad for you. I can see it from a mile away," She cocks her hip.

"Uh, no. You're absolutely wrong about that. He hates me," I blurt out then slam my mouth shut.

Becky throws her head back and laughs. "Fine line. *Fine line.*"

"Ohmygod. You're reading this all wrong, with all due." I shake my head vigorously. Too vigorously. Lack of sleep has me feeling a little woozy. I better dash to my room and take my pill.

She takes the hint. "Alright, forget I said a word. ETA on the buses is fifteen minutes. We'll put out the hot breakfast in batches as they check in."

As I make the short trek to my room, I take comfort in the momentary silence filled with nothing but the crunch of snow beneath my feet. It won't be long before everyone is here and I'll be enmeshed in approximately seventy-two hours of chaos.

I'm glad I've impressed Austin, but I can't let old habits derail me.

I want to do a good job for my own self-worth, not to dazzle someone I'm wildly attracted to who doesn't actually like me as a person.

Wait. Wildly attracted to?

Oh, shit. I'm in big, big trouble.

Chapter Seven

Austin

The Next Evening

Miles and I manage to grab our own gondola for the ten-minute ride up to the Summit House Restaurant for the company detail. It's relaxing. We haven't had a second to ourselves since yesterday morning.

It's been two solid days of intense and meaningful work. We're both quiet. Contemplative. I must say, one of the many, many reasons I've been friends with him for all these years is how alike we are in this respect. There's never need for small talk with us.

Truth be told, it's nice to have a few minutes before dinner to reflect on the retreat, which has been nothing short of inspirational. When we started Hungry Llama, Stodge and I were barely out of our teens. Neither of us knew anything about running a company, we had to figure it all out along the way. Success came early and hasn't slowed down. The two of us shoulder ample responsibility, something we both take seriously.

Maybe *too* seriously.

The thing is, we're not in this alone anymore. With hundreds of employees on our payroll, taking time with the executive team to regroup, refresh, and plan for the future needs to be part of every year's strategic planning. I had no idea getting away from the day-to-day grind of work to focus would be so goddamn priceless.

As we near the summit, the dying embers of the sun cast a pinkish glow on a jaw-dropping panoramic view of Mt. Rainier. I'm not generally emotional about nature-related things, but today I'm appreciative. It's perfect here.

"So, she knocked it out of the park." Miles breaks the silence as we disembark the gondola and start down the pathway to the restaurant.

He's right. Shay fucking killed it. She's been a goddamn beacon of light. Always positive and sunny. Organized. Resourceful. Everything went off without a hitch due to her meticulous planning. "Yeah. She did a tremendous job, Stodge. I'm blown away."

"Is the shit behind us then?" He looks at me hopefully, with a dose of puppy-dog eyes for good measure. "Because her marketing presentation today was possibly the best and most thoughtful approach I've seen since we started the company."

I shove my hands in my pockets. It's freezing and I stupidly left my gloves in my room. "It needs to be. She's definitely changed."

We reach the lodge and I open the door to the restaurant. The tables are meticulously arranged in a U-shape, candles flicker on crisp white tablecloths adorned with subtle Berts. Unsurprisingly, Shay's event staff have done an impeccable job, down to the smallest details.

Stodge's jaw drops. "Wow."

"This place is perfect. So cool." I eyeball the roaring fireplace. "Don't worry. I'll be an adult and talk to her about it at some point. Apologize."

"Soon." Miles slaps his hands together and fixes me with a pointed glare. "From this point forward, the personal vendetta shit needs to stay far away from the office. Yeah?"

I'm about to respond when Mona, our CTO, pulls him aside. Rather than retort, I decide to let Miles have the closing words on the matter. He's not wrong. I've been petulant. Unprofessional. He's shown more patience with me than I would have if the situation were reversed.

I'll do better.

As I approach the fire to warm my hands, Shay walks up beside me, drop-dead gorgeous in a cream, oversized sweater, black leggings with sexy socks that hit slightly above her knee shoved into designer hiking boots. Her hair is loose around her shoulders and she smells like fresh air and vanilla cookies. She smiles tentatively. "Isn't this place breathtaking?"

"It is." I can't help but gawk at the woman whom I've hated for so long. A woman I've tried like hell to ignore since she showed up a couple of weeks ago.

The woman who, despite it all, takes *my* breath away.

Except, every bit of vitriol I still harbored has drained out of my body in the past forty-eight hours. Shay's won me over on her own merits. *Without* Miles's prompting, I might add.

"You impressed me, Shay." I keep my voice low. "You pulled off an extraordinary retreat. *Thank you.*"

Her deep-blue eyes widen and lock on to mine, searching for any hint of sarcasm. Finding none, she visibly relaxes and gives me a radiant, genuine smile that sends my heart into overdrive. "Wow. Okay, then. That means a lot coming from you."

"I give credit where credit is due." I hold her gaze, debating whether I should formally apologize now or wait until we get back to Seattle.

I don't get a chance to figure it out because the restaurant manager announces that dinner is ready. As we take our seats, which are preassigned, Miles and I are on opposite ends of the table. I smile to myself. Assuming she was in charge of the seating chart, splitting the two of us up is another brilliant decision.

Miles is my default. The one person I always have by my side at any company function. The team building exercises forced me outside my comfort zone to get to know the rest of our executives on a personal level. It's something I've never bothered to do which, in retrospect, is a definite shortcoming on my part. Tonight, conversation is animated. Rather than discussing business, everyone is laughing and generally having a good time.

"Hey, everyone!" Anne-Marie, our SVP of Development, taps her wine glass with the end of her spoon to garner everyone's attention. The room grows quiet except for the crackle of the fire. "Before we eat, I'd like to make a toast—to Miles and Austin. This retreat has been truly amazing. I'm proud to work here."

From across the table, Miles stands and holds up his own glass. "No, thank you. We're so incredibly humbled by all of you here today and the contributions you bring to the company. Hungry Llama is reaching new heights. Your hard work, your dedication—it's all appreciated. My toast is to all of you."

Glasses clink all around me. Surprising even myself, I find myself standing too. "Actually, I'd like to thank Shay for pulling this together in such a short time. You're a welcome addition to Hungry Llama and none of this would have been possible without you and your team." I hold my own goblet of wine out in her direction a few seats down from me.

Miles's jaw drops open, but he recovers quickly.

"Oh! Gosh. Thank you. It was my pleasure." Shay's cheeks redden and her voice is shaky, like she's embarrassed by the attention, which surprises me since my comment is consistent with what I told her in private before dinner.

Dessert arrives, which leads to heightened liveliness as some of our team begin talking about their world travels.

"So, I ordered a traditional dish and ended up with indiscernible raw meat. So. Gross." Marie, our CFO, recounts an unexpected culinary adventure on her travels in Thailand.

Vince, our SVP of Sales, who is sitting next to me chortles, "When I was in Venice, I accidentally asked a waiter for a kiss instead of the check. My Italian is...questionable."

Brad, our CRO, replies with a smirk, "Remind me not to let you order if we ever find ourselves in Italy."

"We'll be in Rome next year for the Online Casino Summit." Miles points his fork at Vince. "Maybe we should let Shay take care of the details."

Everyone shrieks with laughter. Shay grins. The camaraderie at the table is palpable, genuine. It feels like a family gathering, the kind where everyone's sharing stories and laughing over past misadventures.

Miles grows sentimental, probably in large part because of the wine he's drinking. "I know I toasted earlier, but I feel compelled to say this. Looking around this table, seeing all of you here. It's humbling. The talent here is unparalleled."

Feeling inspired, I raise my glass again. "To the brilliant minds at this table, and to a future of gaming innovation."

A chorus of clinks follow in a warm and joyful moment followed by pats on the back. Side hugs.

It's glorious.

As the evening begins to wind down, the stars outside sparkle brilliantly. Shay holds out her glass. "I can't express how much tonight and the past couple of days have meant to me. Here's to second chances and new beginnings. We all have our pasts, our mistakes. But it's how we grow from them that defines us. Thank you, all of you. Feel free to hang around and enjoy the wine and company. Gondolas run until ten sharp."

Our eyes meet, and for a fleeting moment, a world of emotions pass between us. I get up and walk over to where Shay's sitting and lean over and speak softly so only she can hear. "I was wrong about you. I judged you based on the past and I shouldn't have. You've shown what you're truly capable of here. Would you be open to having a quick word?"

Shay's eyes widen in surprise. "Austin, I..."

"I'll be out on the patio." I look over at Miles, who nods his approval. "I'd like it if you'd hear me out."

On my way outside, I grab my jacket and scarf from the coat rack, feeling better than I have in a long time. While I'm ready to put this shit with Shay behind us, my heart is beating out of my chest at the idea of being alone with her.

"I'm right behind you." Shay puts on her gloves before buttoning up her coat.

"Shay, I'm heading back down to the hotel, unless you need anything." Cecily runs up behind us. "Thanks for including us in the dinner tonight."

"Of course. And, no, everything is good here. Go hang out with that cute bartender you had your eye on. He's definitely a five-star flirt alert." Shay embraces Cecily and waggles her eyebrows at me from over her shoulder.

All the air whooshes out of my body. Memories from that night come flooding back. Anger bubbles up threatening to explode like a volcanic eruption.

"*Flirt alert?*" I snap, my voice drips with contempt.

Shay looks utterly confused and possibly a bit embarrassed. "Uh…"

"Fuck you, Shay." I shove my way through the glass doors outside and stomp over to a covered seating area at the far corner of the patio. It's nearly pitch black out here, which matches my mood.

I'm such a sucker. I can't help but mutter to myself, "I praised you, complimented you. What a fucking bitch. You haven't changed one bit."

"Austin." Shay taps me on the shoulder, startling me. I didn't realize she followed me out here. "Can we still have a conversation?"

I whirl around. "What could you possibly say to me, Shay? I'm an idiot. You're encouraging the staff to play your little high school games. So fucking unprofessional. Do you know that I kept our secret from him? Despite everything?"

"Uh…" She looks around nervously, as if she's scared Miles is behind us.

"You know what?" I plunk down on a chair and pat the one next to me. "Let's do it. It's time to hash this out once and for all."

Shay gathers her coat around her and positions herself on the edge of the seat closest to me. She looks nervous. Confused.

Fuck it. I'm going all in.

"Why did you fuck me that night?"

Chapter Eight

Ten Years Ago - Age 18

I'm so pissed my parents won't let me drive.

If I had the car I wouldn't be waiting for my BFFs Mindy Smith and Bianca Simpson to give me a ride home. It's Friday, we finished cheerleading practice and I *told* them I was in a hurry. What the heck is taking them so long?

It's not their fault, I guess. They have no idea my anxiety is driving me out of my mind. It's my fault I left my medication in my bedroom and I'm over an hour late for my next dose. It's *probably* no big deal but I can't run the risk of having a seizure here at school.

Hurry. Hurry. Hurry.

I'm trying to stay calm but if anyone finds out... It would *ruin* me.

Nobody knows I have epilepsy but my immediate family. I'm *definitely* keeping it that way.

I can't afford another colossal failure. As my mom always says, "popularity is currency." In high school, the line between friends and enemies blurs every fucking day. I may have been forced to trade pageant competitions for cheerleading, but I'm not about to lose the status I've achieved.

"Hey, bitch." Bianca sashays down the steps in her short little romper to where I'm waiting on the perch. "You ready?"

I slowly rise so I don't seem too pressed. "Took you long enough."

"Oh, you shoulda been there. Five-star flirt alert, no cap." She motions to Mindy, who's behind her, long red hair swishing like the tail of the show pony she is.

A flirt alert is the secret rating system we made up to communicate the hotness of the guys we stan or who stan us. Ratings vary between five stars, which means he's a snack to one star, which means he's cringe AF. I think it's genius—no one knows what we're talking about so we never come across as sus. Mainly, nobody's feelings get hurt.

I follow them to Bianca's red Hyundai. "Who?"

"Austin Andrews." Mindy turns and bats her eyelashes.

Bianca smacks her lips. "I like them smart and nerdy with glow-up potential."

"He's my brother's best friend." I'm a bit shocked that either of my friends would notice Austin, let alone throw down a flirt alert rating above a two on him. Everything inside me wants to squash this before Bianca gets a notion. It makes me consider my brother's nerdy buddy in a different light, though.

Mindy opens the passenger door for me. "If you snooze, you lose beyotch."

"What does that even mean?" I slide in. "The kid's had a crush on me for years but I've never thought about him like that."

"You're too late. I'm calling dibs. I wanna pop that kid's cherry. Make him fall in love with me." Bianca licks her lips.

Mindy chortles. "Maybe I can hook up with Miles."

"My brother?" I yelp. What the hell alternate universe am I living in?

"You're too focused on jocks." Bianca rolls her eyes. "They have it too easy. Too many women. Too many choices. Best to go for a decent-looking dude who will worship the ground you walk on."

Huh. She kinda has a point.

"So, we're coming over? Your folks are out of town and don't Miles and Austin chill at your house most nights?" Mindy pulls out of the parking lot onto the main road.

"Yeah. I guess." I'm not fully on board because I still have to take my meds, but what am I gonna say. No? I glance out the window at the McMansions passing us by on our way to my neighborhood.

We pull into the driveway at the same time Austin arrives on his bike dressed like he and my brother always dress. Ironic t-shirt, zip-up hoodie, jeans. When he sees the three of us pull up I can almost taste his discomfort. I get it. We're a lot.

"Hey, Austin, we meet again. What are you doing here?" Bianca slides out of the driver's seat and bites the tip of her finger seductively.

Austin looks at Bianca, then me. "Uh, hanging out with Miles."

I study him briefly. Bianca has a point. He's on the cusp of handsome if he gains about twenty pounds of muscle, amps up his clothes a bit, maybe grows out his hair on top. He catches me staring, blushes, and looks down.

As we enter my house, I hear the familiar sounds of the zombie video game Miles loves coming from the living room. Austin immediately makes a beeline for the couch where Miles is sitting. "Dude, did you make it past the toxic sewer?"

"On second thought." Bianca's nose is so wrinkled I'm shocked it hasn't disappeared inside her head. "I most likely can't deal with that level of geek factor. Even if he has a big D."

I glance over at them and back at my friends and try not to think about Austin's dick when I have things to take care of. "I've got to pee and then we can get a snack. I didn't have lunch."

I leave Mindy and Bianca in the kitchen and bolt to the bathroom. When I open my pill container to take my dose, I discover it's empty. *Fuck*. A side effect of this stupid medication is it sometimes messes up my memory. I totally forgot that I'm out. Now Miles is going to have to drive me to the pharmacy.

Then I realize, no. My friends are here. They can't know about this, so I can't go until they leave. Rationalization kicks in.

You can wait another day. It's no big deal.

It is what it is, I guess. I return to the kitchen where I see that Bianca broke out the grapefruit-flavored vodka my mom keeps in the freezer. She's poured it into three large glasses and is adding some soda water. She raises a glass. "*This* is what I call a snack. It's cocktail hour, *bitches*!"

"Fine, but we'll need to replace it. My mom will kick my ass." Forgetting I'm hungry, I sit at the counter and take my drink. It's been a stressful day. I need it.

Mindy sits next to me. "So tell me about this crush Austin has on you."

"Shhh." I lean back so I can see where Austin and Miles are battling zombies. "Look, he's always here. He's a nice kid. Immature because of the absolute obsession with video games but..."

"Isn't he eighteen? The same age as us? Why haven't you tapped it?" Bianca chugs down the rest of her drink and pours another.

I'm no virgin. That ship sailed a couple years ago around the time I found out about my situation. I decided life is too short and gave my v-card to Kendall Harrison and discovered I love sex. I'm picky, but not picky enough to go without for longer than a month, maybe two.

"It would be weird. He's my brother's friend." I pretend to be nonchalant, but my wheels start turning. Maybe Austin could scratch an itch. Maybe trying out a nerdy guy who wants to please me might be fun. I've never been with a virgin...

No. Don't go there.

The reality is, my mom has high ambitions for me to follow in her footsteps, marry a professional athlete and have a comfortable life. I guess that's why I've exclusively gone after jocks.

Mindy holds up a portrait of my family that's on the windowsill looking into the back garden. "I still can't get over your dad is Goran Stojanović."

"Stodge is dreamy." Bianca grabs the picture. "I'd do your dad."

"*Jesus*. That's so gross." I swipe it from her and put it back on the windowsill.

"Oh, get over it." Bianca makes a kissy face. "Your dad is the most famous hockey player in the state. There are forums dedicated to erotic fan fiction about him. Surely you have seen them?"

"*Ewwwwwwwwww*," I scream.

"Too far?" Bianca swigs her second drink.

Mindy is doubled over in laughter. "Most def. Should we go hang out with the nerds?"

"We need more alcohol for that." Bianca tops everyone off. We clink glasses and down them like shots.

It hits me hard. I'm drunk as hell by the time we stumble into the living room a few minutes later. Miles and Austin look up in surprise when we plop down on the couch opposite of where they're sitting.

"Do you boys want to put down the controllers and hang out with us? Have a little fun?" Bianca hikes up her skirt and waggles her eyebrows.

I feel a pang of guilt as I see Austin blush but I push it aside and lean over so he can get an impressive view of my cleavage. "Yeah, party with us tonight. We broke into Mom's grapefruit vodka."

"Shit." Miles is up on his feet in an instant. "Shay, you can't..."

"I can and I will." I glare at him and use my twin telepathy to get him to sit down and shut up. I know he's worried about how the alcohol will mix with my medication, but I like to live a little. It's not like my condition is a death sentence. It's time I experience the rite of passage of doing something naughty when my parents are gone for the weekend.

Mindy and Bianca snicker and hold up their glasses in a toast. We clink them together and down another shot.

"Want me to make you guys one?" Bianca asks Austin and my brother as she heads off to the kitchen.

Miles, though, isn't playing along. His disappointment is clear. "Shay, what's gotten into you? Why are you acting like this?"

I shrug, pretending not to care. "What? We're having some fun. Lighten up."

"Maybe we should." Austin's voice is so quiet, I can scarcely hear him.

Miles whirls around. "Get drunk with Shay and her friends?"

"Yeah..." Austin doesn't sound completely convinced. "Maybe...well, okay."

"That's the spirit." Bianca brings back a tray of fresh drinks.

My whole life, I've done everything my mom wanted me to do. I've been the perfect daddy's girl. The good sister. Now, I'm trying to be everything my friends expect. In the process, I've lost myself.

Managing an unpredictable life is exhausting.

Tonight, for once, I'm going to let go.

I want to forget about my problems. My illness.

The night will unfold however it unfolds.

What could possibly go wrong?

Chapter Nine

Ten Years Ago: The Next Morning

My eyes blink open. The tiniest sliver of light peeks through the window shade.

The glow of the television paints the entire room a sickly shade of greenish-blue.

My tongue is stuck to the roof of my mouth and oh, sweet Jesus, my head is pounding.

I'm on the floor, wrapped like a burrito in a blanket. When I try to sit up, the room begins to spin. My stomach lurches and I know I'm going to barf. I don't realize I'm naked until I'm retching up what looks like pizza in the hall bathroom.

What the fuck?

I manage to stand up and splash cold water on my face, swish some toothpaste in my mouth. Try to puzzle together what went down. I have fuzzy memories of drinking vodka shots and battling zombies with Miles. Shay and her two friends dancing together, getting me and Stodge to join them.

Oh shit, we *did* join them. Miles made out with...

Whoa.

Oh holy fuck.

Grabbing a towel, I wrap it around my waist and stumble back to the living room where I woke up. Sure enough, Shay is asleep, sprawled out on the couch, also completely naked. Her head is partially buried under a pillow.

One arm is flung on top of it, the other clutches a blanket that barely covers her stomach. Her gorgeous, creamy tits jiggle a bit in time to her breathing, brown nipples puckered tight in the cool air. One leg is bent and splayed open giving me a view of her pussy, which is covered by fine whisps of light hair. Below, I see a distinct wet spot on the cushion.

My dick instantly grows hard as steel.

Memories of being on top of Shay on the couch flash before my eyes. Pumping into her. Feeling her legs wrapped around my waist. Us kissing. Me sucking on her nipples.

Holy fucking shit. Shay and I had sex after Miles disappeared in his bedroom with her friends.

I'm not a virgin anymore.

Shay stirs. The pillow shifts, exposing her eyes, which squinch in pain. "God, I feel like shit."

"Uh...do you need anything?" I mumble, still stunned.

She jackknifes up at the sound of my voice and winces when her eyes open to no wider than a slit. "Austin?" She glances down, sees that she's naked and yanks up the blanket to cover herself. "Ohmygod! Staring much? What the fuck happened?"

"Uh..." I'm so completely out of my element I have no idea how to say it out loud when I scarcely comprehend it myself.

Shay looks up at me. Her eyes trail down my naked body to the towel around my waist, tented from my boner. Her eyes widen with awareness. "Oh!"

I spy my pants, T-shirt, and boxers balled up at the foot of the couch. I take two steps over to snatch them up before cautiously backing up toward the bathroom. "I'll just..."

By the time I regroup and return fully clothed a few minutes later, Shay's dressed in her low-cut sweater and mini skirt standing in the middle of the room looking off into space. I didn't notice before, but she's a mess. Her hair is like a rat's nest. Black makeup rings her eyes. Pink lipstick is smeared across her plump lips up her cheek.

Another memory flashes before my eyes: my dick pumping in and out of her *mouth.*

My boner returns with a vengeance.

"We can't tell anyone about this, Austin." Shay's words snap me to the present. Her eyes are sad. Ashamed. "I don't want you to get the wrong idea..."

Hurt pierces my heart, but my desire to please her is strong. "Okay. I won't say anything."

She sighs with what seems to be utter and total relief. Like I'm an embarrassment. "Good."

The thing is, I'm crushed and can't hide it. Shay is, hands down, the most beautiful creature on the planet. With the exception of playing video games, having a shot with her is all I've thought about for three years. Now we've actually had sex, I can barely remember what it felt like and she probably doesn't either. This sucks ass.

"Don't be that way, Austin. It's no big deal. We got drunk and I guess we smashed. Forget it happened. That's what I'm going to do." Shay picks up the bottle of vodka and a couple of the glasses from the coffee table. "I've got to take a shower. Check on my brother. You should go home."

I'm not the best at keeping my inner voice quiet though. "Maybe we could go out sometime for real." Shay stares at me blankly, like she didn't hear me. Something about her expression freaks me out. "Shay? Are you okay?"

"I don't know." She drops the bottle and glasses to the floor and furiously rubs her temples with her fingers. "My head feels like someone is pounding me with a hammer."

"I'll get you some Ibuprofen." I dash to the bathroom, open up the medicine cabinet and locate the tablets. I notice there are a few prescription bottles with Shay's name on them, but I don't know what they're for so I ignore them. I stop by the kitchen and get her a glass of water before I return to the living room and hand them to her.

She downs them in one gulp and sinks down into the sofa and shuts her eyes. "Thanks, Austin. You're the sweetest."

"So, what do you think about going out sometime?" I sit next to her and take her hand awkwardly, determined to get an answer. It kind of feels like my life depends on it.

Shay pulls it away and sighs. "Why are you *always* over here?"

"What?" I'm taken aback.

She sighs heavily. "Why don't you and Miles ever play video games at your house?"

Fuck, did Miles say anything about what's going on? I swore him to secrecy. "Uh...does it matter?"

"No. Not really." She opens her eyes and turns to look at me. "I don't want to hurt your feelings, Austin. I'm tired. I need a shower. I want to sleep for an entire day."

"Wha...Wha...What if you're pregnant?" I clap my hand over my mouth. I can't seem to stop myself from saying whatever is on my mind. But...I saw the evidence. So...I need to ask, right?

Shay exhales loudly. "Shit. We didn't use a condom?" She looks around the room frantically, spots the wet spot and winces. "I'm on the pill. It shouldn't be a problem."

"Oh. Okay. Good. Um... Last night...it was, um." I stumble over my words in my attempt to find the connection she and I must have shared the night before. God knows, I want a repeat.

She sits up and leans over her knees on her elbows. "Look. You and I aren't going to be a thing. Don't be a simp. We're not going to cuff. This isn't even a *situationship*. I don't want to DTR because I'm *not* into you that way. Whatever happened yesterday *isn't ever going to happen again*. If you're going to be a baby and go on and on about it, maybe you and Miles should hang out at your house and not here."

My mind whirls from all the cool-girl slang as all the air whooshes from my body. Her words are like ice picks that eviscerate me. I have no response whatsoever. All I can do is fight back tears like my life depends on it.

Shay looks away. "I'm sorry, but it's how I feel."

"Whatever." I stand and head for the door, still trying not to cry because that would be humiliating.

She gets up and follows me. "If it's any consolation, Bianca gave you a five-star flirt alert. You should ask *her* out."

"A *flirt alert?* I don't know what the fuck that is." I stop with my hand on the knob of the front door, but I don't turn around to face her. I can't.

I feel her hand tentatively touch my shoulder. Her voice is soft, consoling. "It means *she* thinks you're hot. To get a five star means she's into you. She'll probably fuck you, if that's what you want."

God. What a total fucking bitch.

Now I'm angry and I can't help but turn to look at her. "Wow. What a great friend, Shay. Didn't that girl Bianca fuck your brother while you fucked me? Probably tag-teamed him with your friend. Oh, I can't wait to go out with someone like that. She's a *real* prize. The ick-factor is off the fucking charts. I'm not interested and it's fucking weird you'd even suggest it."

"*Austin.*" Shay's face falls.

"For the record, I was a virgin," I admit. "I *always* wanted it to be you."

Shay drops her hand and hangs her head. "*Good God.* I said I'm *sorry.*"

"So stop saying it when you're not." I open the door. I feel a surge of anger, not only at Shay but at all the popular, pretty girls like her. They toy with people's emotions and treat people like trash because they're good-looking. My hand is literally shaking.

Shay looks at me with what seems like concern. I don't want it. I don't want anything from her.

I slip through the front door, avoiding her gaze as I leave. "I'm gonna head home. Later."

"Bye, Austin," Shay says quietly before clicking the door shut behind me.

On my walk home, the crisp morning air is a welcome relief, washing over me like a balm for my wounded pride. My thoughts are a jumble of anger, confusion, and hurt. She came on to me last night. She let me have sex with her. Didn't it mean anything? Why did she have to be such a...

Why do girls like her always seem to get away with this shit?

When I arrive home to my empty house, I know I should let it go. Chalk it up to a lesson learned, but I can't. I don't respond to any of Miles's calls or texts because the memory of Shay's callous words fester like a wound that won't heal. By the time I'm lying in bed staring at the ceiling unable to sleep, I know that something has fundamentally changed deep inside me.

My feelings for Shay, once tinged with admiration and lust, have quickly curdled into something darker.

I fucking hate her. I fucking hate everything she stands for. I will *never* allow myself to get involved with someone like her again. She used me and now I'm left to grapple with the fallout.

I can't let this come between me and Miles.

I'm not letting his bitch of a sister mess things up with the one person on earth who has my back.

No fucking way.

Chapter Ten

Back in the Present

"Why did you fuck me that night?"

I stare at Austin in utter and total disbelief.

The cold night air feels like it's piercing my body in a million places. I search Austin's face for any sense of double entendre. Irony. *Anything.*

But no, the soul-crushing tension in the air is real. His brown pupils are dilated with anger. But he also looks lost. Broken. *Shattered.*

He's *serious.*

"I... I...what?" I stammer, unable to comprehend what the hell is happening. I'm wracking my brain to figure out what he's talking about. Tears well up in my eyes and spill down my cheeks. "What do you mean, 'why did I fuck you that night?'"

He slams his fist on the arm of the chair he's sitting in. "Don't play innocent with me. Tell. Me. Why?"

"I don't know what you're talking about," I choke on my words as I crumble into the chair opposite him. His accusation is mortifying, considering my history. "Why would you make that up?"

I can't help it, I begin to cry. I'm so confused. My mind is spinning. Trying to recall some incident between me and Austin. Wondering if I'm in the twilight zone or if he's a psychopathic, gaslighting pig. Neither of which is ideal.

Austin laughs bitterly. "Fucking *typical*. You're going to act like it didn't happen and cry to get out of it."

I take a few cleansing breaths to regain control of my heart rate and emotions. It's been a stressful week. I haven't gotten much sleep. My meds are on point, but I don't want to trigger a stress seizure after being accused of fucking a guy I've never even kissed.

"Let's start at the beginning." I wrap my coat around me protectively, though I know it's not going to do shit to get me out of this conversation. "When did this supposedly happen?"

Austin leans forward and looks at me for a beat. "Do you truly not remember? Were you that drunk?"

"Um..." I suck in a breath and then decide he's not going to bully and berate me for another second. "I'm willing to figure this out, but I'm not going to continue this conversation if you're going to deliberately try to shame me. In answer to your question, *no*. I don't remember having sex with you. Please tell me when it happened, or I'm chalking you up to being certifiable."

"At your house. The night you brought your two friends over and they hooked up with Miles. We were drinking some sort of flavored vodka. You asked me to dance and kissed me..." Austin looks pained. "You sucked my cock. Told me to fuck you. I came inside you. You said you were on the pill. Then you dipped—claimed you weren't into me, I wasn't your type and I should hook up with your friend. In significantly fucking brutal terms, I might add. It was a ten-minute conversation. How in the fuck could you forget that?"

After hearing his blunt recollection, it feels like all of my organs have fallen out my body and nothing's left inside me but shame and confusion. I vaguely remember Miles telling me he lost his virginity to Bianca, but it's foggy like so much of my high school experience is. "I don't remember. I'm sorry. I don't."

"I have a hard time believing you, Shay." Austin stares at me as though he's trying to decipher whether *I'm* a psychopathic liar. His anger is palpable. "You can't brush off what happened by pretending it didn't happen."

This fucking disease. It never ceases to amaze me how much it's fucked up my life.

Continues to fuck up my life.

I draw in a deep breath, hating that I have to explain myself. Humiliated about what clearly happened between me and Austin. Furious that I'm forced to open up about an illness that dictated so much of my life before I got things under control.

So few people know about my struggles and those who do usually run away screaming. I'm well aware my confession won't bridge the chasm between me and Austin, but will likely widen it further. And yet, I owe the man a fucking explanation, even if I'm the one who'll have to deal with the emotional fallout when I'm able to process what I've learned tonight.

"Austin, I'm not pretending. Or playing games. Or *lying*." I feel like I'm about to hyperventilate. Then the words tumble from my mouth in a rush, tinged with desperation and fear. "I...I have focal epilepsy. It's a chronic noncommunicable disease of the brain where seizures create gaps in my memory when my meds aren't regulated. For the first couple of years after I was diagnosed, I was a mess."

He leans forward. His expression is a turbulent sea of pain, anger, and confusion. The bitterness in his eyes tears at my heart. "Miles mentioned you have a health condition on the way up here, but I don't see how it's relevant in this case. You didn't have a seizure that night. You got drunk and we fucked. Sounds like you're making excuses because you're embarrassed you did it with the gaming geek."

"Please, let me explain, it's not that simple," I find myself pleading, desperate to have someone—anyone—understand me. Even if it's *Austin*. "I don't usually have the type of seizures you see in movies. Mine appear like I'm spacing out. Sometimes for a few seconds, sometimes longer. I've been told that I stare off into the distance. In some cases, it appears that I'm alert and I spew a bunch of hurtful garbage. For me, because the seizures originate in a part of the brain that affects my memory, I rarely remember *anything*. Sometimes the gaps are huge—hours. It's a real relationship booster, let me tell you."

The silence stretches between us. A pause loaded with tension. Confusion. I see the moment where understanding begins to bloom in Austin's eyes. Where recognition dawns and replaces the anger and hurt that has been festering for all these years. "Not long after you woke up and we got dressed, that's what happened. You had a hundred-yard stare the entire time we were talking."

Bingo.

And that's when the gravity of what actually happened between us hits me.

Terrifies me.

What else don't I remember about high school?

Oh. My. God.

I tuck my legs up under me and bury my face in my arms. I'm so fucking ashamed. It's moments like this that make it hard for me to live with myself. "I'm sorry. So, so sorry. I don't know what to say." I can't look at him. No wonder he's been so weird with me. The man has been inside my body and I didn't even know it. "I was young, scared, and confused. The meds I was on also made me act so irrationally. Sometimes, I had no control of my actions, my words..."

"I had no idea, Shay." Though I can't see him, I can tell Austin's earlier anger is entirely diffused. His voice is soft and choked with emotion. "I'm the one who's sorry. I wish I had known. All these years I thought you did me dirty, when it was *me* who took advantage of *you*. God. I feel positively sick about it. I cared about you. So much. I really, truly did."

His words are surprising, but mean everything to me. I look up to see if he's sincere. Vulnerability and regret envelop his entire body. Tears continue to stream down my face as I nod and reach for him. He meets me halfway and we cling to each other in a turmoil of regret, loss, and apology for the years of misunderstanding.

We spend the next hour talking. His recollection is detailed. Insightful. As painful as it is to dive deep into a part of the evening I have no memory of, at least it clears up the fog of confusion that has shrouded his opinion of me for too long.

"So, did I come?" I poke Austin in the chest, hoping to lighten the mood.

"Uh." He buries his face in his hand. "I was a virgin. I think I shot my wad the second I realized I was all the way in."

It makes me smile, at least.

"I was a bit, uh, sex-crazy back in high school." We're sitting side by side on the sofa now. "I was so angry at my diagnosis. I wanted to feel good, so I had a lot of sex. You were so sweet back then, you didn't stand a chance with me or the friends I hung out with."

Austin laughs, a sound I realize I haven't heard terribly often. "God, Shay. You were the most beautiful girl at Lake Washington High School. I crushed on you so hard and had no game. When I woke up that morning and realized what happened—for me, it was a dream come true."

Internally, I wince. I know exactly what it's like to have a dream ripped away by someone you love with cruel words and a crass attitude. My heart aches for Austin and I'm sorry for any role I played in it.

"Bianca issued a five-star flirt alert for you. I remember that much." I gaze at his handsome face and realize that he hasn't changed much. Underneath the hurt, Austin is kind and smart. Now, he's also hot as hell.

Austin winces. "God, will you please tell me what a flirt alert means? Ever since high school, I thought you and your friends were using that term to make fun of me. When Cecily mentioned it earlier it sent me back to that insecure place."

"You think?" I raise an eyebrow. "God, Austin. It was just a stupid rating system we came up with to conceal that we had a rating system." I touch his arm. "So, uh...Bianca *was* being serious. If I remember correctly—and we know my memories aren't reliable so take this with a grain of salt—she thought you were hot. She said she wanted to pop your cherry."

He's horrified. "You talked about my *cherry?*"

"Do guys even have a cherry?" I tap my finger to my lip. "Seems like the wrong reference."

Austin grabs my finger and redirects it to my head. "Use your brain, woman. A cherry is a hymen."

His touch ignites the electricity I've felt recently whenever I'm near Austin. We stare at each other for a second, undoubtedly realizing how fast this conversation has turned into something that feels a lot like flirting.

No. It feels a lot like verbal *foreplay*.

We break apart quickly and I jump up. "How long have we been out here?"

"Fuck. I have no idea." He tightens his scarf. "It's cold, though. We should hurry and catch the gondola back to the hotel before it stops running."

Together we cross the patio to the double doors to the restaurant. My heart sinks. The glimmering laughter and camaraderie of earlier is now eerily absent. The doors are locked, the inside lights are shut off and a deafening silence engulfs us. My heart races when I realize I can no longer hear the distinctive sound of the gondola gears screeching.

Holy shit. We're alone on the mountaintop. Everyone's gone.

"Austin, I think we missed the last gondola." I pound on the glass, hoping someone will hear and help us get to the hotel.

Nothing.

Austin darts across the deck, past where we were sitting and looks over at the terminal. "It's dark. Shut down."

"My phone is in the restaurant office, do you have yours?" I pat the pockets on my jacket to recheck.

He shakes his head. "I left it in my hotel room on accident."

"Are you kidding me?" I pound on the windows harder. "We're stuck up here?"

Austin returns to my side. "Looks like it."

Chapter Eleven

A Few Minutes Later

I'm at my breaking point.

Now's not the time to crumble, though. Shay and I have real problems. It's freezing and starting to snow. Hard.

"We have to find somewhere to take shelter." I try the door again. "Maybe even break a window to get in."

Shay puts the hood of her snowy white puffer jacket up. "Can't we figure something out until morning? I'd hate to overreact and cause issues when we're the ones to blame for missing our ride. What about the gondola terminal?"

"I guess it's worth a try." I hold my ungloved hand out to her, blown away by her cool head under pressure. "Let's stick together."

Her blue eyes blink up at me. She's gorgeous with snowflakes melting on her lashes. "Okay." Her voice is trusting as she takes my hand.

The past hour has been emotionally draining and somewhat cathartic. It took courage for Shay to reveal the layers of her struggle with epilepsy after I came at her so aggressively. I'm finding it hard to process how wrong I was about her and what an asshole I've been. I had no idea she was essentially living in her own hidden battleground and warring with her own mind on a daily basis. I can't imagine trying to piece together memory gaps spanning hours.

Moments of her life lost in a fog of unawareness.

Pieces of herself lost in the abyss of time.

Times where she did things she doesn't know about.

Learning that she and I...

What a mind fuck.

We trudge through the snow to the terminal and discover it's locked down as tightly as the restaurant.

There's even less of a shelter here than at the seating area on the patio where we've spent the past hour.

"Crap. Now what?" Shay looks around frantically.

I glance up the hill and see what looks like a ski patrol shack. I point to it. "What about there?"

"We should try." She wraps her arms around herself, shivering.

I know the feeling. I can barely feel my hands. "Let's go."

We hike the hundred yards or so up the hill in the powdery snow. My feet are soaked. Aside from the short walk from the gondola to the restaurant, I didn't plan on being out in the elements tonight. I'm not dressed for this. *At all.* The shack is tiny, about the size of a small tool shed. I try the handle and nearly shout with relief when the door opens.

"Let's get inside." I gesture to Shay, who follows close behind. "Hold it open for a sec so I can see if there's a flashlight or matches."

Shay leans against the door so it won't slam shut. "Wait. Here's a switch." She flicks it and the little hut is bathed in a dim but illuminating light.

"Well, that's a bonus." I glance around. It's quite sparse but there's a counter with a coffee pot. A small fridge. A bunch of fences, ropes, bamboo poles, and signs are propped against one wall, ready for the morning. A few jackets and helmets are on pegs on the back wall. A square fold-out table and some metal chairs are the only furniture. Aha! A heater. "Let's warm this place up."

I flick the switch and the orange glow makes me sigh with relief. This isn't going to be so bad. In fact, it's perfect. Shay and I can spend some time together and quash all of this shit once and for all.

Taking two seats and pulling them closer to the heater, I swallow hard and sit down. Shay takes her snow boots off and tosses them against the door, then sits sideways facing me as if she's ready to dive back in. Her cheeks are red from the cold but her tears have dried. She's strong. Resilient.

Stunning.

The lump in my throat seems insurmountable as I find the words to form questions that remain unasked. "So, how did you find out...um..." My words trail off.

"My original episode happened at the Miss Teen Washington qualifiers when I was sixteen, I had a grand mal seizure in the dressing room. I spent two days at the hospital because I bit through my tongue. Word got around quickly on the circuit." She winces as she recalls the incident. "I'll never forget what Salvio, my coach, told me the day he dumped my ass, 'Sweetheart, facial beauty matters, body proportions matter, your fashion sense matters and your inner diva matters. You might check all those boxes but, unfortunately, the harsh reality is you're not winning anything if you start convulsing on stage. I've got to focus on girls who can *place*.'" Shay rolls her eyes. "He wasn't wrong, but what an asshole."

I can't help it. I reach over, hug her tightly then release her. "I'm so sorry, Shay. That's inexcusable."

"Yeah. The thing is, without Salvio, I didn't have a chance in hell of competing at the top level, so I quit. What was the point if I couldn't be Miss Washington and get the scholarship money? It's not like I loved the pageants themselves, there's something ridiculous about walking across a stage in a bikini and six-inch heels." Shay rests her head on her arm, which is draped along her chair.

"I vaguely remember you being in the hospital. I also remember you talking funny for a couple weeks." I mirror her position to see her better.

She smiles. "God. It sucked. Particularly because my mom didn't want anyone to know because she saw how awful the pageant people were to me. We made up a story about how I fell down to explain how I bit my tongue. I'm surprised no one ever found out at school."

"How did you handle it?" I stare into her blue eyes that seem to hold so many secrets. "I'd never have known you were dealing with something so traumatizing. To me, you were the popular, unattainable sister of my best friend. I was always tongue-tied around you."

Shay crosses her eyes then laughs. "Smoke and mirrors. It took a few years for me to find the precise concoction of medicine to control things. Luckily, we were able to stop the grand mal seizures immediately—they're the type most people associate with epilepsy. The problem is, my incidents are so subtle I didn't realize they were consistent with my diagnosis. I thought things were under control so I was too casual about taking my medication."

"What do you mean?" I'm fascinated. I had no idea about the nuances of epilepsy. Never had reason to.

"Well, for instance, for a long time I was actually blacking out without realizing it. It took some time to recognize what was happening. It's kind of like losing consciousness in my own brain but to everyone around me, I seem perfectly functional. When I'd come out of an episode, I'd be confused and groggy. Conversations and activities wouldn't register at all." Shay scrunches her nose. "It was freaky. I thought I was going insane because I wouldn't remember chunks of time."

My mouth drops open. "How did you figure it out?"

"It took a while for me to piece it together. People would tell me I did something. Or said something. I'd have no memory of it so I was immensely defensive—I thought people were definitely fucking with me. They thought I was lying. When it started happening more often, I was scared." She shudders. "I didn't want to deal with it, though. I used the skills I learned in pageants to cover it up. Laugh it off. Cause chaos to divert attention elsewhere."

"Is that what happened that night?" I reach over and cup her face. She leans into me. "Did you have a blackout?"

She nods sadly. "Yeah. It's the likely explanation. Plus, we were binge drinking, which is a big no-no. Back then, I didn't care. I wanted to be normal. I didn't realize how grave the implications were."

"And you do now?" My thumb strokes her cheek. We stare into each other's eyes and I feel like I've never been closer to anyone in my life.

"Yeah. That summer before college. Miles figured it out. He convinced me my behavior was erratic and unpredictable and did some research online and suspected it related to my epilepsy. He started keeping track of things I'd said and done that I had no recollection of. Scary? Yes. Dangerous? Undoubtedly. Hilarious? Sometimes!" Shay stares off in space and chuckles. "My mom and dad took convincing. They thought I was being a difficult and rebellious teenager. Eventually, they listened to Miles and took me to a new doctor who got to the bottom of it. The official term is 'complex partial seizures.'"

Shay shifts positions and leans toward the heater, rubbing her hands. "Over the years I've worked with my doctors to find the perfect cocktail to control it."

"So you're better now?" I bend down and untie my wet shoes. Take off my socks and extend my toes toward the warmth.

Shay shrugs off her coat. "I'll never be cured, but I manage it through various wellness mechanisms. Medication, of course. I don't drink except for an occasional glass of wine or champagne. Get a lot of sleep. I eat clean and stay away from carbs." She peeks up at me. "Except for mashed potatoes with lots of butter. Oh, and hot chocolate, because *yum*. A girl's gotta have at least a couple of indulgences."

She's so goddamn beautiful. Now that I know what I know, I'm not sure how I'm going to stop myself falling in love with her all over again. I can't take my eyes off her. Everything inside me has shifted and I'm spinning out of control.

It's not like I'll have a chance in hell with her. After how I treated her for the past couple of weeks, there's no way she'd ever reciprocate my feelings. Not in this lifetime.

"Are you okay?" Shay reaches over and taps my knee. "You look freaked out. Did I scare the shit out of you with all of this?"

I cough and shake my head. "Uh...no. I mean, yeah. I mean no. *Argh.*" I clear my throat. "What I mean to say is no, you haven't freaked me out. You've been through so much and I have to apologize for what a complete and total fuckwad I've been. I feel like the biggest asshole that ever walked the face of the earth in how I've treated you."

"Well, give yourself a break." She squeezes my knee then resumes rubbing her hands together in front of the heater. "I feel like a complete loser for finding out you and I had sex and I don't even remember it. It's no wonder you hated me."

Suddenly the entire room is charged with an energy that's hard to deny.

Shay looks at me and I see unmistakable attraction—no, desire in the depths of her eyes.

Without thinking, I lean over, cup her face between my palms, and press my mouth to hers with little finesse. She moans against my lips and launches herself against me, straddling my legs, winding her arms around my neck and slashing her tongue against mine.

We pour everything into the kiss as she writhes against me. My cock throbs against her hot center and I grip her ass to yank her closer.

When we eventually come up for air she rests her hands on my shoulders and cocks her head.

"So, let's make this time one I'll remember."

Chapter Twelve

Minutes Later

Austin looks at me with trepidation.

One thing I've never been shy about is sex, and I haven't had any since Devon broke up with me.

Austin's the hottest guy I've ever seen in my life. Now that I understand why he's been acting so...shitty, it makes perfect sense. I'm used to dealing with this part of my illness. He isn't the first person and won't be the last who's experienced one of my episodes. I can't hold him responsible for feeling the way he did. Or hating me because of it.

I could choose to be upset about the gaps in my memory, the parts of my own life that I've missed and can't remember but, as my therapist says, what good will that do? And what good would it do to blame Austin for hating me for something I have no recollection of?

Now he knows my secret, so I'm free.

We're free.

I'm going to live in the present and enjoy every single opportunity that comes my way.

Tonight, he and I are stranded in a ski patrol lodge. How fucking hot is that?

I move off his lap and back up a few steps. Grab the bottom of my sweater and pull it up over my head, leaving me in my bra, panties, leggings, and knee-high socks. I shake out my hair and lick my lips. "I want you to fuck me, Austin."

"*Shay.*" His eyes bug out.

"I'm not having a blackout episode, if that's what you're worried about." I take a step toward him and brace my hands on his thighs so he can see down my hot-pink bra. "Let's give this another shot."

He grabs one of my hands and places it on the bulge in his jeans. "Yeah. Let's give it another shot."

The moon shines through the window behind Austin, blurred against the snowstorm outside this little hut. His hand slides around my head and he brings my face to his, kissing me softly. Sucking my bottom lip between his. Our tongues meet and slide in a languid rhythm as he grows bigger and harder under my palm.

"Back in high school, I had this plan," he says between kisses, "you'd fall for the nerdy guy," he nuzzles my cheek and sucks the spot behind my ear, "and you'd be my girlfriend," he drags his lips down my neck to the swell of my breasts, "and I'd make love to you every day," he dips his tongue down the front of my bra and licks my puckered nipple, "and worship every inch of your beautiful body."

I squeeze his cock through his jeans. "Oh yeah?"

"Ah, Shay. *Jesus*. Fuck it." Austin releases my hand and pulls the cups of my bra down. Ravenously devours my breasts, sucking then lightly grazing my nipples with his teeth. One after the other.

Oh, it's on. I straddle him again and sink down on his lap. Rub my pussy all over his bulge. Wind my arms around his neck as he feasts on my breasts. I want to drive him to the edge. "Do whatever you want to me. I'm going to love it. I *know* it."

"Oh, I intend to." He reaches behind me to unhook my bra and tosses it on the ground. Cups my breasts with his hands and smashes them together. Licks my nipples. Buries his bearded face in my cleavage. "I fucking fantasize about your tits, Shay. You have no idea. Before tonight's over, I'm going to fuck them. But not before I fuck your sweet pussy. I've never forgotten your tight, wet heat and tonight you're going to remember *everything* I do to you."

I nearly come when I hear Austin talk dirty.

Seconds later, we're standing. Austin hooks his thumbs in the waistband of my leggings and yanks them down to my knees, along with my hot-pink panties. He sinks to his knees and pulls my knee-highs off one by one, then disentangles my leggings from my feet and tosses them on top of my socks, leaving me fully naked before him.

I've never been so turned on in my life.

Running his hands up my legs, he widens my stance so he can kiss my inner thigh. I nearly collapse when his tongue dips between my folds. He grips my hips to hold me in place and I can't help but cry out when he lifts my leg and bends it over his shoulder. The tips of his fingers spread me apart and it feels like he's French kissing my pussy from my opening up to my clit, which he captures between his lips and sucks on gently as he slides one finger into my opening.

"God, Austin. Oh...*Oh*..." My leg starts to tremble. I grab a fistful of his hair and buck against his face. He swirls his tongue furiously around my little bud and I'm about to explode when he pulls his finger out and stops licking me. I'm stunned when he cups my ass and he presses kisses along my stomach and waist. My pussy clenches around nothing, leaving me frustrated.

When I'm about to protest, his hands slide up my back and around to my breasts. "Patience, baby," he murmurs against my belly as he looks up at me and pinches my nipples hard.

"Oh, God. *Yessss*." I nearly fall over but catch myself on the chair behind him. Undeterred, Austin trails kisses along my hipbone, down the thigh bent over his shoulder and back again, all while strumming my nipples into diamond-hard points.

As my body gets used to this rhythm and I relax, he grabs my ass with one hand and slides two fingers into my dripping core and pulls them out gradually. In and out. In and out. His kisses down my belly to my clit and sucks on it gently, then harder as he pumps his fingers inside me, working me into another hip-thrusting frenzy as I fuck his face.

It's not long before my body starts to shake and I'm on the brink of climaxing when he, once again, pulls away abruptly.

This time, I'm pissed and remove my leg from his shoulder. "Oh, my *God*..."

Austin stands and yanks my leg back up under his forearm and wraps it around his waist. Holding me in place, he kisses me and I taste myself on his tongue. "*Please . . .*" I beg. He's making me crazy with how badly I want him. Every inhibition I've ever had is out the window. I grind myself against his cock, seeking contact.

Seeking release.

"Please what, Shay?" Austin smirks as he pulls off his shirt, revealing sculpted pecs and an eight-pack that rivals any athlete I've ever seen.

I can't stop myself from reaching out and palming his chest. Glide my fingers down his carved core. He's so incredibly hot. More attractive in every way than anyone I've ever been with. I tilt my head up to him and kiss his soft lips. Suck on his tongue a little. Whisper, "I need you."

"Then tell me specifically what you want, Shay." His fingers sneak back up to my nipples and twist them, sending a bolt of ecstasy straight down my core.

I lower my leg and undo the buckle on his belt. I understand the assignment. He likes it when he's given some direction via dirty talk. "I want your cock to be buried inside my pussy when I come..."

His lips crash down on mine as he takes over, pulling his belt off and then stepping out of his jeans. He bends slightly to remove his socks, then peels his boxer briefs down his legs so he can kick them aside. When he stands, I gasp. His cock flush against his stomach, long, thick, and harder than steel.

Immediately I reach between us and wrap my hand around him. "It's a crime that I don't remember this beauty."

"I'm gonna make sure you never forget it after tonight." He steps close, reaches around to grab my ass, bends his knees slightly and lifts me up off my feet.

Gripping his shoulders with both hands, I wind my legs around his waist so the undershaft of his dick slides between my pussy lips. He effortlessly moves me up and down the length of him, positioning his crown perfectly so it hits my clit with each pass. Our mouths meet desperately, teeth clashing, tongues dancing. As we kiss, he lifts my body up slightly so the tip of his cock breaches my opening—just a little—but not quite enough.

"Like that?" He buries his face in my neck. "Or do you need more?"

Without answering, I hook my feet together, bear down and squeeze my inner thighs against his legs. I'm wetter than I've ever been in my life, so within seconds I'm impaled all the way to the hilt. He's so big that it takes a minute for me to adjust, but it's glorious.

I've never been filled so deliciously.

I lean back slightly to catch his gaze. "More."

"If that's what you want," Austin growls as he slaps my ass hard. "I'm going to give it to you."

Chapter Thirteen

Seconds Later

I thought I remembered how it felt to be inside Shay.

For years, I've tried to conjure up the memory, fantasizing about her every time I've fucked another woman. Every time I've beat off. Every time I've even thought about sex...

It's always been *her*.

Reality blows fantasy away by a mile.

Never, in a million years, did I dream I'd fuck Shay again. Now it's happening, I'm going to stay in the moment and enjoy every single minute we have together. Revel in how perfect it is to be buried in her hot, wet heat.

She opens her eyes to find me watching her. I press my lips against hers and slide my tongue over then into her mouth and explore her with little nips, licks, and kisses. As we make out, I back her against the whiteboard, giving me leverage to bounce her on my cock. My hands slide under her thighs and I roll my hips up and into her, ensuring my pubic bone hits her clit in exactly the right place.

Shay moans and clings tightly around my neck. "Austin, yessss...right there."

"Do you need to come, baby?" She's so wet and slick, I've kept her on the brink for a while.

She sucks my bottom lip and clenches around my cock. "So badly."

"Look at me," I command and her blue eyes meet mine. "I want you with me when you break apart."

Shay bites her lip when I reach between us and circle her swollen clit. I'm pumping into her, searching for the angle that will take her to nirvana. Her legs squeeze around my waist and she uses her heels to deepen each thrust. I know I've hit the spot when her mouth drops open and she gasps. Our eyes are still locked as we move together, building to something that feels life changing.

I was dead serious earlier. She's never going to forget the way I fuck her tonight. I want to burn myself into her skin. Into her memory. Ruin her for anyone else. God, the way her tits feel pressed against my chest. I have to break eye contact for a moment when I bend to kiss along her cleavage then gently bite the soft, sensitive skin between her breasts.

"Ohmygod. Austin. What are you doing to me?" Shay wails and digs her nails into my shoulders as she thrusts against me, desperate to find release.

Knowing I give her this much pleasure conjures up possessive feelings. I want to be the only man who touches her. Tastes her. Fucks her. Makes her come.

I try to keep control the best I can, but I'm at the brink. Her walls squeeze and contract around my cock. The scent of our sex permeates the air. *It's time.* I need her to go over so I grind my hipbones against her and thrust so deeply Shay makes a guttural sound then shudders around me, sucking in air. Another cant of my hips conjures a moan so uninhibitedly carnal, I can't stop myself from shooting my load deep inside her.

We continue to move together for several minutes. Kissing and groping and coming down off the greatest orgasmic high I've ever had.

"Are you okay?" I tip Shay's chin up to look at me when I let her legs down and slip out of her.

She draws me to her so we're wound together, leaning against the whiteboard. "Yeah. Austin. Wow. That was incredible." Abruptly, she breaks free and pulls on her sweater. "Should we try to get a little sleep?"

I can't help but feel dismissed, but I don't want to overreact. "Sure, we can conceivably use the ski coats to put together a makeshift bed by the heater."

"Yeah, great idea." Shay grabs the clothing off the pegs on the wall and we lay them out in a crisscross pattern on the floor.

I find a storage box tucked under the cabinet. Inside are several first-aid kits and a bunch of emergency thermal blankets. I hold one up. "Aha. We can use these to stay warm."

Silently, we unwrap them and lay them out on top of the coats. I haven't bothered to put my clothes on but Shay doesn't say anything as she gathers the rest of her clothes. I'm disappointed, maybe what happened wasn't as exceptional for her as it was for me. It's like the energy between us has fizzled into nothing.

I plunk down on the coats and sit cross-legged, unable to stop the heavy sigh from escaping my lips.

"What's wrong?" Shay glances down at me.

I shrug and wrap a fluffy blanket around me, deciding to be honest. "Was that okay for you? Are you freaked out because I came inside you? I'm clean."

"It was great, and no. I'm on the pill. Have been since I was sixteen. Can't have any mistakes..." She looks around the cabin.

"Shay." My voice is harsh. "Look at me."

She stills and drags her eyes to mine. "What?"

"Tell me what's going on with you. You're kinda freaking me out. Are you having an episode?" I can't understand the difference in our energy from when we were making love and now.

Shay's eyes fill with tears. "No, what makes you say that?"

"Come here, sit with me." I motion for her to join me. "That was the best sex of my life, I want to be close to you. After all that's happened tonight, I want us to have this time together. You can trust me, Shay."

She takes two steps forward and kneels before me. "You want to be close to me?"

"So much." I gather her to me and pull her onto my lap. Kiss her temple. Eyelids. Then her lips.

Shay opens her mouth and relaxes into my chest as we kiss. My arm is wrapped around her shoulder angled so I can run my fingers through her soft, blonde hair. My other hand finds its way under her sweater where I cup her breast and thumb her nipple. Her fingers graze my chest. I lean back, taking her with me and we reposition ourselves in the makeshift bed.

"You must be an utterly terrific boyfriend." She kisses my chin and looks up at me.

I stroke her hair on her forehead with my finger. "I haven't had many girlfriends. Nothing serious anyway. Quite a few FWB because I love sex—I wonder who got me hooked?" I boop her nose. "Though, there hasn't been anyone in a while."

"Well, you've upped your game considerably." She giggles. "I think you rattled my brain with that orgasm."

Kissing her forehead, then her cheek, I find her lips again. "I liked making you feel fantastic."

We make out for a long time cuddled up together. Sweet kisses. Loving pecks. Feathery nuzzles. Her hands lightly roam all over my torso. I keep her cocooned in my arms, threading my fingers through her hair. When her hand cups my face, I cover them with mine. Her blue eyes bore into mine. Every now and then our lips meet in a long, drawn-out smooch.

"It's cozy in here." Shay runs her nose along my jawline and reaches down to grip my stiff cock in her fist. "Maybe we should go another round."

Her touch sends me into another frenzy. I caress her nape and pull her face to mine, this time our kiss is hungry. Demanding. My tongue sweeps over hers as she strokes me from root to tip. "Let's take your sweater off."

"Okay." Shay sits up and pulls it over her head.

Seeing her taut nipples flips a switch. I cup her breasts in my hands and bring my lips to them, lavishing kisses and little bites across her cleavage. "I worship these tits. My God, you're perfect."

Shay winds her arms around my head, holding me in place. "I swear, there's an excellent chance you'll make me come by sucking on my nipples like that."

"You think?" I drag my teeth across one of the peaks. "Should we try?"

She shakes her head. "I like your cock too much."

"Well, then lie down and tell me to fuck you." My voice is hoarse, oozing with desire.

Shay unfolds the thermal blanket and smooths it over the coats. Lies back, bending one arm under head and skimming the other deliberately down her torso between her parted legs. She circles her clit, occasionally dipping lower into her wet channel, which is still filled with my come. I'm mesmerized and can't look away from her pretty pink pussy on display for me.

"I want you to fuck me," she whispers.

My eyes are riveted to where she's fingering herself. "Lick them," I demand as I kneel between her legs.

Her blue eyes flash. Languidly, she drags her fingers through her folds and brings them to her lips. Her tongue darts out for a long lick before she places them against my lips and I suck our tangy juices.

Shay writhes below me, pointing to my dick, which juts hard and proud from my body. "In me. Now."

"Bossy." I grab Shay's ankles and raise her legs until her calves are pressed against my chest and her ankles rest on my shoulders. Her tits jiggle when I reach for her waist and pull her body against mine. Sink all the way inside with one thrust.

She cries out, "*Yesssss*," fueling me to push in as deep as I can go.

Feeling her velvet wetness unleashes something wild and untethered. My hips rut against her, driving my cock into her perfect little pussy. I bend Shay's legs so her thighs press against her tits. She digs her nails into my back as I continue to drill into her.

I let myself spin out of control.

No thought about the cold. Or being caught. Work. Nothing.

All I want is Shay.

Something tells me, tonight's going to change my life.

Chapter Fourteen

An Hour Later

I feel like I'm in a warm, safe cocoon that I never want to emerge from.

I'm also disoriented and my arm is killing me.

Austin snores softly against my neck, his arms snug around my middle. I feel his erection nestled in my ass crack. Good Lord, the man has *stamina*. Holy hell. His cock is like a homing missile. Not that I'm complaining. Well, maybe one small complaint. I haven't slept on the floor in, well, ever. After tonight it's memory foam beds for the rest of my life, that's for positive.

Careful not to wake him, I turn in his arms and watch him puff little breaths of air in his sleep. A day ago, I'd never have expected to wake up nestled next to Austin

Andrews in a makeshift bed of emergency blankets and ski patrol gear. Spilling my guts. Getting stranded on the top of a mountain. Passing time by fucking the guy who used to hate my guts.

Why does it feel like so much more than that?

Why does it scare the life out of me?

The air is thick with shared warmth and confessions from the night before. I run my hands along his cut chest. Hot damn. He's beautiful. "Your body is amazing. I want to lick you from head to toe," I rest my head against his chest and whisper.

I feel his lips press against my temple. "Being licked *anywhere* by you has been a spank-bank fantasy of mine for years."

His hands roam across my skin until I'm tingly. Turned-on. I feel close to him and I definitely want to be intimate with him again, but so much uncertainty still lingers.

Gazing up into his deep, soulful brown eyes, a silent oath blooms between us. This is a safe space where we can venture deeper and unlock the hidden chambers of our pasts. Discover the events that have molded us, shaped our fears and aspirations. "I poured out my soul to you yesterday, but I don't know much about you. How did you get to be so ambitious at such an early age?"

He hesitates, a flicker of pain crosses his eyes. "It's...not a topic I enjoy. I'm not close to either one of my parents. I don't exactly have a family of my own."

"What do you mean? You lived down the street with your family." I'm confused. Austin always seemed so pulled together.

The tremulous vulnerability in his voice tugs at my heart. "Yeah, I lived with my mom, shithead of a stepdad and their devil spawn—*kidding*. My biological father deserted us when I was ten. He up and left for Florida and started a new family. I haven't talked to him in almost twenty years."

"My parents have this picture-perfect marriage, at least to the outside world. Dad is a famous ex-hockey star. Mom is a former model. I was raised in this en-vironment where I was expected to be flawless, to be a certain kind of perfect." As I say the words I realize how much I long to be free from such high expectations. "I've always craved my own identity, separate from the glamour and the spotlight. It never felt like Miles had similar stress."

"You had too much pressure. I didn't have any." Understanding blossoms in Austin's eyes.

I stroke his eyebrow with my thumb. "My brother became your family. That's why you were always over at our house."

"He and I have always been simpatico. Our shared passion for technology. The desire to build Hungry Llama proved something to everyone who ridiculed and bullied us for being computer geeks. We did okay. I'm happy with my life." Austin touches his lips to mine. "Even better now."

In the dappled orange light of the heater he sips from my lips and entwines his fingers with mine. We're wrapped together tightly. Whispers of the past give way to the potential of a future. Austin drops gentle kisses all over my face like I'm the most beautiful thing he's ever seen. His intensity is staggering. Humbling. He makes me feel like a fucking goddess.

His sweet, gentle kisses turn hungry as he moves down my body. I'm lost in the sensation of his beard against my skin. Lazy flicks of his tongue trace the curve of my breast before he rakes the edge of his teeth across my nipple. My head lolls back when he slides one arm up my torso as he kneels back between my legs.

Every part of me is hypersensitive. Each cell comes alive with desire as he kisses and touches my body. I'm ready for anything he's willing to give me. I reach up and thread my fingers through his hair, gripping the side of his face to pull him closer. This kiss isn't sweet. It's the promise of passion buried deep inside me.

Austin holds the key to unlock it.

His cock nudges my opening and I'm shameless, rolling my hips to grind my pussy against him. Austin's eyes roll back into his head when he slides through my folds. "Not quite yet," he grits out. "I want to make you come first."

"Yes please." I drape my arms around his neck and let him have his way with me. I mean, why not? The man knows what he's doing.

Austin kisses down the hollow of my throat as I dig my nails into his shoulders. He teases my nipple to a hard point as he continues down my body. Every one of my muscles flex with pleasure against his as he progresses down my body. Licking over my sensitive skin, he approaches my needy pussy, pausing to kiss my hip bones and nibble around my belly button.

He presses my thighs wide and studies my most private parts. With a guttural groan, Austin spreads me open with his thumbs and takes a long, slow lick. Then another. And another. My muscles tremble as he licks and kisses my pussy like he's addicted to my—our—taste. Brings me to the edge...

"Fuck my mouth." Austin shoves his hands under my ass and holds me against his face.

Holy shit.

Is he for real?

I don't shy away. I'm all in. I roll my hips against his lips. Grip a handful of his hair and guide him to where I need him. I'm writhing and moaning. Bucking and grinding. Clamping my thighs against his ears when I shudder through my release.

I fall back on our makeshift bed in an orgasm-stunned state. There's no way I'll be moving anytime soon. Austin rests his head on my belly and traces my opening with his thumb. My fingers stroke through his hair. "You're phenomenal at that. My entire body is tingly."

Austin moves up beside me and lies down sideways, facing me. "Mission accomplished."

"When did you become so profoundly sexy?" I kiss down his ridiculously carved abs to the trail that leads to his impressive cock.

He massages my head, watching me. "You think I'm sexy?"

I trace my fingertip from the tip to his root, spreading precum down his shaft. "Oh, yeah."

My gaze locks with his and I slide my hand up and down a few times before bending to lick around his crown. Austin growls when I suck on his head then snarls when my tongue wiggles in his little opening. Feeling extraordinarily satisfied with his reaction, I change positions to get a better look at his beautiful dick. He's big enough that I can't fit him entirely in my mouth, but I do the best I can, licking and sucking until he's writhing under me and thrusting his hips against my lips.

When I dip my head down to suck on his ball sac, Austin yelps. "Oh, God. Shay. I've never done that...it feels incredible but I want to be inside you when I come."

"I'm on board." I sit up. His expression is of utter and total ravenous desire. I'm ready to fuck his brains out again. Or, for him to fuck mine out. Maybe both.

"Ass up." His voice is ragged. Rough. "Brace yourself on the floor."

A shiver skates up my skin as I turn over and present myself to him. My sensitive nipples rub against the ski patrol jacket. I haven't been this exposed and vulnerable during sex—ever. Austin aligns his body behind me. The hair on his thighs brushes the backs of mine. I turn my face and moan when I feel the tip of his cock breach my entrance.

I feel every inch of him as he presses inside me. Gradually. Carefully. His hands pet up and down my back and over the curve of my ass. Instinctively, I push back against him as he ultimately makes his way inside. The edge of burn at his invasion wisps away into pleasure as I adjust to this position. Then it takes all of my control not to shove myself back as hard as I can.

"Patience," Austin whispers for the second time tonight. He swivels his hips, sending sharp zings of pleasure through my body before bending over me and kissing my spine. "You're the one who's sexy, Shay."

Austin continues steadily thrusting in and out of me. He controls the speed. Depth. Angle. His body dominates me. I'm in some sort of trance that allows me to fully let go and enjoy what he's doing to my body. I'm safe with him, of that I'm positive. Primarily when he begins to go harder. Deeper. Faster. I drown in the sensation of being stretched. Worked over. His hand reaches around and strums my clit and the orgasm that's been building is deep and all-consuming.

"You're so beautiful. My every dream," he moans, leaving me speechless. I've thought this man hated me with every fiber of his being, but I know the truth now. It was the opposite. It's always been the opposite because he thought I brutally rejected him all those years ago.

My head falls forward as I tighten around him and words slip out. "You're magical, Austin. Everything I've ever wanted."

His fingers work my little nub faster in time to his thrusts. Moments later I explode and he follows, both of us overwhelmed with how amazing we are together. Austin's face is in my hair as we fall in a heap. He holds me against him, still pulsing inside me.

When he slips out, I sling my leg over him and look up at him sleepily. "Part of me never wants tonight to end."

"All of me thinks this is only the beginning." Austin tugs me to him until I'm fully enclosed in his arms.

As perfect as tonight has been and as much as I'd like to believe him, I can't help but feel unsettled.

He's had this fantasy of me for years.

What if I'm not enough?

Chapter Fifteen

Three Hours Later

The sound of a loud crash wakes me up.

I bolt up, freaked out that we've been caught.

"Ohmygosh, I'm so sorry." Shay scurries over and crouches next to me. She wears nothing but her sweater and sexy knee-high socks. "I didn't mean to bang into the chair. I'm straightening up. I don't know what time the ski patrol report to work, but I'm guessing early since they have to set up the course."

Relieved, I pull her down into my lap. Lightly grip her face. "Relax. I'll help. We have time."

Shay relaxes into me. She's scrubbed the remnants of makeup off her face, leaving her fresh and clean. My lips find hers and we softly kiss. Her hands rest on my shoulders as our tongues move together. I don't know where we stand, but having her in my arms on a regular basis is what I want.

"You're insatiable." She wriggles against my stiff cock. "How many times did we fuck? Four?"

"He likes you, what can I say?" I turn her in my lap so her back is against my front. Cup her breast over her sweater. "I bet we have time for another round, or are you too sore?"

She leans her head back against my chest and pulls my hand away. Looks up at me. "I'm going to be completely honest with you. I didn't get much sleep this week and my meds are down in the hotel room. I'm feeling stressed about getting back down as soon as possible."

Shit. How could I forget everything she confided in me?

"I'm an idiot." I shift out from under her and stand, grab my boxer briefs and pull them up. "Let's get moving. Your health is the most important thing."

She looks up at me and licks her lips when my cock is covered up by my underwear. "On second thought, it's a real shame to put him away."

"You snooze, you lose." I tilt my head.

We dress quickly and finish restoring order to the hut. In fact, it looks better than it did when we arrived. Our tidying up is interrupted by gropes and stolen kisses that give me hope our newfound connection might lead to something meaningful. I don't want to lose our bond forged in shared vulnerabilities, whispered dreams and a night of the hottest goddamn sex I've ever had.

Now we wait. Shay and I position ourselves at the window where we have a view of the gondola looming up the mountain against the backdrop of approaching dawn. I stare out at the terrain. Last night it easily snowed a foot or two. My shoes are essentially dry, I'm not looking forward to the short trudge back to the terminal.

"Whatcha thinking?" Shay stretches her long legs on either side of mine and leans in to stroke my beard.

"The inevitable return to reality." I turn toward her and cup her hand to my jaw.

She loops her arms around my shoulders and scoots forward until she's in my lap, straddling me. "Do you think this is the new normal?"

"Hopefully." I rub my cheek against hers. "I'd like to see where this goes."

"Officially?" Her blue eyes catch mine, confused.

Old feelings of insecurity wash over me. Maybe she thought this was a one and done. My defenses automatically activate. "*Oh.*" I bite down the acid of disappointment and look back out the window.

"Hey." Shay grips my chin between her thumb and forefingers and wrenches my face back around. "Don't do that."

I sigh and look at her, feeling a little sick to my stomach. I still fucking love this girl and...

"I think this could be something special." She kisses my nose. "But, I'm a lot to handle. I know that. Devon broke up with me because..."

I grab her ass and pull her against me. "We don't talk about other men. Or other women. We're the only two people in this room."

"Austin, I was with him for almost a decade. I'm rebuilding my life. You haven't been around me for years and until two days ago you fucking hated me because I—" She stops herself, letting her fingers thread through my hair. "We're clearly sexually compatible. I also find you to be the most fascinating, handsome, incredible man I've ever met. I want to do this, but we should take it slow."

I squeeze her ass cheeks. "I forgot to remind you I was a virgin that night. I told you back then but..."

"Wait...I popped your cherry?" Shay smacks my chest. "God, now I'm super pissed I don't remember. Did you come in two seconds or did you at least get me off?"

I shake my head sadly. "Seriously? Dunno. Might have been three seconds."

Shay throws her head back and laughs with utter abandon. I join in. The goddamn absurdity of our situation is hilarious. Laughter turns into a sexual charge when I grow hard against her core. What can I say, naked or clothed, she does it for me. Our lips meet and we move together, working ourselves up yet again. I'm mentally calculating how fast we can get the job done when the unmistakable mechanical sound of the gondola gearing up for its daily operations sends a pulse of reality rushing back into our veins.

We stop what we're doing. I suck in a breath and smell the lingering scent of our intimacy intertwined with the earthy aroma of the cabin. A tinge of sadness surrounds us. The night is over. Responsibilities loom.

So do the inevitable questions about our whereabouts.

My hands find her waist and I draw her closer. "This. *Us*. It's real, isn't it?"

She nods furiously and leans in so her forehead rests against mine. "Austin, it's incredibly real, more than anything I've ever felt. But we need time and space to explore who we are without the prying eyes of anyone else. *Especially* Miles."

The sincerity in her eyes grounds me, though uncertainty niggles at me.

Then, as I look into Shay's eyes, the depths of various hues of blue which hold oceans of sincerity and genuine affection, I find myself calm. Trusting. "You've got a point. Considering our history, we owe it to ourselves to steer clear of external pressures. Can you promise me this isn't a fleeting thing for you? That you'll give us a real chance?"

"I *promise*. I think this is the beginning of something beautiful. Let's protect and cherish it." Her radiant smile infuses me with faith that I may, after all these years, bag my dream girl.

A slew of voices snap us out of our reverie. We pull apart and grab our coats. Shay pulls on her boots as the outside world intrudes into our love hut. Together, we emerge out the door and walk to the gondola. The operators give us curious glances as we board, but we ignore them and settle in for the ten-minute ride back to reality.

When the door closes and we start down the mountain, I find myself reaching out, my hand finding Shay's. Our fingers intertwine. She leans against my shoulder as we look out at the wonder of and beauty of the mountain. It's quiet. Peaceful. I'm lulled into a state of contentment...

"Shit. We didn't grab our stuff from the restaurant." Shay springs away from me, panicked. "My purse. Planner. Everything is up there and I have to teach yoga in half an hour."

"I'll ride back around and get it." I pet her hair to soothe her.

"But I'll be late..." She whirls toward me.

I wrap her in my arms and kiss her forehead. "Shhh. I got you. When we get down, go to your room. Freshen up. I'll bring it to you. It's fine."

"I can't believe I forgot." Her eyes fill with tears. "Are you mad?"

Her words are like a gut punch. For the past two weeks I've deliberately made her life hell. Made her feel less-than. Incompetent. When she's anything but. This retreat proved it. "Shay. Baby. No, I'm not mad. We need a reset on this working-together thing too." I kiss her sweet lips. "I've got your back. That's how we roll at the company. I'm so sorry that I treated you differently."

"Okay." She relaxes. "Thank you."

I reassure her. "Don't worry about a thing."

***

"So you got stuck on the mountain with my sister." Stodge slugs me in the arm. We're finished with the Appreciation Awards and are grabbing lunch before heading back to Seattle. Shay is nowhere to be found, but I assume she's busy closing out all of the retreat paperwork.

I load up my bowl with rice, spicy tuna, and salmon. Toss on some edamame. Pickles. Crispy wontons. Extra sauce of course. "We hashed things out. It's fine. She's great. I think all of the shit is behind us."

"How in the fuck did you miss the gondola?" His eyebrows furrow. "More importantly, how in the *fuck* did no one notice?"

I hate that I can't tell Miles the full truth. "We were in an intense conversation on the patio and didn't even notice. We were resourceful, though, and holed up in the ski patrol cabin. It even had a heater."

"What's that smile? Don't tell me you're crushing on her again." Miles laughs. "God, you're a sucker for punishment."

Crushing. I should be the one who's laughing. Not that I'm going to tell my best friend I fucked his sister all night long. That wouldn't be ideal. Not even a little. "We talked a lot. She told me about her epilepsy. Slept. It wasn't a big deal."

Stodge's eyes widen. "Wow. That's huge. Practically no one knows. Not even Devon knew."

I try hard to contain my shock. The man she dated for nearly a decade didn't know about her *epilepsy?*

She and I are going to have a conversation about that.

"Anyway, I'm glad you worked it out. Your attitude was getting to be a real pain in the hole." He shakes sesame seeds on his poke bowl concoction.

We take our seats together. The attendance is sparse. Most of the team are either skiing, packing, or sleeping.

"I'm sorry. I should have been a little more mature about all of it."

"Forgiven," Miles says through a mouthful of raw fish. He swallows and adds, "Don't get any bright ideas about you and her being friends. Or dating. She needs to work on herself for a while. Deal with some shit."

"Yeah..." I cover up my discomfort by shoving another forkful of poke in my mouth.

I'm in real trouble if Miles is seriously laying down the law.

If I'm not careful, I could have a real shitshow on my hands.

Because I'm not giving her up.

Not even for Miles.

Chapter Sixteen

The Next Day

I'm exhausted and I can still feel him inside me.

For hours, I've relived every minute Austin and I were together. The way he held me. Kissed me. Went down on me. Thrust himself in between my tits so I could suck on the fat head of his cock.

How he fucked me.

I've never felt more in tune with someone in my life.

Not that I'm acting like it.

True to his word, Austin fetched my stuff and brought it to me so I could take my meds, change, and teach the yoga class. Word spread fast about our overnight adventure, which was expected and also embarrassing.

Mainly when the jabs and teasing started.

As a result, we were both awkward for the rest of the sessions and acted really weird around each other. Avoided eye contact. Didn't speak. I don't know how Austin felt, but—teasing aside—I was *terrified* everyone would figure out we *actually* fucked each other's brains out.

I had bigger problems, though. My head started aching during the award presentation. To avoid an episode, I had no choice but to go to my room and take an emergency Xanax. While I waited for it to kick in, I sent a Slack to my team explaining I wasn't feeling well, together with my checklist. Then I fell asleep.

By the time I woke up ten hours later, everyone was gone. I decided it was best if I stayed the night and rested in my cushy hotel room with a kick-ass room service menu. Pure bliss after living with my parents for the past few months. After two of the most stressful weeks of my life, I turned my phone off, ate a burger, and curled up in bed to watch a *Real Housewives of Beverly Hills* marathon.

On my drive home, I spent two hours talking to my therapist—lots to unpack between the forgotten sex with Austin to the more recent developments over the past twenty-four hours.

"Shay. I'm talking to you." Mom points at me with her fork. "You need to eat."

God. She's such a worry-wart. It's been nonstop all day.

I sigh and take a bite of salad. "*Okay*. I'm still tired, though."

Annika Stojanović, my mother, has always been a formidable force who matches perfectly to my larger-than-life hockey player dad, Goran. They love me hard. Too hard. Overwhelmingly after my diagnosis. They're relentless with their opinions of what's best for their little girl and what my life should be like living with epilepsy. It's why I moved to LA, but their overprotectiveness has picked back up again ever since I got home.

The contrast between how they view me and my brother is startling. Miles is treated like an adult, they leave him alone. I guess it's because he's a billionaire living in a ginormous house on Mercer Island.

Since I'm broke and live at home, I'm still their baby.

"Jesus. Shay. Your mother is speaking to you. Pay attention." Dad tosses his napkin down then grows worried. "Unless...*are you?*"

My body feels weighed down. Exhaustion paints every fiber of my being. When I'm here with my parents every fucking thing is about my epilepsy. "No, Papa. I'm fine. I took a Zannie yesterday when I felt it coming on."

I hate how they still assume I can't be bothered to advocate for my own health. Like I'm too stupid to follow my doctor's advice. I have a seizure action plan that I keep in my purse and in my medical alert app on my phone. As I told Austin yesterday, I take care of myself. Sleep. Eat clean. Take supplements. Pay attention to my body...

"Maybe that job is too much." Mom shakes her head. "I don't know what Miles was thinking giving you so much responsibility. And *Austin*, I'm going to give that boy a piece of my mind next time I see him."

"*Mommm*." Stupid me. Since I moved back home I've fallen back into my old pattern with her—spilling every detail about my day. Well, not what happened at the retreat—getting stranded and fucking Miles's best friend is most definitely not her business. The point being, I give them too much information and they use it like parental weapons.

My dad leans back in his chair. "If she's not in a relationship with someone to look out for her, she needs to find her way, Annika. We won't always be here."

Back and forth. Back and forth. My head swivels to and fro as they spew out everything they think I should and shouldn't do. Whom I should do it with—or not. When and how.

"I like working with Miles. The projects are fulfilling and fun...I'm spending so much time with my brother..." When I manage to get a word in, I'm tongue-tied as I try to navigate the minefield of their expectations. Their ideas of what's right for me always seem to overshadow my own ambition. Aspirations.

"Darling, you know we merely want the best for you." My mom reaches over and grips my hand. "Hungry Llama is Miles's success. Don't get too attached and ride on his coattails."

Ouch. I'm hurt and frustrated by her assessment of me, but that's nothing new. Why do people keep underestimating me?

I force a smile that feels as flimsy as the threads holding my composure together. "Yeah, well, I'm convinced I'm already making a difference there."

"Oh come on now, Shay," my father interjects, his robust voice fills the room with commanding authority. "Don't exaggerate. You've been there two goddamn weeks."

My mom squeezes her fingers around mine. "Devon called a couple days ago. The poor boy is falling apart without you. He feels terrible about how things ended. Doesn't know why you still have him blocked. The two of you were together for so long and he took such great care of you. Maybe you two can patch things up?"

My heart tightens. A vise of conflicting emotions squeezes it painfully at the mention of Devon and how he eviscerated me. "He doesn't know anything about taking care of me. He never even knew I had epilepsy."

"You *couldn't* tell him before you were engaged, Shay." Mom brings her hand to her mouth in horror.

A fist pounds the table. "Bullshit. She should have told him from the beginning. I can't *believe* you gave her that advice." The vein in my dad's forehead quivers.

"I'm sick of it being such a dirty little secret." I also hate being caught in the tug-of-war of my parents' arguments about Devon.

As hurt as I was when Devon dumped me, he was accurate about one thing. I *didn't* love him.

I loved the idea of him.

I know this because one night with Austin was more romantic, more intimate, more *everything* than my entire relationship with him. "I... I appreciate that you both worry about me, but Devon and I are in the past. I have nothing more to say to him. I'm not sure why he keeps calling you, Mama."

I can feel my body trembling. An unbearable pressure builds as the dining room seems to close in. My parents' voices merge into a maelstrom of comments and opinions that drown out everything.

Suddenly, I find myself on the verge of crumbling. Events of the retreat hit with a force that threatens to shatter me. The connection I forged with Austin is precious—and now the tender beginnings of something beautiful feel like a distant dream. A fragile bubble burst by the realities of my current situation.

No one knows about me and Austin—hell, I don't even know if there *is* a me and Austin—yet my parents are still caught up in my past relationship with Devon. I've got to get away from this conversation. Stat. I push away from the table. "I don't feel well, I have to get more rest. I'll see you in the morning."

Once I'm back in my room, my mind drifts to Austin and the night we shared. Even more than the sex—which was phenomenal—I think about how wonderful he was with me. Warm and reassuring about my illness. Enthusiastic about a relationship with me built on mutual understanding and respect. The look of awe and wonder on his face when he moved inside me. How determined he was to give me pleasure.

Austin is so far above anyone I've ever known.

We belong together.

A swell of shame and regret bubbles up when I remember we haven't spoken in nearly twenty-four hours. I'm not surprised when I power on my phone to find dozens of messages that cycle through an evolution of emotions. Teasing and playful. Then annoyed. Pissed. Increasingly frantic. The latest one, sad. Resigned.

> **Austin:** I'll stop bugging you. It's clear you don't feel the same way. Don't worry, I'm not going to give you any more shit at work.

Tears well up and spill like a river of unshed frustrations, fears, and yearnings as I sit on my bed feeling smaller and smaller under my failures. Failure to appease my parents. Failure to be what Devon expected. Unable to give Austin what he needs.

Inability to stand up for myself.

My heart aches for understanding. For a space to be myself without judgment. Without the constant pressure to fit into a mold that feels more like a straitjacket.

I *must* talk to him.

He answers on the first ring. "Hey."

"I wasn't avoiding you." I pinch my nose between my fingers.

Austin sighs. "Coulda fooled me, Shay."

"I almost had an incident, but I caught it in time." Saying the words somehow makes me feel like a pressure valve has been released.

"What? Are you okay?" I hear the tinkly sound of the video chat being activated. I press accept and his gorgeous face fills the screen, contorted with worry.

I hold the phone up high and pout. Try to make light. "All good here."

"Let me come get you." He scrubs his chin with his fingers.

I nearly drop the phone in horror. "Ohmygod. No. Don't you dare. Annika and Goren would blow a gasket."

"You can't tell me that you nearly had a seizure and not expect me to want to take care of you." Austin is earnest. Sincere.

I can't help but smile. "I can take care of myself, you know. I've listened to my parents argue about what's best for me for the past two hours. It was excruciating."

"Of *course* you can take care of yourself." He relaxes back into the gaming chair he's sitting on. "You can take care of everyone, that was fairly evident over the past few days."

I lick my lips. "Well, I know who my *favorite* person to take care of is."

"Well, if you wanted me to be hard as a rock, you got your wish." He laughs.

"Ah, you're such a wonderful, obedient genie." My entire body relaxes from hearing his voice. I lie back on my bed. "Video sex?"

He shakes his head. "Real sex. Come over. Stay with me for the weekend."

"What would I tell my folks? Miles?" I feel like a naughty teenager, not a grown woman who lived on her own for almost a decade until she was forced to crawl home to Mommy and Daddy.

Austin taps his finger to his chin. "Hmm. How about the truth? You're going away for the weekend to get a little time for yourself?"

"Will there be orgasms?" I cock my head. "Because there's no way I'm leaving the sanctuary of my childhood bedroom unless there'll be dozens and dozens of orgasms."

"You only want dozens?" He bugs his eyes out.

I jump up and run to the closet, careful to show him my overnight bag and my car keys.

"Text me your address."

Chapter Seventeen

One Hour Later

The pulsating heart of Seattle sprawls below my penthouse on the 24th floor of Madison Tower, two blocks away from Hungry Llama.

My business manager—it still feels weird to say that—convinced me to buy a home two years ago. I figured, I'm young and single. Why not lean into an urban sophistication vibe. With floor-to-ceiling windows, my panoramic view of Puget Sound and the Olympic Mountains isn't unlike the one at my office. This space is much more me, though. I hired a designer to transform the sleek and contemporary living space into a comfortable and functional retreat.

The living room is bathed in the warm glow of a rare winter sunset, which casts long shadows on the dark oak hardwood floors. I'm humming with anticipation. Dying to know what she'll think of my place. My heart beats erratically at the thought of having Shay with me for the entire weekend.

The doorman buzzed her up a minute ago.

I'm not certain what I did I in my life to deserve this, but holy fucking hell. Every one of my fantasies is about to come true.

Well, maybe not every single one, but a lot are going to get checked off the list. I'm rather goddamn sure of it.

I'm trying to look semi-cool as I wait by the elevator doors in anticipation of seeing her, but it's probably no use. No matter how many times I've thought of wrinkly grannies, my cock's still hard as steel, it's a dead give-away.

The elevator doors open directly into my condo. Shay enters wearing a white, oversized sweater, jeans, and another pair of the knee-high socks tucked into a different pair of ankle boots. She carries a buzz of excitement with a hint of apprehension as she looks around at my art collection, which lines the walls and shelves.

"Whenever I travel for work, I buy art. Mostly modern. I've collected paintings, sculptures, textiles—you name it. If it speaks to me, I don't question it." I stand next to her. "It seems I have superb taste, though I know virtually nothing about the artists. Some of the pieces have doubled and tripled in value."

"Wow." She traces her finger along a hand-carved sculpture.

I motion for her to follow me and I lead her to the open-plan living room adjacent to the kitchen and dining area. "Let's catch the end of the sunset." I sit facing the windows and pat the seat next to me.

Shay sits in a graceful cascade of limbs that seems both effortlessly elegant and innately shy. Every fiber of my being vibrates with the desire to bridge the small distance and take her in my arms, if for no other reason but to affirm the realness of what's blossoming between us.

With a concerted effort to keep the atmosphere light, I give her a goofy grin. "So, here we are. Back in the real world."

"Yes, the *real* world." She gestures around the room and then between me and her. "Just two normal people."

I reach over and trace a line on her knee. "What did you tell your folks?"

"Exactly what you said. You should have seen mom's face when I left." Shay shakes her head, bemused. "You'd think I was sixteen years old again."

"Isn't that the year all of the stuff started?" I cock my head.

She nods, looking down, then glances around the condo. "This place is bomb. Reminds me a little of where I lived in LA."

"Thank you." I decide to ignore her reference to the life she shared with Devon. "It's been my refuge. A place to escape when the world gets too...noisy."

She smiles, blinking up at me through her long lashes. "Noisy? Up here? It seems so serene."

I tap my head. "Not that kind of noise."

We fall silent and gaze at each other. The tension between us is palpable. The kind you can't shrug off because it's borne out of raw emotion, confusion, and unspoken words.

After what feels like an eternity, Shay breaks the silence. "Austin, about that night—"

I cut her off with a raised hand. "I can't stop thinking about it. More than I'd like to admit."

Her voice is shaky, uncertain. "What happened between us...it wasn't a fluke, was it?"

I lean in and brush the hair off her face. "No," I admit. "But it terrifies me."

"Why?" Her voice trembles, revealing a vulnerability that touches my soul.

"Because," I pause, searching for the proper words, "from the day I met you when I was a teenager, I've felt a pull. Like gravity. It scares the hell out of me because I can't resist it and I hope you finally feel it too."

Her mouth opens, clearly shocked by my raw honesty. "Austin, yes, I do. But, how do we keep this...*us*, under wraps at the company, primarily from Miles?" Shay's eyes convey a depth of vulnerability—a plea for reassurance that it's possible to forge a path through the complexity of our situation.

I lean in and kiss her. "We'll take it one step at a time." My voice carries conviction. "For now, we'll build trust. Trust in one another. Trust in what we have."

Shay slides her fingers through my hair, pulling me closer. I can't help but smile against her mouth as we kiss, sealing our promise. She's delicious, all vanilla and sunshine. I suck on the spot behind her ear that I've learned makes her crazy. Venture down her neck, leaving her quivering. I pull away to find her thoroughly blissed out.

"If you stop, I'll maim you." She yanks me back to her. "You need to kiss me some more."

I quirk a brow and gladly move over her and kiss her chest, her heart, gripping the bottom of her sweater to pull it off over her head. She's bare on top, except for a whisp of a sheer black bra revealing her taut, brown nipples.

"Jesus, Shay. How can I be expected to resist your tits?" I cup and squeeze her breasts and she arches into my touch.

Shay reaches down to stroke my dick through my jeans. "How can I be expected to resist your cock? I want to fuck you so badly it's a little embarrassing."

"That's the best news I've heard all day." I slide off the couch and kneel between her legs.

Her hands trace down the front of my shirt and she makes short work of the buttons. I shrug it off and stroke the inside of her thighs up and down, gliding across her pussy every now and then. She wheezes, "Oh, *shit*...do you want it as much as me?"

"*More*." I push her back against the cushions and she looks down her body at me as I roll off her sexy socks and peel down her jeans. My desire for her is so powerful my hands shake a bit. It takes everything I have not to rip off her panties and plunge my cock inside her to the hilt, but I also want to worship her. Show her how precious she is.

Still on my knees, I lean up and over her to press my lips against hers. One hand strokes her hair, the other thumbs her nipple. Shay's arms encircle my upper body. Her fingers dig into the muscles of my shoulders in time to our kisses, which turn from sweet to passionate to ravenous. I can wait no longer, so I pop the catch at the front of her bra and her gorgeous tits spill out.

I lavish attention on her breasts, rolling and pinching her nipples. She arches into my hands, moaning and begging for more, so I give it to her. Pinch harder, eliciting a whimper, which turns into a snarl when I dip my head down and slide my tongue over the same nipple. I kiss over to her other breast and repeat the pinching and licking until she's squirming.

I continue kissing and licking down her rib cage and belly, over her hip bone to the hollow where her leg meets her body. Hovering over her pussy, I breathe in the sweet scent of her arousal and kiss her mound through her panties. My finger dips in through the side to find her soaking, swollen, and ready. "You're so wet. You smell so delicious. Damn, Shay."

Without thinking, I rip her panties in two and toss the remnants over my shoulder. Shay brazenly allows her knees to fall open as she watches me from above. I'm mesmerized by her perfect, glistening pussy. I drag my tongue through her folds and drink her down.

"It's guaranteed I'll masturbate to this exact moment whenever we're apart." Her voice is ragged, sexual.

Taking it to the next level, I pick one of her legs up and kiss the sole of her foot, then her ankle. Flick my tongue behind her knee. "Put your arms up over your head and let me feast on you, baby."

"Ohmygod. I may come purely from your words, Austin," she gasps, but does as she's told.

Shay closes her eyes and moans when I drag my beard against her pussy and spread her open with my fingers. I take long, quick licks to drive her to the brink and then back off again. When I look up at her she reaches for my head to push me back down, but I catch her hands and kiss them. "Oh, no you don't. Back above your head."

She complies so I nuzzle her belly and caress her inner thighs, pushing them up and out so she's wide open to me. I bend my head and kiss her pussy long and slow, exploring every part. Flatten my tongue against her to tease her clit, then I suck it between my lips as I plunge two fingers inside.

Her orgasm crashes into her. I watch her tremble and shake. She clamps her thighs to my ears, but I don't stop until she's utterly spent. I look up at her through her parted legs.

The rawness of the moment is overwhelming.

Shay's chest heaves. Her nipples are so tight.

When she looks down at me, she smiles. "God, that was *marvelous*. Now, I want you inside me."

Chapter Eighteen

Minutes Later

Austin drives me wild.

I've never had someone be so entirely focused on my pleasure.

I'm desperate to reciprocate.

"Your turn." I pat the cushion next to me.

He waggles his eyebrows and sits sideways, raising his leg and resting it on the back of the couch behind me. "I like the sound of that."

I turn between his legs, unbuckle his belt and unzip his jeans. He shifts, allowing me to pull them along with his boxer briefs down and off, before resuming position. Crawling up his body, I caress every muscle in his torso and hover my tits above his lips.

"I must have done something significant to deserve this." He catches a nipple in his mouth and sucks.

I can't help but laugh as I pull back, causing him to release my breast. "Oh, you did. That orgasm was...*wow*."

"Dozens to go." Austin smiles, then he groans when my hands smooth across his thighs and I bend and kiss down his body, stopping to lick his flat, brown nipples and give them a little chew. Hisses when I feather kisses all over his stomach muscles and fist his cock, which is flush against his belly button. I watch him watching me when I put the head in my mouth and suck him deep. Feel him methodically drag his shaft across my tongue until he's nearly free, then repeat.

"Holy shit, Shay." He threads his fingers through my hair. "Soooo fucking good."

Keeping his shaft wet and slick, I slide my fist up and down as I lave him. My other hand reaches under to palm his balls. His hips buck gently against my mouth and I allow him to slide down my throat so I can swallow around him.

"Christ, if you do that again I'm gonna come." He pushes against my shoulder. "And I positively want you to be fucking me when I do."

I release him with a pop and watch him grip his thick shaft and stroke it, transfixed. "Your cock is a thing of beauty."

"Oh yeah? Why don't you ride my beautiful cock then?" He holds it up and ready for me.

Slinging my leg over his hip so I'm straddling him, I allow him to feed his girth into me as I slowly lower myself down, adjusting to his size. I lean down and kiss him slow and long—our combined taste is intoxicating—before taking his cock in as deep as he'll fit. Getting into a rhythm, I push myself upright and slide my pussy up and down until he winces with pleasure and groans, "You're so *fucking* bomb."

"Oh, so you like this?" I circle my hips, bracing my hands on his thighs behind by body so I'm arched toward him with my head back and my tits jiggling a bit. I love to create an outstanding visual.

"God, yes." Austin runs his hands over every part of my body he can reach, dipping his fingers to my clit. "Come again for me." Watching him squeeze my little nub gently between his thumb and index finger with his cock buried within my walls makes me gush with arousal. "You like that, baby? You're so, so wet. It feels amazing." He thrusts up into me from below, hitting my inner wall with accurate precision.

"Oh sweet Jesus," I groan and reach up and pinch my nipples hard, the way he did earlier. He, in turn, furiously rubs my clit as he pumps. My pussy tightens and flutters, sensation zings all the way through my core—I'm on the brink.

My orgasm hits me all at once and I fall forward, bracing my hands on his pecs, never wanting it to end. Clamping around him, I thrust my pussy against him harder and harder, faster and faster until he grips my hips and gives me the leverage I need to grind my pubic bone against his. I scream his name when I begin to come again, this time ten times as intensely.

Coming twice during intercourse has never happened before and, I swear to Jesus, it's life-changing. Austin furiously bucks up into me, which keep the aftershocks going—I'm hanging on for the ride. A few seconds later, he cants his hips off the sofa and goes over, roaring when he spurts deep inside me.

We move together until I think I'm going out of my mind with the most intense pleasure I've ever experienced. When I shudder through my aftershocks, I slump down against him and lazily undulate my hips, squeezing my muscles around his cock to milk the last of his release. Austin buries his face in my hair, his arms band around my waist.

Lying together this way, with him still buried inside me, I feel like I'm home.

I never want this to end.

<hr>

"What are we on, twelve?" The next evening, Austin butters toast while I scramble some eggs.

"Twenty-four hours. Twelve orgasms. I'll never recover." I laugh as I ladle the eggs onto plates. "A little breakfast for dinner? Maybe a sexy shower and we still have tomorrow to double our money."

Austin has fucked me in every room of this condo. The living room, of course. In his bed a few times. On the kitchen counter where we're eating now. On the sink in the powder room. Against the window overlooking the city. Out on the balcony in a lawn chair. Bent over the edge of his desk. On the floor of his closet. Each time more inventive and incredible than the previous encounter.

In between, we've talked for hours. Morphing from serious discussions into playful banter. It's incredible how our individual quirks and nuances mesh. We always seem to find a playful rhythm as we dance between flirtation and deep connection.

He teases me about my impeccable taste in fashion. I razz him over his shocking well of pop culture knowledge. We kiss. Touch. Fondle. Cuddle. I've never been so content in my life. I've never felt so myself.

We've had so many moments where our eyes lock and the world narrows down to the overwhelming connection we share. I find myself lost in the depth of his gaze, when the rich tapestry of his soul is laid bare. I've never been so open and honest with anyone, even Miles.

It's hard to fathom how much comfort we seem to find in each other's presence, when a few days ago we were, basically, enemies. Now there's a natural ease between us that speaks of a kinship of souls. Hopefully, a shared vision of a future. Together.

"You're a sex goddess." Austin takes a bite of toast. "I love how you ask for what you want and how you want it. Then I can give it to you. It's fucking awesome you don't make me guess."

"Well, I feel the most confident in my own body when I'm having sex," I blurt out.

He chews thoughtfully. "I wonder why. You're such a force in everything you do. You never seem insecure."

"Oh, that's the fake it until you make it pageant girl in me. Truthfully, I'm still figuring myself out." I grab our empty plates and rinse them in the sink. "I think when I'm having sex, I'm so present in the moment. The pleasure. I'm not thinking about anything else. Or my problems. Nothing. Only how pleasing it feels. How I can satisfy my partner."

His jaw clenches. "Can I be honest? That comment bugs me. I don't wanna be some rando sex partner, Shay. I'd like to know if this connection we have is unique. Not merely because of us, but because of Miles. I can't risk my friendship with your brother over something that might be only physical to you."

His words sting but I realize I've slipped into my default mode of generalizing things to protect myself. I keep my voice even. "Physical? You think I think our connection is about sex?"

"No. That's not what I meant." He rakes his fingers through his hair. "Every time I'm near you, the world fades away. I want to know this is real—not some fleeting thing for *you*."

I move closer. My fingers itch to touch him, but I resist. "I'm sorry. My comment was flippant. Careless."

"No, *I'm* sorry," he murmurs, his voice laced with regret. "I can't keep being defensive about what happened years ago. My feelings for you are *huge*, Shay. I'm terrified of making a mistake. Of losing Miles. Of losing you."

We stand close, the air between us thick with tension and desire. The pull between us is undeniable. "Austin," my voice warbles, "I can't promise how things will unfold, but the truth is I'm falling in love with you."

A tumult of emotions play out behind his eyes. Without another word, he closes the distance between us and his lips meet mine in a searing, all-consuming kiss. "Thank Christ, because I'm falling in love with you too."

I reach out and trace a gentle path along his hand. Our fingers intertwine in a silent pledge of commitment to figuring it out.

"Shay." Austin's voice carries a tremble of vulnerability, a raw openness that has been rarely directed toward me by anyone. "I want this—us—to work. I feel like this is, truly, once in a lifetime."

My eyes well up with tears that carry the weight of hope after a year of incredible disappointment and struggle. I'm scared, though. Is it wise for me to jump into another relationship with someone who has the power to crush me? This feels special, distinct from how it was with Devon, where everything—and I mean everything—revolved around him.

Austin seems to truly love me for who I am.

Not what I can do for him.

Am I ready for this?

"Let's go watch a movie or something." I hold out my hand. "Enough with all of this serious stuff. I want to snuggle my boyfriend and fuck in a room that remains unchristened."

As I lead him to the back room where his giant television and gaming command station is set up, Austin finally catches on. "Wait, so I'm your boyfriend?"

"Well...yeah. Even if we're not broadcasting our relationship to the public. I'll cut any bitch who tries to get her claws into you. Now that I've had your cock, no one else is allowed near it. *Ever.*" I look back and stick my tongue out at him.

Austin lunges for me and throws me over his shoulder firefighter-style. "Good thing my cock wants one woman and that's you."

"Only your cock?" I spank his ass as we enter the room.

"*All of me.*" He puts me down and cradles my cheeks in between his hands. Guides my face to him and sips from my lips. "Every." Kiss. "Single." Kiss. "Part." Kiss.

Hours and several orgasms later, I lie in Austin's arms in his bed as he sleeps.

For the first time in nearly a year, I feel thoroughly happy.

Chapter Nineteen

Two Weeks Later

Last year, I met Less Than Zero's lead singer, Tyson Rainier and his wife Zoey, when they pitched me an idea for their foundation, which provides arts education to school programs in underserved communities.

To say I was starstruck is an understatement. LTZ is the biggest band out of Seattle since Limelight back in the nineties. We're all around the same age though, and I realized he and I weren't so dissimilar. I'm famous in the gaming and tech community because of Hungry Llama's success. His notoriety is more public because he's a Grammy-award-winning rockstar.

His kindness and humility cemented the notion in my mind that people are people.

Money is money.

We were pretty far along the path of working together when things fell apart. Ty had some sort of breakdown and his band broke up. The baby was born. The band reunited and went on tour. Now, LTZ is on a short break so we're picking things up again.

It's the perfect project for Shay, who's joining me for the meeting.

"Hey." Shay slips into my office wearing the skinniest black slacks, a V-neck purple sweater and her trademark high heels.

Ever since she and I started our, um, thing, I've regretted having floor-to-ceiling glass walls in my office. I'd love to be able to kiss her and touch her without prying eyes. "Hey. You look stunning."

"Thank you." She faux-curtseys and takes a seat at the conference table in my office. "My mom lost her shit with me this morning. Demanded to know where I'm sleeping."

Shay's spent most nights at my place since we declared our love. I've asked her to move in but she claims she's not ready yet. I know I'm speeding ahead in my own mind, but I also know what I want—and I want *her*. "I think we should reconsider when we're going to tell your family."

She nods. "Yeah. I know…it's not fair to keep my folks in the dark. They worry."

We're interrupted when Angie, my assistant, leads Ty and Zoey into my office. Their security guard, Sergey waits outside.

"Hey, man. Good to see you." I clasp Ty's hand in a bro-shake and turn to Zoey. "Whoa, when are you due?"

Zoey is a tiny, blonde dynamo of a woman who is sweet but tough as nails. She rubs her prominent baby bump. "A couple months. Ty knocked me back up right after Oliver was born."

"Hi, I'm Shay Stojanović, Vice President of Marketing and Events." Shay sticks her hand out. "I'll be joining you today."

I shake my head. "Shit, that was rude. My apologies, Shay." I nearly put my arm around her but cover it up by gesturing to the conference table. "Let's sit over here."

"Oh, it's understandable when the famous woman who spurred a million love songs walks in." She winks at Zoey, who laughs. At this point, everyone on the planet knows

Ty and Zoey broke up when they were young and LTZ's hit album *Z* was about Zoey.

One thing I love about Shay—and there are many—is how unbothered she is about fame. I guess it's because she grew up with a famous athlete, so notoriety doesn't faze her. She treats everyone alike.

When we're all seated, Ty holds his hand up. "Before we begin, I want to apologize profusely for the delay. It wasn't due to a lack of desire or interest—we're very excited. Life got in the way a bit." He puts his arm around Zoey's shoulder. "And thank you for having the meeting here, we're trying to keep things low key with our pregnancy."

"I get it." Shay nods. "Social media was brutal to you guys for a while. I'm so glad everything's turned around."

Zoey shakes her head. "When the band's on break, all of the families like to be on break too. Be normal until the madness starts again."

"Oh, I remember. My dad is Stodge Stojanović. It was the same in between seasons. We had security growing up. It leveled off a few years ago." Shay shrugs like it's no big thing.

It's something I never knew about. Miles certainly never said anything. Huh.

Ty leans toward her, eyes wide. "No shit? That's rad. I'm not exactly a sports guy, but Stodge is an hockey icon."

"Try growing up with him." Shay rolls her eyes. "Strict as *fuck*. I got around it though. I'm convinced he went bald because of me."

I cough to get things back on track, not wanting to relive the...past. Also, I have a million meetings today. "So, we were close to finalizing the term sheet where Hungry Llama would provide grant money to expand your arts programming into tech. Things have gotten worse with the programmer shortage. I'm excited to see how we can diversify to get more women and members of the BIPOC and LGBTQIA+ communities interested in STEM."

"Yes, we love the idea." Zoey shows me her tablet. "As promised, here is my plan to unite tech and arts and implement that into our work."

Shay scoots closer to me and looks over my shoulder. Instinctively, I lean in to kiss her then realize where we are and try to cover it up by whipping my head back around. Make it even worse by awkwardly moving my chair and dropping the device.

Ty and Zoey exchange glances and look between us, trying not to smile.

Shit.

"Let me take a look." Shay notices my gaffe but pretends to ignore it all by taking the iPad and scrolling through Zoey's presentation. "Oh, cool. Yeah." Her eyes flick up and down the screen. "It's completely doable. I like this a lot."

My office door opens and Miles strides in and takes a seat at the table and holds out his hand. "Hey, Miles Stojanović. Cofounder. You can call me Stodge."

Ty and Zoey graciously introduce themselves. Shay looks at me, rolls her eyes and mouths, "He's a big fan."

"Are you two siblings?" Zoey points between Shay and Miles.

Shay nods and looks over at Miles. "I already told them about Dad. Now they know you have twin nicknames and hence, there are two famous Stodges. Congratulations."

I snort with laughter. Ty joins me followed by Shay and Zoey. Miles clearly feels a little stupid, but he's so laid back he's able to laugh at himself too.

"I'm such a *dick*." Miles chortles.

For the next hour, the five of us hammer out a timetable and plan to collaborate. When they leave, Miles stays behind with me and Shay.

"Mom and Dad want you to spend Thanksgiving with us. I assume you aren't going to your mom's?" Miles taps a pen annoyingly on the table.

It takes all I have not to look at Shay. I don't plan on attending the dinner, she and I will have our own Thanksgiving after she puts in time with her parents. Our plans don't involve food though. We're looking forward to a four-day weekend of being naked. "Uh, I'd planned on gaming that day and being on call for the release."

"Ah, c'mon. You and I haven't hung out with my family in a while. We haven't even had a beer together since the retreat. What's going on? Do you have a girlfriend or something?" Miles leans back in his chair and grins.

Don't look at her. Don't look at her.

Shay slugs him in the arm. "Shut up, *Miles*."

"God, *Shay*. Why you gotta get up in our business?" Miles mimics her like they're eight years old.

"*Seriously?*" It's hard enough to keep our secret without the two of them acting like idiots. "Thanks, Stodge, but I'm gonna stick to staying in."

Miles sighs. "I hate that you're not seeing your own family. Hasn't it gotten better?"

"Uh…" My eyes flick to Shay, who knows the scoop. Her eyes soften with empathy. "My stepfather asked me for a loan. Said I owed him the money to repay him for everything he spent on me as a kid. So, no. It's not gotten any better."

Our eyeball exchange doesn't go unnoticed. "Is there something going on here I should know about?" Miles glances back and forth at us. "You're awfully eyebally."

"Don't be cray. Austin and I have become friends, Miles. We put our differences behind us at the retreat when we got stranded." She juts her chin out defiantly.

I marvel at Shay's eloquence and fervor. There's a reason I've fallen for her, beyond the physical attraction. She can diffuse any situation, yet stand her ground.

"So what do you think about working with The Rainier Foundation?" I try to move Miles out of the dangerous territory of me and Shay. "They want us to gamify music education. But I'm thinking broader. Arts and coding are similar. It's all about pattern recognition. In music, you have notes that form patterns and rhythms. In visual art, there are patterns of light, color, and shape. In coding, it's patterns of logic, commands, and responses. All require critical thinking, problem-solving, and creativity. And, most importantly, they allow an individual to create something novel, unique, and expressive."

Miles nods thoughtfully. "So, you're saying we could teach kids how to code and, in the process, tap into their creative potential?"

"Exactly," Shay affirms. "And by integrating computer programming into their curriculum, we're equipping these kids with valuable job skills and offering them an innovative medium of artistic expression. Think of the video games we create. They're a blend of technology, storytelling, art, and sound."

"It's high time Hungry Llama gave back to the community." I'm sincerely excited about this collaboration. It feels...legitimate. "I'm a firm believer that when you are successful it's great to share the wealth."

Shay nods. "The gaming industry is massive, yet lacks representation from diverse communities. I love that we'll be able to reach people who may not have ever dreamed of this type of opportunity."

Miles's head snaps back and forth between us as we babble on and on.

"I like it but it's your call, let me know how to staff it." Miles stands and heads toward the door. "I'm heading out. See you tomorrow, Shay."

"Have a great holiday," I call after him.

Miles raises his hand but doesn't look back as he walks away.

Shay and I both let out huge, cleansing breaths.

I notice the floor is practically empty and feel a little annoyed until I realize we let people off early for the holiday. "What time is it? I think most people have left already."

"At least an hour ago." Shay glances at her phone and bites her lip. Peers up at me. "Should we live life on the edge and get in a quickie?"

My dick instantly hardens. I nod, leaning in for a clandestine kiss. "I almost blew our cover..."

"I know." Shay slaps at me playfully before kissing me again, this time with tongue. "Where should we..."

"What the hell is going on here?" Miles shouts. We both look up to find him standing at the door.

Well, *sheeee-it*.

Chapter Twenty

Shay's Perspective

The world around us seems to disappear when we're together.

Oh, I know it sounds like a sappy love song. A line from a romance novel. A trite Hallmark card. Until Austin and I started things up, I had no clue.

Now I do.

The taste of Austin's kisses are addictive and I'm fully immersed in the euphoria of our romantic-moment love when the hair on my neck stands up. Austin and I pull apart the second we both realize we're no longer alone.

Then whirl around to find the door to his office is wide open, and there, eyes burning with anger, is my twin brother, Miles.

I feel like I've been doused with ice water. Austin stumbles away from me, knocking his chair backward. He's as shook as I am.

"Miles…" I bolt toward him, my voice trembling.

"What the hell is this?" Miles's voice is low and controlled, which is scarier than if he were yelling.

Austin takes a deep breath, attempting to defuse the situation. "Stodge, let us explain. We—"

"You took advantage of my *sister*?" Miles takes a threatening step toward Austin.

I've never seen him like this and I don't know what to do.

Austin holds up his hand in surrender. "*No*. It's not like that. Shay and I… We've grown close. It's mutual. We were going to wait to tell your family…"

"You expect me to believe that? With your track record, Austin?" Miles sneers and directs his attention at me. "Do you *know* where his dick's been? *Huh?*"

I file away the comment to discuss with Austin later, deciding to compartmentalize. Focus on the matter at hand.

"I'd *never* do anything to hurt Shay." Austin crosses his arms over his chest. "*Never.*"

Before either of them can say anything more, Miles turns his fiery gaze to me. "And you? We talked about this, Shay. After what happened with Devon, you said you were focusing on yourself. You came crying to me begging for advice. Telling me you're going to take a break from dating. From sex. This is how you do it? Fucking the guy who treated you like absolute *garbage* for the first two weeks you worked here?"

I feel my face heat up with humiliation. "It's not like that, Miles. Austin isn't Devon."

"Of course, he's not! He's supposedly my best fucking friend..." Miles trails off and his voice grows quiet as he shakes his head in disgust. "You're going to take that away too. You ruin *everything* in our family."

Austin's jaw tenses. "I know this is surprising, but don't take your anger out on her."

"Oh, you have no idea how angry I am." Miles is reinvigorated. He points at me. "Did you forget about your condition? Or did he?" He swirls his finger around his head . "A few lapses in memory and you throw yourself at the next guy."

The dig stings. Tears burn behind my eyes, but I refuse to let them fall. "Miles, stop it. This has nothing to do with my epilepsy."

"You're in over your head. *Again.*" Miles's voice drips with condescension.

I've never, ever hated my brother until now. Then again, he's never been anything but supportive of me, which is why the sharp taste of betrayal lingers. I'm caught in the crossfire of a storm I knew would come when he found out about my relationship with Austin. I certainly didn't anticipate it would go quite this badly.

Austin, however, stands resolute. "Miles, whatever issues you have with Shay or with me, throwing them out in anger isn't the solution. That's not how we roll."

Miles scoffs and throws his hands up. "Not how we *roll*? You think I didn't know about that night in high school when we all got drunk and she took your virginity? You moped about it for a long time. For the past few years you fucked any woman that showed even a hint of interest; none of whom look like Shay, I might add. The reason I felt comfortable giving her a job at our company was because I thought you *were* over her."

Austin's eyes widen slightly, but he says nothing. I want to go to him, but my feet feel like they're bolted to the ground.

"Shay might not remember what happened that night, but I do." Miles slaps his leg. "I chose to stay silent, thinking it was best she didn't know."

"Miles, that was years ago. We were kids. It's in the past." Though I'm reeling from my brother's pent-up resentment about my illness, my pageant training kicks in like I'm on autopilot. I'm not going to let him see me fall apart. I stay measured. Calm. I want this to end quickly so Austin and I can pick up the pieces.

Hopefully.

Miles's gaze softens a little, but there's a clear pain behind his eyes. "Ever since you got sick, you've been...unpredictable. I never know what you're going to do next. One minute you're here, the next you're gone. I thought if I gave you some stability..."

His condescending tone takes me aback and I lose my cool. "*Wow*. Okay. *Patronizing* much?"

Miles winces but is undeterred. "It's always got to be about you. Doesn't it? Whatever Shay wants. Whenever she wants it. I'm so sick and tired of this."

"It's her life, Miles. Not yours. You can't control her decisions." Austin moves next to me and grips my hand in solidarity.

Miles's gaze darkens. "I've had to watch out for her and pick up the pieces since we were kids. *Especially* after her diagnosis. She's destroyed our friendship and she'll destroy you too. Don't you realize that, Austin? It's infuriating."

I feel like I'm watching this conversation from above. Like it's not really happening. Like we're not going to have to deal with the fallout of this angry tirade. I hear myself blurting out, "I can find another job."

"Yeah. Good. I think that's best." Miles gestures with his arm for me to leave.

Austin's arm tightens around me. I look up and see the hurt in his eyes, but he stands by me. "She's not going anywhere."

Miles laughs. "Oh, but she is. As you said, 'you can't control her decisions.'"

"What I meant to say is, I can find another job but I don't want to leave," I find my true voice amidst the storm of emotions. "You're being so disrespectful and cruel. I don't even recognize you."

Miles deflates. "I've reached the end of my rope."

Austin steps in front of me. "Okay, that's enough, Stodge. You've said your piece. I think we should all head out. Let cooler heads prevail in the morning."

"I trusted you, Austin." Miles shakes his head. "I *trusted* you."

Austin pulls me against his side. "You *can* trust me with Shay. I *love* her."

The room goes silent. I look between the two most important men in my life, praying for a resolution. But it seems Miles has had enough. "*Fuck this.*"

He storms out.

I slump into a chair, burying my face in my hands.

Austin crouches beside me and wraps an arm around my shoulders. "We'll get through this," he soothes. "It's out in the open now."

Realization dawns on me. "Miles is correct. I'm *not* stable."

He takes my hands away from my face and rubs the backs of them with his thumbs. "Do you know what I think?"

I look into his golden-brown eyes. "Nope."

"This might be a better conversation for you to have with your therapist, but it seems like your family likes to keep you in a role you outgrew years ago—they take care of things for you." Austin kisses my fingers. "When you left to forge your own life, you went the opposite direction. By keeping your illness to yourself and taking care of Devon, you got control back—though it didn't turn out the way you planned. Either way, Shay, *you're* the strong and capable one and there's no reason you can't have want you want."

I shake my head. "I'm not feeling either of those things. I can't believe what happened with Miles."

"Move in with me." Austin threads his fingers through mine.

"I don't think that's the solution," I sigh. "I should find my own place. I'm also inclined to find a different job."

Austin pulls me up and holds me against him. "Well, at least come spend the weekend with me. We'll have time to let things settle down and you can make a plan."

"I need to get out in front of this. Will you come with me to my folks' house? Might as well rip the bandage off if Miles hasn't done it already." I lean my cheek against Austin's chest.

"Of course." He tips my chin up with his finger and bends down to kiss me.

We stand that way for a while, taking comfort in our togetherness during the calm before the storm.

I hope we're not finished before we could get started.

What we have feels monumental.

Still, I can't help but wonder if I'm heading for disaster.

A repeat of my past mistakes all over again.

Chapter Twenty-One

One Hour Later

The air is heavy with tension as Shay fumbles with her keys before managing to unlock the door.

We walk inside, me following Shay. The familiar, sprawling living room is dimly lit. Annika and Goran, Shay's parents, sit on the couch watching *Deadliest Catch*. Annika's feet are curled up under her. She's scrolling through her tablet, barely paying attention to the show while Goran is transfixed.

I try not to think about what Shay and I did on that couch back in high school, but every time I'm over here the memories flood back. It's still freaks me out a bit that she has no recollection and doesn't seem bothered by it, but I've chosen to take her at her word.

"Hey, I hate to interrupt your show, but we need to talk." Shay's voice shakes slightly.

Annika, who looks exactly like an older version of Shay, tilts her head. "Oh God, you're not pregnant are you?"

I nearly choke. I'm certain my expression is one of abject horror.

Goran's gaze sharpens, a protective edge evident when he looks at me. "Austin? What happened?"

Shay takes a deep breath and looks to me for support. I take her hand and squeeze it in reassurance. "Miles saw Austin and me…together." She kicks the carpet with her toe. "He wasn't happy."

Annika raises a knowing eyebrow but remains silent.

Goran doesn't mask his surprise. "*Together*? As in….?"

"Dating," I interject. "Shay and I are dating."

Goran leans back, assessing me with a scrutinous gaze, while Annika's lips curl into a slight smile. "Well, we suspected she was seeing someone. So, now we know it's *you*."

"We didn't want to keep it from you." Shay pulls her hand from mine. Her voice is laced with anxiety. "The plan was to let everyone know after Thanksgiving. After

214

Miles's, uh, negative reaction. I didn't want you finding out from him."

Annika and Goran exchange glances, and for a moment, there's an uncomfortable silence. Then, to my surprise, Goran shrugs. "Well, it's your life, Shay. As long as you're happy, we're happy for you."

My heart swells with gratitude. "Thank you, sir. I promise I have nothing but the best intentions for Shay."

Annika's voice is less supportive. "Austin. You've been half in love with my daughter for years. Not that long ago, she got out of a long relationship. Now's perhaps not the time—"

"*Annika.*" Goran cuts her off with a glare.

"What?" She squints at him. "I'm saying the truth."

Their opposing reactions are disconcerting to me but Shay forges ahead. "We've been broken up for months, Mama. I'm over Devon. Austin and I are special..." Her voice trails off, and I can sense the uncertainty. Which hurts.

"Austin, I hope you understand Shay's condition requires patience. Understanding." Annika directs her attention on me. Goran does too.

I nod, swallowing the unease that's settled in my stomach. "Shay's been thoroughly candid about her epilepsy and I've been reading up on it. I'll support her in every way I can."

Goran strokes his beard. "She has good days and bad days. There'll be times she might not remember things, even important ones."

"Dad, it's not that bad. It hasn't been like that since I was a teenager." Shay's face crumbles as if she's realizing my observation is accurate. In this house, it's like she's frozen in time at the maturity level of the teenager who left for college years ago.

It's also clear her parents love her. Worry about her. Her dad's eyes soften. "Shay, I know you want to pretend everything is perfect, but Austin should know how to help you if and when you need it."

I appreciate Goran's honesty, but I'm also going to back Shay. No matter what. "Look, whatever happens, I'll be there for her. No matter what."

Shay's hand finds mine. "I'm ready to go back to your place and chill. I've got to pack a few things. Austin, can you wait here?"

"Of course," I reply, watching as she heads upstairs to her room.

Once she's out of earshot, Annika's voice drops to a whisper. "Shay is strong but she likes to sweep things under the rug. The diagnosis has taken a toll."

I take note because Annika's version of how Shay's dealt with epilepsy is so disparate than how Shay sees it.

"What happened with Miles?" Goran stands, walks over to the stairs and looks up before returning to the couch. "We suggested he give her a job at your company so he could look out for her. He told us you weren't happy about it. What the hell has changed?"

"Shay proved me wrong, I was originally upset about not being consulted, but it's all good now. With respect to Miles, unfortunately he saw us kissing and utterly let us both—mostly Shay—have it. It almost seemed like he'd been holding in his feelings about the situation for all these years." Goran and Annika have become like my surrogate parents, which makes all of this trickier. "Cooler heads should prevail after everyone takes a break."

Annika gets up and joins us. "If I know my Miles, he'll be particularly upset about all of this. Maybe we can get it all out in the open tomorrow at dinner."

Shit. I nearly forgot tomorrow's Thanksgiving. "I'm not coming for dinner. You'll have to ask Shay..."

"Of course you're coming." Goran folds his still-massive arms across his chest. "You spend holidays with your family."

"We're not." Shay is on her way down the stairs with her suitcase. I dash over to help her with it.

Annika literally stomps her foot. "I've spent the better part of the day prepping food for all of us. I won't hear of you abandoning me on Thanksgiving when you've been away for so long."

"Uh..." I glance at Shay, who shakes her head.

"I think it's best I stay at Austin's this weekend." She glances between her parents and me. "I'm not putting you guys in the middle of anything, but Miles said some very, *very* hurtful things. Launched personal attacks that I need to process. I don't want to be around him."

Goran puts his hand on Annika's shoulder. "We'll talk to him tomorrow."

"Let's go." Shay looks up at me and I can tell she's wiped out emotionally.

Her parents are sad, but resigned. "If you change your mind remember, no matter what, we're always here."

As we head out, Shay clings tightly to my hand. I open the door for her and she climbs in. By the time we're on the road, she's curled up in the passenger seat, staring out the window.

"Are you okay? We'll pick up your car next week." I reach over and squeeze her shoulder.

She shakes her head. "Oh, I know. I have so much on my mind after today."

"Yeah. Fine. I'll give you room in my closet, I have plenty." I try to lighten the mood.

She doesn't react. Stares out the window.

"I'm not going to treat you like a pestering parent about the epilepsy, Shay. I'll be here to lift you up when you have a rough day. I'll be by your side if you have an incident." I stroke the side of her neck with my finger. "If you need me to help remind you to take it easy if you've had a stressful day at work or aren't feeling well, I can do that."

Shay turns to face me. "I'm glad you know. It's such a relief."

"Yeah?"

"A couple days before he broke things off with me, Devon asked me about a conversation we'd had at dinner with the Raiders' coaching staff before he signed his contract. I couldn't remember a word of it. I tried to play it off, but I was busted by my short-term memory problems." Shay looks down at her lap.

This is a conversation I've wanted to have. "Wait, so Devon *did* know?"

"No, I never told him. The whole thing perpetuated on itself. At the time of that dinner, we'd been together for so many years, what would I have said? 'So, crazy story, Devon, I have epilepsy and it makes it hard for me to remember things sometimes, nothing personal. Sorry I didn't tell you years ago.'" Shay laughs bitterly. "I played it off and basically gaslit him. Made him feel like he was making shit up. But, I could tell by his face that he knew something was wrong. He found my meds a few days later. I lied about what they were for—pretended they were anti-anxiety."

The revelation is surprising considering how honest and forthcoming Shay's been with me. "Why would you keep it from him?"

"I can't defend myself, not really. Although, you have no idea what a stigma it's been. Plus, the drugs kept everything at bay for the most part until..." She wrinkles her nose. "Until it was manifesting in weird ways and made me seem more like a charm-school dropout than a loser who forgot important conversations. Another example? Devon and I were at I fancy dinner with a group of players and their significant others in Cincinnati. Everyone was chatty. Apparently, I began banging my butter knife on the table demanding that the waiter bring our food. Repetitive bodily behaviors like that are some of the ways complex partial seizures can manifest, but of course no one knew that. Everyone genuinely thought I was being funny. Devon left a generous tip, though."

I'm overwhelmed learning more about what Shay has been dealing with for so long. It can't be easy living in a body you can't control. Still, if Shay has unresolved business with the man she hoped to marry, I need to know. "Do you think that's why things ended? Because you weren't honest with him?"

"Possibly." Her eyes fill with tears.

I suck in a breath. I don't want to be someone's sloppy seconds. But goddamnit. I love this woman so much. My voice is ragged, pleading, "You don't want him back?"

"No." Shay shakes her head vigorously. "I want *you*. Only *you*. Understand, living my truth is the one way for me to live authentically. I never want to feel like I'm about to get caught again. If he hadn't broken up with me, I don't know what would have happened—well, I do. I'd be faking my life. Every second of it. Even though I'm going through loads of painful shit currently, it's real. You and I...we're *real*."

"We are," I confirm as we pull into the parking garage of my building.

I believe Shay, I do.

Still...I wonder—if Devon knew the truth about her illness, would he have thrown their relationship away so casually?

And, what would she do if he wanted her back?

Chapter Twenty-Two

A Few Minutes Later

One thing most people with epilepsy have in common is that we look like healthy people.

Until there's an episode.

It's difficult to talk about. To explain. Particularly if you don't understand it yourself. For me, living with epilepsy is an emotional, difficult, and lonely reality. Though I've tried to remain positive and unbothered by it, the side effects are brutal—and I've been through them all. Bad reaction to medication. Concentration and memory problems. Fatigue. Learning difficulties. Sluggishness. Insecurity.

Yeah. Insecurity. It's why I lie about it. Why I keep things from people. But lying doesn't make me feel better. In fact, the guilt and shame is overwhelming.

And yet, I've done it again. At least this time it wasn't about my condition. Maybe it's worse. I lied to my twin about falling for his best friend. When all he's done is help and support me. No wonder he let me have it.

Undoubtedly, I deserved everything he said.

"Hey..." Austin takes my hand and gently pulls me into his arms when we're on the elevator. "What's going on in that head of yours?"

My eyes flick to his lips. He backs to the wall and presses his body along the length of mine. I link my arms around his neck as he grips my waist, his fingertips dig in to pull me against his stiff cock.

"This." I lean up on my tiptoes to crush my mouth to his. I need Austin in order to breathe these days. Taking control, I turn us around and slam him against the wall of the elevator as we kiss.

I trail my hands down his body and kneel before him. Tug at his belt, pop the button on his jeans and lower his zipper so fast he doesn't have time to protest. His giant bulge tells me there's an excellent chance he's on board. I reach into his boxer briefs and pull out his cock, stroking his length a few times. When I look up at him, he's watching me. His eyes are glassy from arousal.

This. This is what I need. I want to make Austin feel fantastic.

Keeping my eyes fixed on his, I run my tongue along the length of him then take him all the way into my mouth until he bumps against my throat. I can't help but moan. I've never been one for blowjobs, but something about giving head to Austin sends zings of arousal all through my core. I'm so full of lust and need, I want to suck his dick like a porn star.

We're nearing the end of the elevator ride to his condo, so I double down. Austin grips my face on either side now, holding me in place while he fucks my mouth. With a guttural growl he comes down my throat until he's empty.

I push away, rock back onto my heels and smirk up at him as he tucks his dick back into his jeans. He's a bit out of breath. "Well, that was a bit of a bonus."

Before I can reply, Austin hauls me up into his arms and smashes his mouth against mine. He reaches down the front of my leggings through the side of my panties and begins to fuck me with his fingers. I'm drenched, of course and buck against him. Or mouths are frenzied and desperate, lashing together in time to his thrusts. I moan against his lips when he pulls out, runs his wet fingers along my clit then shoves them back inside me, finding a rhythm that drives me out of my fucking mind.

When he curves his fingers and hits my magical inner wall, I throw my head back and scream, "Ohmygod, *yesssss*."

"Come for me, baby. Let go." Austin trails his lips to my neck and sucks behind my ear as he relentlessly pumps into me.

My fingers claw at his shoulders and dig in, riding his hand shamelessly. I don't care who's watching as long as I get there. It hits me in waves. "Oh fuck," I stammer. "Oh yes, yes, yes. I'm coming, I'm coming, I'm *coming*!"

The orgasm is so overwhelming, I slump against him as he methodically flutters his fingers back and forth through my folds to drag it out. I shudder and pant through several little jolts and nearly come again when he pulls his fingers out and sucks on them just as the elevator opens into his unit.

"The best finger bang ever had by anyone ever in history." I pull my pants up and follow Austin out into his living room.

"Good to know." He winks, then takes the handle of my suitcase and rolls it into his condo. "We should order in dinner, don't you think?"

"Sure, you pick." I'm not even remotely hungry, but I know Austin is.

He jogs over to the kitchen where he keeps a bunch of takeout menus and rifles through them. He holds one up. "Chinese?"

"Sure. Get me some Almond Fried Chicken and fried rice." I give him a thumbs up.

While he orders our food, I stand at his floor-to-ceiling windows overlooking Puget Sound. It's still early in the evening, but aside from the traffic of people heading out for the long weekend, the city is rather quiet. Today's been a rollercoaster. From meeting Ty and Zoey to the confrontation with Miles to dropping in on my parents, my emotions are all over the map.

Plus, my clit is still pulsing from our intimate moment in the elevator.

The sex part is most definitely my favorite part of today.

I click the button on his remote and the shades close, shutting out the outside world so I can enjoy the bubble of Austin's condo. This place has become such a refuge for me. He and I can be in our own world here.

I feel the electric touch of his lips against my neck. "That elevator move was...unexpected," he whispers, a hint of playfulness evident in his tone.

"I was hoping you wouldn't think I was a psychopath for wanting to blow you after the day we had." I arch back into him.

Austin wraps his arms around my waist and pulls me close. "Well, after everything we went through tonight, I think we deserved a little...fun." His thumbs trace circles on my lower belly and begin to travel farther south.

I lean my head back against him and look up. "My parents can be too much. It's hard to figure out how to make them see me as an adult. They seem to think I'm still a defiant eighteen-year-old who refuses to take her meds."

"Yeah, well, your family was intense today. I'm not gonna lie. There're a slew of mixed messages, that's for sure. At the end of the day, though, I'd rather have my people looking out for me than ignoring I exist. I like that they're so protective of you."

The pressure of everything related to my condition niggles. "Does my epilepsy scare you?"

"Not exactly." He searches my eyes from above, taking a moment before responding. "Except for one thing."

My heart beats faster. This is usually when someone tells me I'm too much. "Tell me."

"I'll preface this by saying your condition is only one aspect of who you are. It doesn't fully define you." He kisses my temple. "The one thing that scares me is how much you've lied about it. I'd like you to always be honest with me, even if it's hard. No matter what."

"I will." Suddenly feeling uncomfortable, I break our embrace and flip around and down on the couch. "Tonight was a perfect example of why I do lie, though. Why I never told Devon. The second I got my diagnosis, it's been all my parents focus on with me. Now that you know, I don't want it to define our relationship, Austin. I don't need you to take care of me or hound me about medication. As long we operate on the premise that I'm a normal girl with a condition that I'm perfectly capable of managing, we'll be golden. Can you promise me that?"

Austin sits next to me and pulls me into his lap. "Of course I can. As long as you let me be a perfectly normal guy who wants to be assured the girl he loves is protected. It's a testosterone thing." He kisses me softly. "But, I see where you're coming from. Your health was all your parents talked about tonight. Have they even asked you about your job and what you're doing?"

"Well, of course. Though it always comes back to the epilepsy. It's so weird to be so one-dimensional to my family. First I was the pretty pageant girl. Then the erratic epileptic. My mom loved the idea of me being the quarterback's wife, I think she thought somehow that would protect me." I grab his thigh and squeeze. "She's was on board when I decided not to tell Devon, by the way. That was in the beginning and then...well, it became hard to come clean as time went on."

Austin sucks his lips all the way in and looks away. Nods.

"What did I say?" I cup his face and move it toward me so he's looking at me.

He narrows his eyes as if he's thinking about how to say what he needs to say, then comes out with it. "I'd like it if we put Devon in the past. Whatever you had or didn't have with him is irrelevant to me. I'm focused on our future as a couple. I don't need to hear why things didn't work out with you and him. It makes me feel…"

"Jealous?" I cock my head.

"Not exactly." He runs his hand up and down my thigh. "Annoyed. Because I can relate to how he presumably felt if you were keeping things from him. Like shit. I don't want you to treat me that way. It would make me feel like I don't matter enough for you to get real with me."

His words hit me deep in the gut. Is that how Devon felt? I certainly don't think so. Everything revolved around him, not me. Either way, I definitely don't want Austin to feel like he doesn't matter to me. Because he does. So much it scares me.

"I love you, Austin. I'm truly glad all of this is out in the open." I curl up in his lap and rest my head on his shoulder. "Devon is my past, I bring it up because I want to learn from the mistakes I made in a relationship that mattered to me so I don't screw things up with you."

Austin tips us over on the couch and cages my upper body in with his arms. Kisses me long and deep. "You won't screw things up. We're each other's future."

"Speaking of which, how far in the future will the food be here?" I blow a raspberry on his cheek.

He reaches for his phone to check the delivery status.

This beautiful man has become so important to me in such a short period of time. He allows me to be myself and loves me for it. He's stood by my side in the face of some heavy family drama.

I'm not going to let anyone—or anything—come between us.

Chapter Twenty-Three

Austin

The Next Afternoon

After such an emotional and weird day, Shay and I slept in.

Admittedly, we were up most of the night because I can't keep my hands off her. When she's curled up next to me naked in my bed, what am I supposed to do? I can't help myself.

My head is also spinning because of how quickly my plans changed. Yesterday, before Miles found out about us, I planned on spending the day on my own playing video games. Now, Shay and I get to make a memory of our first Thanksgiving together—and she's staying all weekend, if not longer.

I'm relieved she doesn't want to go back to her parents' house. I'm not ready to see Miles and I don't want to re-live the "are you going to take care of Shay" conversation with her folks. I want a normal day with my girlfriend.

For now I'm breathing in the warm aroma of roasted turkey mingling with the rich scent of buttery mashed potatoes, herb-infused stuffing, and tangy cranberry sauce. We also have caramelized brussels sprouts and a creamy green bean casserole topped with crispy onions. I can't wait to dig in.

Shay suggested we eat our leftovers from last night for dinner, but I wanted to have a real feast. I called in a favor and Canlis sent food over this afternoon together with a sous chef to finish cooking. Everything is ready, all I have to do is take the turkey and side dishes out of the warmer.

My housekeeper popped over earlier and set two place settings on one side of my enormous dining table. I'm convinced she bought updated place settings because I've never seen the gold-rimmed plates and crystal glass-es before. There's also a beautiful arrangement of au-tumn flowers. A perfect decoration for a perfect day. I set up the food on the opposite side of the table.

Shay enters the room wearing an oversized sweatshirt and not much else. Her eyes wide with amazement. "Wow, Austin. So fancy. This looks incredible."

"I wanted it to be special for us." I pull out a chair for her.

She sits and takes in all the food. "We'll never need to buy groceries again."

Pouring a glass of sparkling cider for her and one for myself, I raise my glass. "To us. To new beginnings and to finding happiness in unexpected places."

She clinks her glass against mine. "Amen. To us."

"Should we watch the Seahawks game?" I say through a bite of turkey.

Shay's face brightens. "Yeah. It's been a while since I've cheered for the home team."

The game hasn't started so we concentrate on eating. The food is absolutely delicious, which distracts us—it isn't until the players take the field that I realize I've inadvertently set a potential landmine into our day. The Raiders make their entrance through the tunnel and the camera zooms in on their star quarterback, Devon, as they take the field.

My stomach roils when I see his face. The idea that this guy had his hands on Shay kinda kills me. He lived with her. Spent nearly a decade with her...

Shay is quiet, her attention on the screen and not on my reaction. "I didn't know they were in town."

"Yeah," I try to sound casual. "Me neither."

The tension in the air between us is palpable. Her ex is in the same city as we are. Rather than rehash the conversation we've already had, I decide to try to distract myself by focusing on the food. I get up for another helping of stuffing and gravy and sit back down.

The rest of the game is intense. Scores trading back and forth with both teams showing incredible prowess. Every time Devon appears on the screen, I can't help but glance at Shay, wondering if she's reminiscing about their time together. The fact that the woman I'm in love with could've easily been this guy's wife gnaws at me.

And then, to my dismay, the Raiders pull off a victory.

Post-game, the commentator approaches Devon, microphone in hand. "A stunning victory tonight. How do you feel about playing and winning against Seattle?"

Devon's eyes bore into the camera. "The Seahawks are formidable—it just went our way today. There's a bigger reason Seattle will always be special to me. Not because of football, but because the woman I love is from here. Shay, if you're watching, I want you to know that I made a mistake and want you back."

Shay's fork clatters onto her plate, her face is pale.

I clear my throat. "Shay...you don't have to say anything."

Her eyes glisten with tears. "Austin, I'm not taking him back. I haven't spoken to him since the day I moved out of our place. I changed my phone and blocked him on social media."

Her phone, which is on the dining table next to her, begins to buzz uncontrollably.

"He's clearly not over you," I mutter, feeling sick with jealousy and fear. "You should see who's trying to get ahold of you."

Shay grabs her phone and throws it across the room. "I don't give a shit about whoever is trying to reach me. What he said is most likely all over the media, goddammit." She pounds her fist into her palm. "I'm so fucking over him. I told you that last night. What you and I have is unique. *Special.* You've shown me what real love feels like." She gets up and moves around the table to sit in my lap. "Please don't be the kind of guy who reads into something I have no control over and makes it my fault."

Am I doing that? I lean against her chest and look up at her. Search for reassurance in her eyes. "Sometimes it feels surreal that you and I are in this place after so many years. Knowing you were with someone like him—it's hard not to feel like I'm in his shadow."

"Austin, I know you possibly still have some residual worries about me because of what happened in high school." Shay combs her fingers through the long part of my hair. "You said you wanted to leave it behind. What matters is us, here and now. *You're* my present and future. Not Devon."

We sit in silence for a few moments. I know I've got to take her at her word. Unfortunately, there's the part of my brain that excelled in programming that knows something is off. Or, I'm missing a piece of information. At the same time, I have a choice. Get fucked up in my head by petty shit or enjoy my gorgeous, sweet girlfriend who's sitting in my lap.

It's undoubtedly an easy decision.

"I have a few ideas on how to leave all of it behind." I grab the bottom of her sweatshirt and pull it up and over her head, tossing it on the floor next to me. Then, I reach behind her and sweep my dinner plate, silverware, and glassware to the side.

Shay smiles when I lick across her cleavage, which is level with my mouth. "Oh. Yes."

Back and forth I suck and lave her nipples until they are puckered into stiff points. She shifts so she's straddling my lap and arches against me, grinding against my cock. I rip my own shirt off in a flash and she leverages her thrusts by gripping my shoulders, her nails digging in until it stings. I love it and hope she leaves marks. It's cool to see evidence of our passion on my skin.

I grip her waist and push her back against the table and kiss down her ribs. "I don't want to wait, I want to be inside you."

"That's terrific news, because I want you in me." She slides her hands up my sides and scores her nails over my ribs, sending shivers all over my body. "*Now*."

I reach down and see a dark, wet spot on her panties causing my cock to lurch. I move the slip of fabric to the side to reveal her pink pussy lips, glistening with arousal. I slide my thumb through her folds, fascinated by her beautiful little cunt. Swirling my fingers into her moisture I swipe up to her clit, which is engorged and pokes out of its hood. I lightly rub it and watch her contract around me. Her stomach muscles ripple.

Shay's arms are over her head, draped along the table. "God, how you touch me," she cries.

I can wait no longer. I clasp her hips and lift her so her entire back and ass is on the table. I stand between her legs and yank down my joggers so my achingly hard dick is free. Shay reaches down between us and grabs my cock and angles it toward her opening. "In me."

"I love it when you turn into a demandingly cock-hungry temptress." I cant my hips and impale her to the hilt with one thrust.

Shay sucks in a breath and locks her long legs around my hips. I lean over and kiss her mouth and make my way to her throat. She rolls her head up and back, giving me access to her entire neck like an offering to a vampire. I taste the softness of her skin and breathe deep. Her muscles flex as she moves with me to meet my slow thrusts.

There are no words, just gasps and groans as we move together, her tits jiggling in time to our rhythm. She grabs my ass and digs her fingers in, holding on. I smooth my hands along her thighs and hike her legs up to the sides of her stomach, angling to lick and kiss the back of her legs. Shay moans loudly and I can't take my eyes off my engorged cock sliding in and out of her channel.

Holy shit. Shay reaches down and circles her clit with her middle finger, causing her to tighten around my cock with each motion. Every time I thrust, she squeezes. Her hot, wet heat is sending me to a blissful oblivion when her inner muscles begin to tremble and clench. I know I can't hold back any longer.

I drive harder into her like a battering ram and she screams bloody murder when her pussy clamps down on my cock. Her eyes nearly roll back into her head when she shatters around me. With one final thrust, I cry out her name and join her, filling her with my release.

As spent as I am, I'm in a sexual haze when I pull out and sit back down, gripping each of her feet and placing them on my thighs. I lean over and spread her pussy lips apart and have a bird's eye view of my come spilling out of her. She's the most delicious all-you-can-eat buffet ever. I want to gorge and gorge on her. So, I do. I dive in and clean her with my tongue. Savor every inch of her pussy. Drink our combined liquid down like wine as I circle her sensitive clit with my finger.

I glance up to find her propped up on her elbows watching me, pinching her nipples between her fingers. "This is the hottest thing I've ever seen," she pants.

I don't answer, I keep enjoying her deliciousness. Her inner thighs begin to shake and quiver. I thrust two fingers inside her as I lap her up. Soon she's bucking against my lips. Undulating her hips. Hissing and swearing. Then she jackknifes against my face and let's go like I've never seen before.

It takes her ages to stop writhing and moaning.

I pull her back down into my lap to pet her back. Soothe her. Show her how much I worship her and her body.

When she recovers a while later, Shay blinks up at me and smiles.

"You definitely know how to throw down the gauntlet, don't you?"

Chapter Twenty-Four

I press the elevator button to the top floor, feeling nauseated.

Last weekend with Austin was everything I hoped for. A supercharged version of the night we were trapped in the ski patrol hut. The two of us in our own bubble of sex, laughter, and togetherness.

It's Monday, though and it's time to be back in the real world. The first thing on my list is to squash things with my brother. We've had a few days to cool off. I'm hurt. He's hurt. I know this conversation is crucial.

I approach his office and see he's behind his desk. Taking a deep breath, I open his door. "Miles? Can I come in?"

He doesn't look up, nods. "Sure."

Natural light filters through the floor-to-ceiling windows. It's a typical dreary, gray winter day which, hopefully, won't match his mood. I can't stand being at odds with Miles, my twin, and I'll do nearly anything to make amends.

I close the door behind me and take a seat facing his desk. "I know we all have a full day today, but I came to talk about...everything."

He runs his hand through his thatch of blond hair and raises an eyebrow. "Missed you at dinner. I can't believe you didn't come over."

"Austin and I stopped by the night before Thanksgiving to let the 'rents know about us being together. I didn't want them to hear it from anyone else but me." I lean back in the chair and keep eye contact. I don't want us to have any further misunderstandings.

Miles shakes his head. "I heard. Shay, I feel like an ass. I said stupid shit I didn't mean. Um... I worry about you so much. It's exhausting sometimes."

"I know you're concerned about me. And I get why. You said some profoundly hurtful things last week. But in case you're not clear, Austin and I—we're serious." I tug at my skirt. "I *know* it seems sudden..."

He scoffs. "Sudden? It's been, what? Three weeks since the retreat? You have to admit, considering what a dick he was being to you this so-called love connection seems a little suss."

"Yeah, I know. We genuinely worked things out when we got stranded. Austin was hurt because of what happened back in high school. He didn't know about the memory loss and the med situation. I didn't remember that we, uh...had sex that night." I wince. Miles and I are close, but not so close that we share details about our romantic interludes.

Miles shuts his eyes and then opens them. Sighs. "He and I both lost our virginity that night. We both were dumped the next day. It was a bit traumatizing for a couple of geeks like us to have the beautiful girls use us for our bodies and then utterly ignore us."

"You've done fine. So has he." I laugh. "He was telling me about your smooth ways in college before you dropped out."

He covers his face with his hand. "Yeah, yeah. We did okay. Can we *please* change the subject?"

"Fine. I came here to make up with you and ask you sincerely, from the bottom of my heart, what can I do to stop all of the resentment that's built up? Most of what you hurled at me came from a place of truth." I wrap my arms around myself protectively, ready to take whatever he's going to give out.

Silence hangs in the air. I watch as Miles leans back in his chair, a myriad of emotions playing on his face. "I...don't want to see you hurt again, Shay."

"You've always been protective. I mean, we're twins and you were born first. It's kinda your job, I guess." I try to keep my voice even.

His gaze turns distant. "It was...until pageants came along. And then your epilepsy diagnosis. Then cheerleading and the popular kids at school. Then there was Devon. It felt like you kept moving into worlds where I didn't belong."

I bite my lip, guilt washing over me. "I didn't mean to push you away. Pageants were a way for me to build confidence. Mom made me take up cheerleading after the diagnosis. It wasn't about leaving you behind. It was about me keeping up with smart, destined-for-greatness Miles."

"You seriously thought that?" Miles looks at me like I'm nuts. "I always thought I was the loser of the family."

My heart aches. "Hardly. Look what you've built." I gesture around the room. "I'm always going to win the title of 'most fucked up' in our family. I'm so sorry about anything I've done that hurt you, I never wanted us to drift apart. For so many years I was trying to cope but I've grown, I've changed. And Austin...he's going to be a part of my future."

"Look, I don't want to be the bad guy. But I'm scared for you. I know I hurled petty, spiteful things at you—but the truth is I'm worried. What if Austin breaks your heart? What if things don't work out?" He clenches his hands together.

I shrug. Smile. "It's a risk I'm willing to take. For love, for my happiness."

"Do you know about Austin's childhood?" Miles clears his throat. "When he and I became friends?"

I shake my head slowly. "Some. Not enough. He's indicated things were tough for him, but he hasn't shared the details."

Miles takes a deep breath. "There were many afternoons when I'd find Austin at our doorstep, crying. Once he had kids with Austin's mom, the stepdad made it brutally clear that Austin wasn't part of their family unit. And it wasn't only the blatant exclusions during family events, it was the little things too. The way he'd speak to him, the way Austin would sometimes flinch at sudden movements. And worst of all, Austin's mom, she never once defended her own son."

The knowledge feels like daggers to my heart. I can't believe anyone could treat any child that way, let alone someone as special as Austin. It makes so much sense now. When we talked about having kids, he was passionate about how important it is to show them love. "Don't say anymore. I want to know, but I want to respect him enough to let him share all of this with me when he feels safer in our relationship."

Miles shakes his head. "Good luck with that. Austin is extremely proficient at focusing on you and terrible at having you focus on him. Take it from me. He hates being a burden to anyone."

I want to cry. I don't want him to think anything he could tell me would be burdensome. "It's heartbreaking."

"Yeah." Miles nods. "Austin leaned on our family—mostly me and Dad, an awful lot. We were his sanctuary, a place where he felt wanted."

I digest what Miles has shared. "Do you think he thinks I can't handle his past? Is that it?"

"It's not about what you can handle." Miles pauses, choosing his words. "It's about Austin. He tends to immerse himself—no, lose himself in distraction from his personal life. With you, I'm worried he'll lose himself entirely because you're so...extra."

I feel exceedingly defensive at my brother's comment. "In my relationship with Devon, I molded myself to be what I thought he needed—what *he* said he needed. I thought I wanted to be like Mom. Marry someone with fame and wealth. Be taken care of. Bend over backward to be the perfect partner. If there's anyone who understands losing one's self in a relationship, it's me. I won't let that happen again, not to me and certainly not to Austin."

"Shay." Miles leans forward and rests his elbows on the desk. "I know you've been through a lot. And I know you and Austin are in the honeymoon phase. But you need to understand something. This isn't about what you've been through; it's about what Austin has endured too. He's sensitive in ways you might not fully grasp yet."

The insinuation stings. "You think I don't understand sensitivity? After all my years of dealing with epilepsy, of being stared at and whispered about? I know sensitivity, Miles."

"Sure, but Austin's brand of sensitivity is tied to abandonment, to never feeling worthy. I've seen it. When we were kids, he was bullied. Other children excluded him because of rumors about his family. He'd get teased after his stepdad publicly reprimanded him. He's always felt the need to prove himself, to be seen. You have to understand that it's the same, but different." Miles gets up and walks around to where I'm sitting and crouches next to me. "What I'm trying to say is, take care of each *other*. He needs a little TLC too."

Miles' revelations press heavily on my heart. "Okay. I need to fully digest what you're saying to me."

Miles takes my hand. "Look, I may not know a lot about love but I do know it's not only about finding refuge in someone else. It's about being a refuge for them too."

"I think that goes for you and me too." I get up from my chair. Miles stands and we hug. "I promise to do better.

Speaking of which, aside from the company, what's going on with you?"

Miles pulls away. "You know Austin wants to sell Hungry Llama when we're at our peak so he can get involved in venture capital. I think if we make stupid money from this thing I'll potentially go in an entirely unconventional direction."

"Oh, really?" I jab him with my elbow. "Like what?"

"I'd like to get married, have kids. Maybe start a farm or something." Miles purses his lips. Shrugs.

I'm thoroughly blown away. "A farm? That's cool."

Miles nods. "Look, I'm genuinely sorry about the other day. I want to be the best brother to you, Shay."

"And I want the best for both of us. Let's bridge this stupid gap between us, Miles. For the record, I like working here and I think I'm making a difference. Please tell Mom and Dad I'm not some pity party." I hug him again.

A small smile appears on his lips. "It won't be easy."

"Since when do we do things the easy way?" I chuckle.

He laughs, and in that moment, we're back. I get up to leave.

"Promise me you'll be careful and always be honest with him about your health," he says to my back.

I turn and hold up my hand like I'm swearing in on the witness stand. "I promise."

I leave feeling like our twin bond has been mended. The road ahead might be uncertain in many ways, but with my brother's hesitant blessing, I feel better.

For today, that's enough.

Chapter Twenty-Five

Austin

A Few Hours Later

The annoying hum of the office heater does nothing to ease the tension in the room.

Shay encouraged me to talk to Miles after her meeting went well, which of course it did. They're twins, for fuck's sake.

I'm merely the rent-a-brother.

Through the glass walls of his office, I see Miles sitting behind his desk, he's facing away from me, staring out the window. I hate what happened last week and wish Shay had felt comfortable telling him about our relationship status after we hooked up. But, what's done is done.

The thought of losing Stodge is unfathomable. We're not solely business partners, as far as I'm concerned we've been brothers in all but blood for nearly two decades. It's time to repair whatever damage I caused by falling in love with his sister. This is uncharted territory.

I clear my throat when I open the door to his office and jump in without any fanfare. "Stodge, I understand your concerns regarding Shay. But you need to know this isn't a casual fling."

He whirls around and glares at me. "And?"

"Uh…" I stammer. "I love her."

Miles slaps his desk. "I have to ask, is it lust or love, Austin?"

"Both?" I wince. He doesn't need to know about our sex life. So much ick.

Miles looks like he's smelled something rancid. "I walked right into that one, didn't I? Sit down, let's hash through this shit."

"Yeah, let's." I take the seat across from him. "Let me have it."

He nods. "She's my twin. We shared the same womb. When she hurts, I feel it. And when she's happy, that's my joy too."

"I get it. And you know my history, you're worried I won't be enough for her." It makes sense, it's not like

I have stellar role models modeling romantic relation-ships.

He stands and leans over his desk, pointing his index finger at me. "Don't be an idiot. You're so off base it's comical. I actually think you're perfect for her, but between the two of you there's a load of baggage to sort through. And I *don't* mean Devon."

"What do you mean then?" I'm relieved to hear he approves of me but the baggage comment has me worried.

He turns to his computer and pivots the monitor around so I can see a website with a ton of informa-tion about epilepsy. "Shay's condition... It's not always predictable. She's found the correct meds, but there are certain protocols you need to know if she has an episode. My guess is she hasn't gone over any of this with you."

I raise a hand, halting him. "Wait a minute. I've been researching. Reading up on it. I will be there for her, every step of the way."

His eyebrows furrow. "It's beyond knowing what to do when she has a seizure. It's understanding that even if things are controlled now it can change. If she's tired. Agitated. Stressed. Her hormones are out of whack. Have you talked about having kids?"

"Whoa, whoa." I shake both hands at him. "We've been together for less than a month. Only on a surficial level."

He lifts his shoulders. "Don't put those conversations off. I'm just sayin'."

"Miles, I can assure you, whatever challenges lie ahead, we'll face them together. I won't let her go through any of it alone." I place my hand over my heart.

He watches me for a long moment. "Okay. Because if you ever let her down, it won't only be her heart that breaks."

A heavy silence settles between us. But there's another topic to address. "We need to talk about Hungry Llama and where we see ourselves in the next few years. Do we sell or keep going?"

"You're still thinking we should sell?" Miles leans back in his chair, his fingers drum on the desk. "That's your part of the business, I pump out the games."

"Fire up your Slack." I watch as he pulls it up on his desktop. "Open up that spreadsheet." He clicks and opens the document I worked on for the past couple months. Columns of numbers, prospective buyers, and market data come into view. The possibility of selling Hungry Llama suddenly feels real.

"Okay," Miles begins, tapping a cell on the spreadsheet that lists out potential buyers, "We've got a few options to consider. Private equity firms, strategic buyers, and maybe even a few industry giants might be interested."

I frown, considering. "Strategic buyers? You mean our competitors?"

"Precisely. Sometimes it's easier for a competitor to buy us out than to try to outpace us in the market." Miles nods.

"Well, well, well. Listen to you! There are pros and cons to all of these options." I love that Miles has done some homework. "Our team has been with us through thick and thin. I want to be confident they're taken care of. Especially after the retreat."

Miles gives me a knowing look. "Agreed. A competitor might have redundancy but a private equity firm could restructure and lay off staff. If we're not in any rush, let's take the time to find the appropriate industry buyer so our team might get a better deal. More resources, better benefits."

I nod cautiously. "Alright, so how do we approach this? A bidding war?"

Miles grins, the glint of challenge lights up his eyes. "I think so. We'll need to generate buzz. Make Hungry Llama seem like the hottest ticket in town. A business everyone wants to own."

Leaning forward, I consider this. "I'm not so sure. We're a unicorn of gaming companies. Whoever acquires us is going to want us to be part of a portfolio—and keep the management team intact. Or, they're a bigger media company that wants a gaming arm."

Miles chuckles. "So more like a down-low outreach then."

"Yeah, I think we'll garner a bigger payout if we keep it quiet. Publicity could eliminate a key leveraged position of being stealth. If the perception is we don't want—and don't need—to sell, we become coveted." I tap out of the spreadsheet and into our financial management program. "We can't forget the due diligence. Our books are in pristine order but any buyer will go through our financial records and key strategic contracts with a fine tooth comb."

Miles leans back and puts his hands behind his head. "I'm assuming you're doing this already?"

"Yup. I have a system in place." I nod.

"You're thinking big." Miles smirks. "I like it."

"Go big or go home, right?" We fist pump across the table then I click to another spreadsheet I'm working on. "Early next year, I'd like to meet with a few investment banking firms that specialize in our sector. They can help us work on a valuation, set a price and make introductions. I'm leaning toward Morrison & Co. because they brokered the deal for TechGrid last year, but I figure we should stay open."

Miles taps his finger to his lips. "What about Jacoby International? Joar Jacoby seems to be gobbling up media properties. I hear he's a decent guy."

"Yeah, we should meet with him." I close out all of the windows. "At the end of the day, I love running Hungry Llama so if nothing seems suitable, we stay the course."

Miles gets up and walks over to a cabinet where he keeps a couple bottles of whiskey. "I think this calls for a celebration." He takes out a limited-edition bottle of Midleton. "When we started this company, did you ever think we'd be worth over a billion dollars?"

"Not in a billion years." I throw Miles a cheesy grin.

There's a long pause as Miles pours us our drinks. I know him. He's wrestling with emotions and practicalities. This is a big deal. Ultimately, he nods and hands me a glass. We clink them together and take a sip. "Alright. We need to explore it. We'll meet with a few of these firms. Get a feel for who might be the best fit."

I grasp his shoulder and pull him in for a bro hug. "If I don't say it enough, building this with you has been the greatest thing I've ever done. It wouldn't mean anything without you."

"Same, dude. Same." Miles pounds my back with his fist. "It's not a business decision, is it? It's about Shay. Wanting to create a future with her."

I can't deny it. "Sure, yes. But also, maybe it's time for a new adventure. Both professionally and personally."

We both sit in silence, lost in our thoughts. After what seems like hours, Miles speaks. "I'm glad you've finally seen the real Shay."

I clasp my hands together. "Me too. I feel like such a dick for being so hard on her those first couple of weeks. You weren't wrong to call me out on the way to the retreat."

"It's what partners do. I didn't mean for you to sleep with her, but I guess what's done is done." He laughs then grows serious. "Remember, whatever happens with Hungry Llama, or with Shay, we're in this together. You're my brother in all the ways that count."

Our bond reaffirmed, I leave his office feeling lighter.

Having Miles's blessing is everything.

I can't wait to see Shay.

Chapter Twenty-Six

Christmas Day

The soft glow of Christmas lights spills across the living room, illuminating Austin's handsome face with a warm, gentle light.

The air around us carries a mix of holiday scents—pine, peppermint, and freshly baked cookies. My parents are buzzing around, making certain everything is perfect for the Christmas feast. Neither of them will let us lift a finger.

Miles is upstairs fixing Dad's computer, leaving Austin and I drinking hot cocoa in the living room opposite the ginormous tree decorated in silver, green, and gold.

Despite the external cheer, Austin's quiet demeanor has my attention. I can sense an underlying sadness, though he's trying to hide it.

"You okay?" I nudge him slightly.

He offers a weak smile. "Yeah. Of course."

"Austin," I press gently, intertwining our fingers and bringing them to my lips. "Tell me the truth."

He takes a deep breath and looks down at our entwined hands. "I stopped by my mom's house before coming here to drop off gifts for my step-siblings. No one was home. The entire place was dark."

I squeeze his hand, feeling a pang of sorrow. "Wow. I wonder where they are?"

"Who knows." He shakes his head. "I'm so fucking happy, I wanted to share it with my own family. I keep forgetting I don't have one. I wish I had answers. What the fuck did I do to them?"

"I'm so sorry." I nestle into him. "I'm happy to share mine with you. Someday, maybe we'll have our own family, so you won't have to feel so alone."

He shrugs, attempting nonchalance. "It's ...odd. Like I've been erased from their lives."

My heart aches for him. Austin has always strived for connections, a sense of belonging. And to be shut out from his own family, especially during the holidays, must be gut-wrenching. "You're not erased from this family," I whisper, kissing his soft lips. "You're a part of us now."

He smiles at me, though the sadness doesn't fully leave his eyes. "Thank you, babe."

Before we can continue our conversation, my mom sweeps into the room, her usual efficient energy filling the space. "Austin, help me with the roast? It's a bit heavy and Goran has disappeared into the garage for some reason."

Austin rises to his feet. "Of course, Annika."

I bring my knees to my chest and sip my cocoa, watching them interact. It's incredible how seamlessly Austin has integrated even further into our family. They share laughs over the kitchen counter as they get the food put together. My dad reappears, chiming in with his own jokes. Even amidst the laughter, I can't shake off the cloud that hangs over Austin. I want to do something about it, but I don't know what.

Yet.

"Shay, go get your brother. Dinner's ready," Dad shouts from the kitchen.

Miles bounds down the stairs. "I heard you. Computer's back up and running."

Miles and I join my folks and Austin in the kitchen to bring the food to the dining room. As we settle down for dinner, my dad raises his glass for a toast. "To family," he starts, his voice deep and filled with emotion, "to those we're born into, and those we choose. Austin, you may have felt like an outsider in some parts of your life, but here, in this home, you'll always belong."

Tears sting my eyes as I watch Austin, his face reflecting a mixture of gratitude and lingering sadness.

The room erupts in a chorus of "cheers," but the significance of my dad's words hangs in the air. I wonder if the toast made Austin feel better or worse.

I'll talk to him about it when we're alone.

***

Dressed in my comfortable, oversized white sweater that Austin loves so much, I snuggle closer to him on the sofa, cherishing the warmth of his embrace. My parents and Miles sit across from us, sipping on mulled wine. The aroma of spices fill the room. It's so cozy and comfortable, I'm almost hesitant to bring up the topic at hand.

His sadness from earlier has been replaced by nervous energy as we prepare to broach the subject of my moving into his penthouse.

Mom's gaze meets mine. "Are you staying here tonight, Shay?"

"Well, now that you mention it..." I start.

Austin gently clears his throat and interrupts. I know it's important for him to have my parents' blessing. "Shay and I have been discussing the possibility of her moving into my penthouse. Obviously, we're adults and don't need permission, but we wanted to discuss it with you both before making any final decisions."

"Well, that's a significant step." Dad's eyebrows rise, a flicker of concern flashes in his eyes.

Austin nods, gripping my hand tightly. "I understand, Goran. But Miles and I had a long talk and I've taken the time to discuss Shay's epilepsy journey with her. We created a Seizure Action Plan."

"You did?" Mom looks surprised. My family has one, but it's been such a secret since none of us let anyone know about my condition.

"I brought Austin to my appointment with my neurologist. She spent time with us to help Austin identify my potential seizure triggers and the most beneficial response," I jump in to explain. "Obviously, I knew about things like stress, lack of sleep, or certain stimuli. We also learned episodes might be related to hormonal fluctuations as I approach thirty—which means, if I'm going to have babies, we're potentially on a shorter timeline."

"We've also enlisted a medical facility familiar with Shay's condition closer to Seattle," Austin says. "I'll text you the emergency contacts. Oh, and I've been through basic training on how to assist during a seizure."

"Babies?" My mom flutters her hand over her heart. "Don't toy with me, Shay."

I can't help but laugh. "We're fast tracking our relationship a bit."

"Before we get there, I'll be asking you a profoundly important question." Austin points at my dad.

Dad's stern gaze softens, clearly impressed by Austin's commitment. "I'm not only fine with this, I'm happy about it. Shay, your well-being is paramount to us. Honestly, this is the first time in a long time I feel relieved, knowing you'll be in excellent hands."

"Thank you, Goran. Although, Shay is perfectly capable of taking care of herself. I want to be there for her in every possible way." Austin cuddles me closer to him.

There's a brief silence, the soft crackling of the fire filling the void. Miles breaks it with a pointed question, "You're both confident about this step?"

I nod, drawing a deep breath. "With Austin, I feel safe, loved. Our relationship has grown immensely. We've discussed our dreams, our fears, and our hopes for the future. Living together feels like the next step for us."

Dad raises his wine glass. "To new beginnings and unwavering love. I guess this is your official welcome to the family, Austin."

We all join in the toast, the sound of clinking glasses is music to my ears.

After dinner, Austin and I steal a quiet moment away from the festivities to sit on the porch, wrapped in blankets against the winter chill. The night sky is clear, stars shimmer brightly.

"I'm sorry about earlier." Austin kisses my temple. "I didn't mean to bring a downer to the celebration."

"No, don't apologize." I shake my head. "You should never hide your feelings from me. I seriously want to go tell your mother off."

He pulls me close, resting his chin atop my head. "I always hoped that, one day, things would change. That they'd see me. Accept me. But I guess some things aren't meant to be. I'm not going to try anymore, it sucks every fucking time."

I tilt my head up, and gaze into his eyes. "You know, families come in all forms. It's not only about blood. It's about the people who show up for you, who stand by your side no matter what. And I know I said it earlier, but it's true. My family is your family."

"Your dad's toast unquestionably hit me. I've never been welcomed like that before." He brushes his lips against mine. "You can never break up with me now. You're stuck with me."

"It's no hardship. You deserve all the love." I press a soft kiss to his lips.

We sit in comfortable silence for a while, taking in the serenity of the night. In the distance, we can even hear friggin' Christmas carols. I feel like I'm in a *Lifetime* Christmas movie. Minus the murder and kidnapping.

"Shay?" Austin nuzzles my ear.

"Hmm?"

"Maybe it's time for a change." He kisses the soft spot on my neck that drives me wild. "A fresh start, somewhere we can build our own traditions, our own family. Miles and I are going to sell the company."

I blink, processing his words. "What?"

He grins. "It's time to move on to bigger and better things. Together."

"I think that's a beautiful idea, Austin." Warmth floods my chest, excitement bubbles up within me.

Of course, he hasn't brought up marriage, which worries me a little.

Well, a lot.

"Merry Christmas, Shay." He pulls me close, our breaths mingle in the cold air.

I smile, feeling the utter comfort of this moment, a promise of a future together. "Merry Christmas, Austin."

Chapter Twenty-Seven

Austin

New Years Eve

I don't remember ever legitimately celebrating New Year's Eve, but this year there's a myriad of reasons to revel.

Shay moved in last weekend. All her stuff is hanging in our closet. Her makeup and shampoo and all the little doo-dads she needs to get ready fill the drawers in our bathroom. She's already talking about redecorating a couple of the bedrooms.

It's a domestic paradise.

Tonight, we're hanging out with Miles at a quaint little speakeasy a couple of blocks from our home. It's filled with locals and the room is abuzz with laughter, music, and chatter. Glittering lights reflect off the polished wood and dim, overhead stained-glass lights create a cozy ambiance, perfectly capturing the New Year's Eve spirit.

Shay looks stunning, wearing a little black dress that hugs her curves, her blonde hair cascades in loose waves over her shoulders. She dances facing where I sit on a barstool, swaying slightly to the rhythm of the jazz band playing in the corner. Miles, looking dapper in a crisp white shirt, is chatting with a gorgeous dark-haired beauty who is covered in colorful tattoos.

I tug Shay in between my legs and whisper, "Flirt alert."

"God, I'm glad we reclaimed that word for ourselves." Shay drapes her arms across my shoulder and leans in for a sweltering kiss. "We just got here, though."

I run my hands down her back and cup her perfect ass. "Yeah, I know. Can't help it."

It's funny to me now how much Shay's old high school term used to make me see red.

Now hearing it makes me hard as a rock.

It's still a secret message. Now it's *our* secret message.

Shay hated that something so silly had made me feel shitty for so long. A couple days ago she decided we should repurpose the term. Associate a flirt alert with something positive—now it's our signal that we're hot for each other and need to find somewhere to be alone. *Stat*.

"I love you." Shay presses her body against mine. "Tell you what. Let's ring in the new year and immediately go home and fuck until dawn."

I nearly spit out my drink. "You're trying to kill me. My boner's about to burst through my pants."

"Hmmm." She covertly rubs the heel of her hand against my distinct bulge. "*Maybe* we could go sooner."

Unfortunately, we're thwarted.

Miles slings his arm around both of our necks, nearly causing the three of us to bang our heads together. "This is the best night ever. I'm with my two favorite people in the world." He raises his glass and downs it. Slaps his hand on the bar and orders another.

"It's great to see the two of you let loose." Shay sips her cocktail. "Everyone needs to blow off some steam."

When Miles gets another beer, I raise my glass. "To us." I clink it against their glasses. I haven't felt this loose and free in a long time. Our camaraderie is tangible, and it feels like the perfect ending to a challenging year and the promising start of another.

As the night wears on and the bar starts filling up, I'm feeling the effects of the alcohol. The atmosphere is electric. Everyone is in a terrific mood. The energy seems illuminated with hope and excitement for the midnight countdown. I see a strobe light descend from the ceiling. The digital clock clicks down. In five minutes, we'll be kissing at midnight.

Shay leans into me and I wind my arms around her middle, keeping her close. The lights are flashing. The music is loud. It's so crowded I don't want to risk getting separated when it's time for our new year's kiss. I nuzzle her ear. "It's been a whirlwind few months, hasn't it?"

She doesn't answer. Even though I'm a bit buzzed, I notice a change in her demeanor. Shay's fingers twitch slightly on her glass. Her face contorts into a slight grimace, and she blinks rapidly, looking disoriented. Like she can't speak.

"Shay? Baby?" I question, now extremely concerned.

Miles, noticing my distress asks, "Everything okay?"

In that moment the bar's lighting takes a dramatic turn. Flashing beams of white, blue, and red start darting around the room as patrons begin to shout out the final countdown. The strobing effect seems to heighten her distress.

Trying to stay calm and assess the situation, I know that it's too late to give her a Xanax. My only option is to note the time and keep her safe until this passes. "I ought to get her out of here, can you get our coats and meet me back at my place?"

Before I can do anything, Shay's symptoms escalate. She clutches her head with both hands and winces, looking around. "I'm so fucking hot." Alarmingly, she starts to fumble at her dress, nearly pulling it off.

Miles is on his feet in an instant. We know we're not supposed to contain her but we try box her in gently but firmly, so she won't undress in the middle of a crowded room. The bar noise fades to a muted hum in my ears as my world zeroes in on Shay and keeping my promise to her dad, mom, and brother.

The vibrant atmosphere turns nightmarish as I desperately try to shield her from the surrounding chaos. "Shay, stay with us," I plead, my voice thick with anguish.

Moments that feel like hours pass. And then, as abruptly as it started, Shay snaps out of it. Her breathing is ragged, her eyes bewildered. "Wh-what happened?" she murmurs, looking down at her disheveled dress.

I pull her close, my heart pounding in my chest. "You're safe now. Let's get home."

Miles rests his hand on Shay's shoulder but looks at me. "I'll meet you at your place. Go, I'll take care of the tab and get your things."

As we make our way out, the patrons who were close to us and witnessed Shay's episode, offer words of empathy. They probably think she's drunk, but it doesn't matter. The one person who matters in this moment is my girlfriend.

We walk the two blocks to our building. I know that fresh air will be helpful for Shay to clear her head. Even better, we're away from the blaring lights and noise. Shay leans into me on the short walk, I keep my arm firmly around her until I have her safely on the couch. Thank sweet baby Jesus that we were close to home because I wouldn't have been able to drive us, there's no doubt I'd be over the limit.

"How do you feel, baby?" I kneel beside her and take her shoes off, kissing the sole of each foot.

"This isn't how I imagined ending the year." Shay holds her forehead. "I have a splitting headache."

I squeeze her hand. "Miles will be here soon and I'll go get your medicine. I'm not going to leave you alone."

"Thank you." Tears eke from the corners of her eyes.

Taking a seat next to her, I grab a pillow, place it in my lap and gently guide her to lie down. She brings her knees to her chest and curls up. I lightly run my fingers through her hair. "I'm privileged to have this moment with you, Shay. Good or bad, every minute I spend with you is a moment I cherish."

"I haven't had one of those in a long time," she murmurs against my legs. "What happened?"

I stroke her temples with my thumb. "I think you had a reaction to the strobe light right before the countdown. Your fingers started twitching and then you said you were hot and wanted to take off your clothes. Then it was over. Now we're home."

"Jesus." Shay turns to look at me. "Tell me you stopped me."

"Against my better judgement, yes." I lean down and kiss her forehead.

Miles arrives and holds up Shay's purse and our coats. "I'll drop these off. How are you, sis?"

"Clothed, thank God." She raises her arm and gives him a thumbs up.

He approaches. "You're in good hands. Should I come by tomorrow?"

"I think we're fine." I look up at him. "Tomorrow I want to pamper Shay."

Shay props herself up on one arm. "Can you not say anything to Mama and Papa? I'll make an appointment with my neurologist and get scans if necessary. I need to sever that tie."

He nods. Flicks his eyes to mine. Nods again. "Yeah. Okay. But you need to tell them after."

Miles leaves and Shay sits up. "Let's go to bed. I need you to hold me."

"Anything you want." I stand and pick her up before striding to our bedroom. "So, how did I do?"

"Perfect. I've never felt so safe in my life." Shay throws her arms around my shoulders and buries her face in my neck.

I breathe a sigh of relief.

Make a vow to myself: I'm never going to take a chance with Shay's safety again.

I'm all for having fun. For letting loose and enjoying life. But I will not forget tonight. And how quickly shit can go wrong with Shay's condition.

I meant what I said that it is a privilege to be with Shay.

In any moment.

Even the scary ones.

Chapter Twenty-Eight

Three Weeks Later

The chic bistro in West Seattle is bathed in soft sunlight that filters in through the large windows. The hum of conversations, clinking of cutlery, and subdued laughter create a relaxing backdrop. I adjust the pendant necklace I'm wearing, excited to have lunch with Zoey Pearson and get to work on our project. She enters the bistro with a grace that belies her petite stature and huge belly. Her hazel eyes light up when she spots me and her warm smile instantly sets me at ease.

"Shay! Thank you for meeting in West Seattle." She embraces me. "It's necessary for me to stick close to home in case I go into labor. We're trying for a home birth this time around."

I'm fascinated by the woman who's the inspiration for some of the biggest songs in pop culture, but I bet she's sick to death of the association. Since we're quite close in age. I'd like to get to know her as a person, considering we're going to be working together. "No problem. I Ubered over from the office."

"Oh, there's so much parking." She gestures to the lot.

"Yeah." I glance out to where she's pointing. "I currently don't drive. I have epilepsy and recently had an episode. It's not safe for me or others until I go for a bit with no incident."

She leans in and rests her face on her palm. "Really? Full-blown seizures, huh. That must be tough."

"Actually, no. Mine are called Focal Onset Aware Seizures. Occasionally, if I'm triggered, I'll have what's called Focal Onset Impaired Awareness Seizures. They present passably normal to the average person. It's like I space out for a minute, then don't remember what we were talking about. If I'm in a strange situation, sometimes I'll do something weird." I wrinkle my nose. "On New Year's Eve, I was out with Austin and Miles and the strobe light caused an episode where, apparently, I tried to take off my dress in the bar. I have no recollection of it at all."

Zoey's eyeballs nearly pop out of her head. "Wow. Is it scary? Do you know when it's happening?"

"Sometimes I'll get what's called an aura which presents in variable ways. Flickering. Blurry vision. Headache. Seeing things that aren't there. I often feel a bit panicky." I trace my finger on the pattern of the tablecloth. "If I pop a Zannie when it first starts I can head it off usually. That being said, when I was first diagnosed and didn't know the signs I had one or two episodes a month. I went almost four years without episode. In the past few months I staved one off when I didn't get enough sleep one night and then the thing on New Years, so I'm being careful, but my meds are in a stable place."

Zoey nods sympathetically. "Health challenges can be overwhelming. I've struggled with aura migraines for a few years. They're so debilitating, sometimes I can't even get out of bed. I'm now on decent meds too."

"Are you serious?" She's the first person I've ever met who can truly understand what I live with. "Dealing with this stuff can be so scary, don't you think?"

Zoey sighs, "Yeah. And medication can be a double-edged sword. For instance, for me any birth control triggers the migraines so I had to go off it altogether. The timing worked out—we were ready to get pregnant with Oliver. Then everything went nuts with Ty and the band. A rough patch, for sure."

"I'm so sorry you had to deal with so much." I grip her hand from across the table. "And now you're pregnant again. Do you know if it's a boy or a girl?"

Zoey rubs her prominent bump. "We do and we're excited, but not telling anyone yet. It's a good thing I love being pregnant. Ty wants a bunch of children so there's an excellent chance I'll be popping out kids for the next few years—until I can't take it anymore, then one of us will get snipped."

"Wow, how are you going to manage all of that and the foundation?" I'm surprised at her confession. Maybe she has nannies.

Zoey winces. "I'm oversharing, which is unlike me. I guess that shows I trust you, Shay. You get it since you grew up with a famous dad."

"In the vault." I make a zipping motion across my lips. "I'm also fascinated. I definitely want kids but I have some hormonal things that are essential for me to figure out with my epilepsy. I'm also scared to be alone with my baby and have an episode."

"Choose your partner wisely. Ty and I have been in love for our entire adult lives. We had a long separation, but he's my rock." Zoey smiles dreamily. "There's nothing he wouldn't do to help me when I have episodes. He's so understanding and supportive. That's the silver lining of any health struggle, isn't it? Finding out who truly cares about you."

I nod, thinking of Austin. "Absolutely. Austin was there for me during the New Year's Eve incident. He's been so patient, trying to understand my condition and how he can support me. It's the first time I feel like I can still be me and rely on someone who doesn't treat me like I'm fragile."

Zoey smiles knowingly. "So, you *are* an item? Sounds like you've found a keeper."

"Yeah. We were days into it when we met with you and Ty, still keeping it secret." I can't help but grin when I think of him. "Now we live together, although he's away for a few days in Silicon Valley on business."

We both share a moment of understanding, realizing how fortunate we are to have men in our lives who stand by us through thick and thin. We study the menus and place our orders before getting into the main reason why we're here.

"Should we dive into discussions about the Rainier Foundation?" I'm so excited for the incredible opportunity to collaborate with someone as accomplished as Zoey on this incredible initiative, but knowing I also can connect with another woman who understands the unique challenges of balancing work, health, and personal life is cool too.

Zoey drums her pink-tipped fingers on the table. "Ty and I were talking and this may seem presumptuous and possibly a little inappropriate, but would you ever consider working for the foundation?"

"What?" I'm so taken aback I can't even respond.

She shakes her head. "God, I'm sorry to spring that on you. I need someone who's going to give their all. When I took the job as CEO, Ty and I had just reunited. I'd quit my job at the law firm and the idea that he and I could be together working on important shit that was so personal to him was *everything*."

"And now?" I fidget with my napkin, because part of me is so fucking excited I can't even believe it. Another part of me doesn't want to give up working with Miles and Austin. I don't want to let them down in any way.

The server sets our lunch in front of us. Zoey stabs at her salad until she leaves, then looks me in the eye. "I want to shift my role to the board so I can be present with my kids. Go on the road with Ty. We lost too many years, and being with him is of utmost importance to me."

"I'm blown away." I cut my burger in half. "I'll have to think about it. Is there a position in mind?"

Zoey nods. "If you'd consider it, we'd promote our head of marketing to CEO and bring you on to spread the word about the foundation. Or, if you think it's a better fit, we're hiring a director of development too."

"Thank you so much for thinking of me." I gaze out the window, contemplating how weird life can be and find myself spilling my story. "Before I moved back to Seattle, I dated Devon Wright throughout college and into his pro football career. I gave up my ambitions to support his. When he took the job with the Raiders, I figured we'd get engaged, married. All the things. Instead he dumped me because, as he put it, I didn't have enough in my own life going on."

Zoey recoils. "What a total asshole."

"No, he was right." I laugh, for the first time able to have perspective on what happened. "Don't get me wrong, I'm not sad we split up. I've definitely leveled up. But, I shouldn't have given up my own career when I was so young. That being said, I did get a ton of experience working with prominent charities. I chaired galas. Fundraisers. I love that work. It makes me feel so fulfilled."

She rests her hand on her palm. "You have such a refreshing attitude, Shay. Whether you take the job or not, I hope we can be friends."

"I'd like that." Inside, I'm dying. Zoey fucking Pearson wants to be my *friend*?

For the rest of our lunch, Zoey catches me up on the progress and we make plans to touch base after she gives birth. The entire time we're there, I can't get over what a bullet I dodged. A few months ago, I came back to Seattle with my tail between my legs. Now, I have a great job, a soul mate, and now a potential life-changing opportunity.

"Good luck with your home birth. I can't wait to meet the baby." I hug Zoey on our way out. "I'll also talk to Austin about what we discussed. I can tell you I'm unquestionably excited about the possibility, but I can't leave Hungry Llama in the lurch before a game launch and someone else is trained."

She claps her hands. "And that level of professionalism is specifically what we're looking for." She waves. "Talk to you in a couple months."

My Uber arrives a couple minutes later. On the way back to the office, a huge smile remains permanently affixed to my face. As I think about the offer Zoey made me, I'm fairly certain Austin is going to love this opportunity and encourage me to take it.

Miles is likely going to be pissed.

I don't want to let my brother down, but at the same time I can't live my life in fear of disappointing people.

It's time for me to have a meeting with myself and figure out what I want.

Then make it happen.

Chapter Twenty-Nine

Austin

Two Days Later

I'm the luckiest man in the fucking world.

Shay has her earbuds in, shimmying as she puts something in the oven. Her back is toward me and I can see she's wearing nothing but an apron and a pair of tiny panties. When she shuts the oven door, she throws her hands up and sings so off-key it's adorable.

"It's me, hi, I'm the problem, it's me..."

I'm not about to sneak up and scare her, so I make a big production out of throwing my coat on the barstool at the kitchen island. She whirls around and shrieks, "Ohmygod, you scared me," in the loudest voice humanly possible.

Approaching her with one thing in mind, I pull out her earbuds and kiss her ear, nibbling down the outer edge, whispering, "Honey, I'm home."

She shivers at my touch. "I missed you so much."

I lick to the underside of her jaw where I suck a bit until she melts into me. I turn her in my arms so her back is to my front. "You can't expect a man to come home from a business trip to find his girl dancing naked in the kitchen without fucking her, can you?"

"No, and said girl was hoping to get fucked, for the record. I'm so horny." She wiggles her ass against my cock.

My hands stroke up and down her ribs then under her breasts, teasing her. My lips wander along her neck and jawline until she's arching into me, moaning. Patiently, I untie the knot in the apron and spin her back around in my arms. I help her take it off and immediately fasten my lips to her nipple. "You're perfect." I lick over and suck on her other nipple. "So fucking perfect." Back to the first. "Every part of you." I feather kisses down her belly and lick a line from her belly button to her clit.

"God, Austin." She holds my head where she wants me and gyrates her hips.

Releasing her for a second to pull off my hoodie and T-shirt, I lead her around the island to a bar stool and lift her into the seat. "I need a taste."

Shay lifts her leg up and places her foot on the counter. "I think I might come at the idea of this."

I kneel down so my face lines up with her pussy and breath her in. There's no better perfume than when she's wet and ready for me, which is evident by how soaked her panties are. Hooking my finger into the crotch of her panties, I move it to the side and expose her. "I'm going to feast on you, baby."

"So much yes." Shay leans back and drapes her arm over the barstool for leverage and looks down at me. I dive in and cover her entire pussy with my mouth, holding her steady at the hips. My tongue teases and prods her opening. "Jesus, that is...*ohhhhh*."

I love that Shay has no shame, hesitation, or fear. We explore our sexuality without boundaries. She runs her fingers through the long hair at the top of my head and tugs me closer. My fingers dig into the muscles of her hips as I move my face back and forth and to and fro, lapping at her. Sucking her folds between my lips, but avoiding her little clit.

Shay keens and pants and wails because my mouth is all over her, edging her closer and closer. She arches back, hooking her other foot on the foot rest and bracing her body with her forearms. Her hips cant forward to fuck my face. When I hear her moans deepen, I know she's close so I flick her clit with the tip of my tongue rapidly before sucking on it. Then repeating. Her thighs shake when she unravels and screams unabashedly, unable to hold back her orgasm any longer.

Gently, I flatten my tongue and lick from her little puckered hole to her clit, soothing her through a few aftershocks. Shay holds my head against her until she's settled then releases me. I stand up.

I undo my buckle and jeans and step out of them. My hands frame her face and I draw her close. "Taste yourself." I kiss her, tracing the seam of her lips with my tongue, then pushing in to find hers. We make out for what seems like hours. My dick is so hard it's weeping.

"God, I *covet* you." Shay wraps her legs around my waist and pulls me against her wet pussy. I buck against her so her wetness coats the length of my shaft. "I need your cock in me, I definitely do."

I dip my head down to capture her nipple in my mouth, then grip her hips and shift her so I'm lined up with her opening. "I love that idea." I fist my cock, tap it against her clit, and run the head through her folds. "I missed you."

"I missed you too." Shay's hands rest lightly on my waist as she watches me feed my cock into her. "God, there's nothing hotter than watching your fat cock disappear inside me."

I pull all the way out, my cock glistens. "Damn. Your pussy is dripping." I slide two fingers inside her and press my thumb to her clit. Fuck her with my fingers and rub her clit until she cries out and shudders, bucking against me. "That's it. Come all over my fingers, then you can have my cock back."

"Harder." Shay bites her lip, so I oblige and also curl my fingers up to rub her inner wall. I dip my head down to graze my teeth against her nipple and that does the trick, she explodes and whimpers as her muscles flex.

I continue to circle her sensitive clit with my fingertip, but she pushes against my chest. "Austin, fuck me. *Please.*"

"Oh, I will." I capture her little nub between the pads of my fingers and squeeze. Not hard. But with enough pressure to send another wave of pleasure through her.

It's so intense I watch the flush heat her from head to toe in seconds. "Oh, Jesus. God," Shay cries out. "It's too much."

She nearly slides off the barstool, so I help her back into position. Months of marathon sex have conditioned Shay into having as many orgasms as I can give her. I love to see her face slack with pleasure. For her to completely let go and be free in these moments. I position myself at her opening and flick my cock around, not quite entering her. She groans. "You're hungry for it?"

"Yes!" Her fingers slip down to try to take control. "Put it in me."

I can't help but chuckle and tease her, drag my dick through her folds and tap her clit again. It makes her hotter. Makes her want it more. As for me, I'm at the end of my rope, so I push all the way in and hook her legs under my arms so she's wide open as I thrust in and out of her. We both watch my cock disappear inside her with awe, as if we're the only two people in the world who've discovered what our bodies are capable of.

"You're a miracle, Shay. Nothing feels this amazing." I flick her engorged clit because she can take it.

Shay's little breaths turn into moans with every pass. "How do you do this to me, every time," she cries and grips the counter to bear down on me as she comes on my cock.

Now, I have no fucking control anymore. I suck in a breath like a drowning man, sliding my palms over every part of her skin I could reach. The connection between us is so strong and deep. My need for her evident as I fuck her hard and deep. Our skin slaps together. The smell of sex overpowers whatever's in the oven. This feels so phenomenal I never want to leave her body.

"Think you've got another one in you, Shay?" I'm ramming into her so hard my balls are slapping her asshole.

She's holding onto the counter for dear life. "*Yesssss.* I want you to come with me."

I'm on the verge. I bend around her, bringing our bodies close together. "No one has ever made me feel this. It's you. Always you." I brush my fingertips over her thighs and touch her clit gently, knowing she'd be overly sensitive from all of my earlier manipulations. Steadily,

I build her back up as she squeezes my cock. I'm so fucking close.

"I love you, Austin," Shay whispers in my ear.

It's too much. Everything I need. "I love you too."

I bite down on her shoulder and pick up speed, thrusting so, so deep as she rolls her hips to meet me. Shay emits a tortured gasp when she comes yet again and I follow, filling her up with my release. I cling to her so I don't fall over. I don't think I've ever come so hard in my life. I feel Shay's arms around me as I heave. My hips still thrusting my softening cock in her.

"Welcome home." She grips my ass to hold me inside.

I sluggishly return to the real world and capture her lips. We savor each other until I slip out and reach for a towel to clean us up. We've destroyed the barstool, I'll have to replace it.

"Maybe we can be creepy and get plastic covers for our furniture," I joke.

Shay laughs and slides off the barstool, her legs wobbly so I steady her. "I better check on dinner."

"Since when do you cook?" I snap her ass with the towel.

"I don't, I heat up." She opens the oven door. "Or, I burn." She takes out what looks like lasagna, except it's charred black on top.

God I love this woman.

There's literally nothing about her I don't adore.

Chapter Thirty

A Week Later

I'm beyond nervous.

It's my first time leading this particular meeting since I joined the company.

The vast conference room at Hungry Llama HQ is abuzz with anticipation for the quarterly marketing meeting where we set goals for the next three months. Sleek black chairs surround the long, wooden conference table, each seat is occupied by one of my team members. I know I'm not imagining it, the buzz isn't about our upcoming plans, it's about the updated dynamics of the room since Austin and I went public with our relationship.

I stand at the front of the room, waiting for everyone to settle down. Next to me is the huge projector screen showcasing the first slide of my presentation. I know my material inside out, but I'm wary of my staff member, Belinda Charles, who wears a snotty expression. Ever since my success at the retreat, her open hostility is a palpable undercurrent in my day.

"Alright, everyone, let's dive in," I begin, projecting what I hope is an air of confidence. "Our new game has a unique dynamic, and I believe it can be a game-changer for Hungry Llama. However, it's crucial that our marketing strategies align with its innovative features."

I delve into the presentation, talking about target demographics, marketing channels, and potential partnerships. Everyone seems engrossed, except Belinda. She's tapping her pen aggressively against her notepad, eyes narrowed.

When I mention a proposed collaboration with a leading TikTok influencer, Belinda's hand shoots up. "Why would we partner with a TikToker when we could get better visibility through a Twitch streamer?" Her voice drips with condescension.

I remain calm. I know women like Belinda. Hell, I ate them for lunch when I was a pageant girl. "It's about demographic reach, Belinda. While Twitch would be a great avenue, this particular TikToker's audience matches our game's core demographic precisely."

"I think you're trying to push your own agenda. Maybe you can get away with amateur strategy because of personal connections." She sniffs, not so subtly hinting at my relationship with Miles and, presumably, Austin.

Murmurs of agreement and dissent ripple through the room. I feel the atmosphere growing thicker, tension pulling tight. I take a deep breath. I know precisely how to handle this. I'm about ready to open my mouth...

"Belinda," Miles interjects, in his casual yet authoritative way. "Shay has worked closely with the research team on this. Please allow her a chance to explain her strategy before you make judgements."

Belinda scoffs, leans back in her chair and crosses her arms defiantly. "If I'm honest, I don't understand how she's in charge of this department, let alone leading this meeting. I have superior experience and I was the clear choice for the promotion. But no, of course, it had to go to Miles' twin sister, who's now conveniently dating the other cofounder!"

Austin's face reddens. "Belinda, that's enough."

"You're blinded by your infatuation!" she spits back, standing up. "Maybe I should consider a lawsuit, given the clear nepotism and favoritism at play here. I know my rights."

"Wait one second." Miles holds up a hand, still trying to keep things calm. "Belinda, this isn't the time or place for this."

Austin's temper flares, though. "You want to threaten lawsuits? Maybe we should talk about your insubordination and open hostility in a professional setting."

The room falls silent. Everyone's watching the unfolding drama, and I feel like I'm caught in a storm I didn't anticipate. Plus, I'm mortified that Austin and Miles didn't let me handle this animosity with Belinda myself. I'll definitely have words with them later.

"Enough." I try to regain some control. "This meeting is about the marketing plan and isn't a place to air personal grievances."

Belinda gives me a withering look. "Of course, you'd say that. It's easy to be smug when you have everything handed to you."

Feeling my own anger rising, I retort, "I've earned my place here, Belinda. My personal life doesn't dictate my professional decisions."

She laughs bitterly. "Keep telling yourself that." With that, she grabs her stuff and storms out, leaving a palpable silence behind.

Miles exhales deeply, running a hand through his blond hair. "Okay, show's over. Let's take a short break and reconvene in ten minutes."

I'm infuriated.

People begin to murmur among themselves. Some head to the break room. A couple people huddle and whisper back and forth, glancing up at me every now and then.

Austin and Miles approach me. Austin's face is contorted with frustration. "Shay, I'm sorry, I shouldn't have lost my cool."

"It's okay," I reply, though it's not. Now isn't the time for the discussion though, not with all of the whispering going on already. "Can you let me handle this? Please?"

He nods, wrapping an arm around me briefly, which I shrug off. "We will. Sorry for butting in."

The room is still abuzz with quiet conversations as everyone takes a moment to process the scene that just played out. I tap the microphone and all eyes turn to me. It's essential for me to redirect the meeting away from the bullshit Belinda brought to the table.

"Okay, everyone. I understand there was a disruption. But our focus here is to deliver an exceptional marketing strategy for Q2. Let's keep our eyes on the prize." I tap the remote, transitioning the presentation to the next slide, which showcases a heat map of our target demographic online activity.

"As you can see," I continue, pointing to the prominent red zones on the screen, "these are the hotspots we need to capitalize on."

For the next hour, I walk them through every detail, every decision, and every data-driven insight that I've meticulously researched over the past few weeks. I can feel when the team's initial skepticism gradually morphs into appreciation and interest. There are nods, note-taking, and several constructive questions — even some reluctant agreement from Belinda's close allies.

When the meeting wraps up, several colleagues approach me to discuss specifics or to commend the presentation. The tension seems to have dissipated, replaced by a collective professional camaraderie.

As the final few employees trickle out, Austin and Miles approach, both looking apologetic.

"Shay," Austin begins, his voice heavy, "I'm sorry. I shouldn't have tried to take control earlier. I made the situation worse."

I reach out to touch his arm. "It's okay. I get that you wanted to defend me. But remember, if you want me to be seen as a leader, you need to let me lead. I'm not going to let someone like Belinda tell me who I am."

"You handled that situation incredibly well." Miles side hugs me. "Despite everything, you managed to bring it back on track."

I haven't told Austin or Miles about the job offer Zoey floated yet. Mainly because I wanted to figure out how I felt about it first. Today's made me think...if my being here creates such tension with longtime employees, maybe I should let them know. "Guys, I know we have a busy week, but do you have ten minutes? I'd like to talk to you about something."

"Sure, Miles?" Austin turns to my brother.

He nods. "Yeah, should we go to your office, Shay?"

We cross the floor to my office and Miles shuts the door. I take a deep breath. "When I met with Zoey Pearson last week about the foundation collaboration, she asked me if I'd be interested in working at the Rainier Foundation. Her priorities are shifting and she's hoping to build up the team so she can be at home with her growing family. I didn't say anything because, well, I love working here with both of you but I'm beginning to wonder if it wouldn't be better for everyone if I considered her offer."

Austin is shocked and hurt. "Shay, you can't let one incident force you out. We want you here."

"I agree with Austin. We want you here, but you should think about what's best for you." Miles seems contemplative. "Don't decide because of external pressures. Figure out what you want."

I grab both of their hands. "I appreciate that. I need some time to think it through."

"It's time for my programming meeting." Miles extricates himself from me and slips out.

Austin turns to me and looks down at the floor. "Do you seriously want to leave Hungry Llama?"

"No, not really. I love working with you and Miles. But I feel like, no matter how hard I work, there'll always be whispers. Whispers that I didn't earn my position." I take his hand and lead us to my little seating area where I sit across from him. "I connect with Zoey. Working with her at the Rainier Foundation presents a special kind of opportunity. A fresh start, in a way."

He rests his elbows on his knees and buries his face in his hands. "I'll support whatever you decide, Shay. Don't tuck tail and run if you want to be here. You've got the talent, the drive. You belong in this industry as much as anyone else."

"Thanks, babe." The sincerity in his voice warms me. "I'm not quite ready to make any big moves now. I'd like to see the potential impact of my latest marketing strategies and watch Belinda choke when we hit milestones. I'm a petty-ass bitch. Don't try me."

The tension between us is instantly diffused. "God, I love you. I'm being stupid, I know. I love having you with me all the time. At the end of the day, you have to follow your heart, Shay. Whether it's here or at the foundation, I want you to be happy."

"Well , you guys are stuck with me. At least for now." I reach over and grab his hand. "All kidding aside, I do want to see some of my marketing strategies come to life. And, I like to face challenges like Belinda head-on."

Austin smiles. "That's my girl."

While the path ahead might be fraught with challenges, I'm determined to prove my worth, not only to the team but to myself. After all, every hurdle is an opportunity for growth.

However, the incident has made me observant of the undercurrents at Hungry Llama.

I've got to look out for my best interest.

Because I'm not, under any circumstances, allowing anyone—including Austin—to dictate my career.

Ever again.

Chapter Thirty-One

Two Weeks Later

I thought I was ready to marry Shay.

Or, at least ask her to marry me and let the wedding date sort itself out.

Now, with the ring box hidden in my secret safe, I feel the pressure of unanswered questions and unresolved family issues pressing down on me like the weight of every coin in Mario's kingdom.

How can I be an exceptional husband and father if I don't get to the bottom of my own family shit?

Yeah, you could say I'm still pissed about Christmas.

It's fucked me up, big time.

Shay and I talk about our future in such general terms—I want to give her a full-blown commitment. I love her desperately. Picture our kids. Envision growing old. I'm not the asshole who's going to lead her on the way Devon did. I know she's my soulmate and I have no problem putting a ring on it. It's just...

Before I go there, I need to understand why my family abandoned me.

Despite everything, I've built a great life for myself. I can't help feeling like there's a huge hole in my heart where my parents' love should be. They're both still alive. They acknowledge I'm their child. Yet, neither of them seem to give two shits about my well-being. I'm always the one who makes all the effort and I'm sick of it.

The bottom line is, I want clarity before I ask Shay to officially be a part of my life. Her own family may not be perfect, but they love deeply. Have each other's backs. I'd like to clean up my house before I ask Shay to intertwine her future with mine.

As determined as I am to move forward, my heart races as I clutch my phone. Shay's in the bedroom, likely reading one of her favorite romance novels, which is perfect. Gives me some uninterrupted time with my mother.

Taking a deep breath, I dial her number. Each ring echoes in my ears. She'll likely not even answer...

"Hello?" Her voice is familiar yet distant.

I swallow the lump that's formed in my throat. "Mom, it's Austin."

She's silent for a moment before responding, her tone guarded. "How have you been?"

"Uh..." I fight to keep my voice steady, pushing down the flood of emotions. "I've been...okay. I haven't heard from you in months. Why didn't you call after Christmas? I left gifts for you, Caden, and Trina."

She sighs, the sound heavy with something I can't quite identify. "I have a lot going on. You're so busy now I didn't think you'd notice."

"Notice? *Seriously?* Would it have been so hard to drop me a text or leave me a message thanking me for thinking of you? God, why does it seem like I don't have a family anymore?" I sound like a little boy with all my whining.

There's a hesitation, then she replies, "You're a grown man with your own life now. We hate bothering you; it's easier for you to reach out when you have a spare minute. I'm trying to...let you be."

"Easier?" I can barely stop myself from yelling. "Being abandoned by my family is easier for *me*? And, who's 'we?'"

Her voice grows so quiet it's barely a whisper. "Look, Mitch thought it was best. He feels that you need to stand on your own."

"What the actual fuck, Mom? I've stood on my own since you married that guy." I pinch the bridge of my nose with my fingers. "What about my brother and sister? They're my family too. I haven't seen them in over a year."

She pauses again and I can almost picture her biting her lip. "It's ...complicated. They're Mitch's children too and he doesn't think your lifestyle is...appropriate."

"Not appropriate?" A rage begins to build, my voice rising with every word. "They're my *family*, Mom! So are you. How can keeping me away from you guys ever be considered *appropriate*?"

"Austin, please understand. I've had to make some tough choices." She lowers her voice considerably. I can barely make out the words. "Mitch, he has a certain way of thinking. I can't go against him."

I run a hand through my hair. I'm so fucking frustrated and confused. "Mom, this isn't about him. You're my mother. You have a say. Why have you let him treat me like this? Why do you stay silent?"

"It's not that simple." She lets out a shaky breath. "He thinks...maybe it's best for everyone to keep things separate. You have your own life now."

My heart aches. I've always thought that's what was going on but hearing makes my pain palpable. "I've never moved on, Mom. How do you think it feels when your own mother ignores you?"

"Look, I can't talk. Maybe... Maybe I can slip out to see you." She's silent for a moment then whispers, "Let's talk face-to-face."

Swallowing hard, I nod, even though she can't see me. "Okay. Lunch? Tomorrow?"

"Okay." Her voice is small.

"Meet me at the Metropolitan Grill." I check my calendar. "Noon."

When I hang up the phone, the heaviness remains. I'm giving it a fifty-fifty chance she shows up. No, thirty-seventy. I bury my face in my hands. What will I even say to her? It's all such a shitshow.

Feeling a presence in the room, I look up to find Shay standing at the doorway, concern evident in her eyes.

"Babe?" she says softly, "are you okay?"

"I don't know, truthfully." I manage a weak but genuine smile because she makes everything better.

She walks over and sits next to me. Wraps her arms around my shoulders. "Tell me about it."

I rest my forehead against hers, drawing strength from her unwavering support and fill her in on the conversation. I appreciate she doesn't race to judgment and listens as I recount all of the times my mom and dad have let me down.

Tomorrow, I will confront at least part of my past and try to get answers to questions that have haunted me for years. But today, in this moment, I'm grateful for Shay and her support. Building my life with her reminds me that family isn't merely about blood.

<hr>

The Metropolitan Grill buzzes with chatter as patrons dine amidst sparkling glassware and low lighting. I'm a regular here—it's a couple blocks from the office—so they honored my request for a booth in a secluded corner. I purposely arrived early, which might not have been the best idea because I'm anxious. Watching the entrance to see if my mom bothers to show.

Odds aren't in my favor.

At quarter after, I'm about to leave when my mother walks in. It's been a while since I've seen her. She looks older. Wearier than I remember. Her deterioration tugs at my heartstrings. Once upon a time she was my entire world. It was only the two of us after my dad left until she met Mitch.

Everything fell apart.

Our eyes meet when the hostess leads her to the table. As she sits down, there's an awkward silence between us. Ultimately, she breaks the ice. "You look wonderful, Austin."

I stare at her for a beat.

"Thanks, Mom," I reply, steepling my fingers.

She sets her purse down on the booth next to her. "Thank you for meeting me. I know it's been far too long."

"It has, Mom." I take a long, hard look at the woman who gave birth to me. I can't imagine ever abandoning my kids. Ever. No matter how old. No matter what they did. "Are you going to tell me what's going on?"

Her gaze flickers downward. "Things haven't been easy for a while. Mitch is...controlling. It's getting worse. He manages the finances and things aren't going very well. We're gonna lose the house."

I clench my fist beneath the table, remembering a couple of times in the last year he asked me for money. "His financial woes are no excuse for *you* shutting me out. For allowing him to treat me the way he did—still does."

"I feel trapped." Tears shimmer in her eyes. "Today I was able to duck out because I lied and said I had a doctor's appointment. He's made it clear that if I go against him, there'll be consequences. I have two kids to think about."

Three, I think, but don't voice it.

"You could leave him." Anger and concern war within me. "I have more money than I can ever spend. I'll help you, all you have to do is ask."

She manages a wistful smile. "I can't risk it."

"*Convenient.*" The words come out harsher than intended, but I smell bullshit and all of this runaround pisses me off to no end. "Let me guess. He knows you're here and wants you to ask me for money."

Her breath is shaky. "No, Austin. He doesn't know but he'll find out. He monitors my calls, my location. Everything. I live in constant fear. He threatened to cut me off, to take the kids away. I'm... I'm trapped. I wouldn't be surprised if he walks in this door and then it will be all over."

"Wait, he's threatened to, essentially, destroy your life if you see *me*? Your *son*?" The revelation hits me hard. All these years, I'd been harboring resentment, feeling abandoned. But now, seeing the pain in her eyes, I understand the extent of her own suffering, though I still don't understand how it's gone this far.

Reaching across the table, I grasp her hand, offering what little comfort I can. "Mom, you don't have to live like this. There are ways out, resources available. Let me help."

She shakes her head. "It's not that simple. I'm terrified about what he might do if I try to leave and take the kids."

"Are you in fear for your life?" I'll fucking kill the guy myself if he's threatened my mother.

"*Austin*..." she pleads.

"If you want to leave, say so. I'll find a way, I promise." Determination burns within me, but I'm also not going to be played for a fool. This still feels a bit like a setup.

Maybe I'm jaded.

Mom smiles weakly. "I made a mistake marrying him, but I wouldn't give up my kids for anything." She must realize how that sounds and grabs my hand. "No. That came out wrong. Every day, every moment, I regret not being able to be there for you. I'm so proud of the man you've become."

"Look, you and I can hash out or own relationship later. For now will you allow me to help get you and the kids out of this situation?" At this point, she's going to accept my help or she won't. What I won't stand for is Caden and Trina being abused. Mentally or physically. "If my brother and sister are in danger, you need to let me know."

Tears stream down her face. "He won't hurt his own children."

"I don't believe that for a second." I picture the million ways Mitch has berated my mom, which I've seen for myself. He's a shit excuse for a man. "What kind of example are you setting for my sister and brother if you don't get out of this? The man is dangerous. You need to leave."

I'm furious and undoubtedly am going about this all wrong, but I don't know what else to do. I make a mental note to find a counselor to help figure this out.

My harsh words somehow penetrate, though. Mom covers her mouth with her hand. "How?"

We spend the next hour discussing potential solutions and plans for her to regain her independence. As we part, I have a sense of hope. Maybe even a promise of a better future. It all depends on my mother finding some inner strength and allowing me to assist her. If she doesn't, then I'll explore my own legal options regarding my siblings.

When I return to the office, I find Shay waiting. She takes one look at me, envelopes me in her arms, much like she did last night. "Tell me everything."

As I relay what went down at the restaurant, her expression grows grave. "Austin, this is serious. You have to be prepared for this to be a long process. Hopefully when things settle down you can all get some counseling."

I bury my face in her vanilla-scented hair. "I know it's a long shot, but at least I'm doing something."

"I'm so sorry you are going through this." Shay strokes my nape. "Whatever you need from me, I'll give to you. Flirt alert?"

I lean back to catch a twinkle in her eye. She licks her lips.

"You're my little minx." I kiss her nose. "Tonight, I'm not the mood. I'm sorry."

I can't believe I don't feel like fucking my girlfriend. Usually, I can't get enough of her.

The heaviness of today still presses down on me, though.

I hope I can help my mom and maybe get my own family back on track.

Shay deserves everything.

I won't be able to give it to her unless I resolve this.

Chapter Thirty-Two

Four Weeks Later

Soft jazz music plays in the background, muted by the low hum of conversations around me.

I'm seated in a cozy booth at Saffron's, a chic little café around the corner from Hungry Llama's office. Miles is meeting me here for happy hour. It's been an intense month and I need a break to get away from the pressure. There's no one I'd rather hang out with than my twin.

As I sip my green tea, waiting, my thoughts drift to Austin. He's been a ghost these past few weeks. Buried in paperwork. Long meetings. Longer phone calls. It's heart-wrenching to see him grapple with the ghosts of his past to try to free his mother from the clutches of a man who's been a negative presence in their lives for so long.

I wish he'd open up more, but Austin seems determined to handle this on his own.

I can't help but feel shut out.

Miles makes his way through the crowd to the table with a beer. Seeing him perks me up a bit.

"Hey, Shay." He slides into the seat opposite me. "How're you holding up?"

I offer a weary smile. "Hanging in there. Austin...he's struggling. And I want to help, but sometimes, it feels like I'm in the way."

Miles rubs the scruff of his neck, a hint of discomfort in his gaze. "Yeah. It's tough. Austin's always been the type to bottle things up. But with all this stuff about his mom, it's hitting him harder than I've ever seen."

"I get that." I wrap my hands around the warm cup. "Sometimes, I wish he'd let me in, you know? He's been there for me. I want to do the same for him."

Miles leans back, considering. "This is a little different, though. You've got to understand, Austin's relationship with his mother...it's complicated."

"He's your best friend. I don't want you to betray his trust, but if you could give me any insight I'd genuinely appreciate it." I blink up at my brother with puppy-dog eyes. It's an old trick, but it usually works.

He hesitates, but then sighs. "Fine. When we were kids, Austin used to come over to our place all the time. I mean, you know the story. But what you might not know is the depth of it. He wasn't just escaping his stepdad; he was escaping the pressure he felt from his mom. So I don't think this is all on Mitch."

"Pressure? How so?" I blow on my tea.

"Mitch is a dick. There's no denying it." Miles rubs his chin. "Without knowing all the ins and outs, it's hard for me to articulate this but I'll try. I think when Austin's dad left Molly and moved to Florida, she blamed Austin. I didn't know him when that happened, but Austin—as you know—can be focused and intense." He looks up at the ceiling to compose his thoughts. "I guess what I'm trying to say is Austin's parents didn't know what to do with a kid who has an IQ as high as Austin does. Someone who is curious. Asks questions. Isn't easy. When Molly married Mitch, I think it gave her an excuse to immerse herself in what she thought was her new life.

Mitch thought he was weird. Austin represented her old life and was older and self-sufficient. Yada. Yada. Yada."

My heart aches as I process this. "Heartbreaking. I don't understand how she could treat him that way."

"Who knows? It's hard to say. Austin feels like his mom chose her new life over him. And now, even after all the hurt, he's fighting for her. That says a lot about him." Miles sips his beer.

My respect and admiration for my love deepens. "He's trying to be the hero now."

"Yeah, but here's the thing," Miles leans in. "I bet he doesn't see it as being a hero. To him, it's making amends for not being good enough for her back then. He was a kid. Powerless. But being singled out for being different—it's stayed with him."

I feel a surge of anger, not at Austin, at the whole messed-up situation. "She's his mom. She should've protected him."

"Of course she should have. But it's not always black and white." He struggles to find the words. "Domestic situations, especially ones with control and fear at play, they're...intricate. Messy."

My brother is, seriously, the wisest and most intuitive man I know. I take a deep breath. "So, what should I do? How do I help him?"

"Be there. Listen. And when he pushes you away, because trust me, he will, give him space but let him know you're not going anywhere. The thing about Austin is, once he lets those walls down, he loves deeply and for life." He leans forward and boops me on the nose. "But, you knew that already, didn't you?"

"Yeah." I can't help but smile thinking about the many times Austin has shown his vulnerable side to me. God, I love him so fucking much.

Miles gives me a reassuring smile. "Shay, he loves you. Even if he doesn't always show it, he needs you. Be patient."

"I will." It's like a weight has lifted and been replaced by a renewed determination. "You're the best twin ever."

"I know." He smirks.

As we leave the café, I can't wait to get home.

The road ahead won't be easy, but with understanding, patience, and love, Austin and I can face anything.

Together.

Ten minutes later, I unlock the door to our apartment. The dim lighting reveals a familiar silhouette slouched on the couch. Austin's hunched form appears defeated, a stark contrast to the usually confident man I've grown to love.

"Babe?" I call out tentatively, setting my bag down.

Austin looks up. His handsome face is drawn and tired. His hair, usually meticulously groomed, is grown out and disheveled. "Hey." His voice seems to be carrying the gravity of a thousand unsaid words.

Walking over, I settle beside him, wrapping my arms around his shoulders. "Talk to me," I urge gently.

He sighs, pinching the bridge of his nose. "I found a way out for her. I have a house in escrow. A family law legal team. A housekeeper and nanny. More than what she needs to break free." He swallows hard, looking away. "But she's hesitating. Said she wants to think about it. After everything... I don't understand."

A feeling of helplessness washes over me, but I push it aside. Remembering my conversation with Miles, I know this is one of those moments where Austin needs me most. "Austin, sometimes, when you've been in the dark for so long, the light can be blinding, even terrifying."

"I want my mom back. I want her to be safe. To have a life away from that asshole. Why won't she take my help?" He meets my gaze, his brown eyes are filled with frustration and sorrow.

I gently cup his face. "Fear does strange things to people. Maybe she's afraid of the unknown, of starting over. Or maybe she's afraid of what he might do if she tries to leave."

"I've done everything, Shay." Austin's eyes well up with tears, which he hastily wipes away. "Everything I could think of. And it feels like it's not enough."

I pull his head into my lap and rub his back. Thread my fingers through his hair. "You've done more than anyone could've expected. It's her choice now, Austin. You can't make it for her."

He buries his face in my lap, his voice muffled. "I know. I wish I could."

We sit in silence for a few minutes, the soft hum of the city outside our window the only sound.

"You know, Miles and I had a talk today." I scoot down on the couch beside him and nestle in his arms. I stroke his beard and flick my eyes to his. "He helped me see things from your perspective. About your mom, the guilt, everything. And while I can't claim to understand fully what you're going through, I want you to know something."

Austin looks at me, waiting.

"I'm here, Austin. No matter what happens, I'm by your side." I press my lips to his. "Whether she chooses to leave or stay, whether you're filled with joy or battling demons from the past, I'm with you. Every step of the way."

Austin chokes on a sob, his composure crumbling. "I don't deserve you, Shay."

"Well, too bad, because you're stuck with me." I smile and wipe away his tears.

He laughs weakly, pulling me close again. "I'm glad. Because I don't know what I'd do without you."

"I know a way to make you feel better." I snake my hand lower and pull his joggers down to reveal his cock, which curves into my grip, thick and heavy. "Relax and let me take care of you. Sometimes you need to send up a flirt alert so I can make you feel better."

Austin watches me stretch my lips around his flesh. His salty flavor hits my taste buds as he grows hard in seconds. I wrap my fingers around the base of his shaft and knead his thigh, inching my fingers lower to graze his balls with my nails.

"God, Shay. That feels amazing." Austin's arms are above his head as he stares at me bobbing up and down on his length.

I grip his sac in my palm and flatten my tongue as I work him. Relaxing my throat, I prepare to take him deeper. As he slides down past my gag reflex, I try not to choke, but he's so big it's hard not to. To get better control, I grip the base of his cock and take hold of him firmly. His hips buck into my hand as I work him over and over again, sucking, licking and teasing his entire shaft.

Sensing he's close, I hum and go faster, enclosing him tightly in my lips. It sends him over the edge and his salty-sweet release coats my mouth. I love how he tastes, so I lick up every last drop before tucking him back into his pants.

Austin's face is serene now. He even has a hint of a smile.

We stay cuddled on the couch for a long while in a moment of solace amidst the chaos.

In this moment, everything feels okay.

Chapter Thirty-Three

Austin

Two Weeks Later

The crisp spring evening sky paints the vast windows of our penthouse in muted hues of blues and purples.

Despite the sanctuary our home provides, a thick cloud of tension hangs in the air. It's been a few days since my mother agreed to leave Mitch and since then the backlash has been relentless. Legal threats. Veiled warnings. Security guards. Threats of going to the press. It's enough to drive anyone to the brink.

Through it all, Shay has been my rock.

Yet lately, I can't help but notice a shift in her demeanor. The fiery passion she once held in her eyes seems slightly dimmed. Her once-radiant smile, though still present, appears less frequent.

Pacing back and forth in our living area, I grapple with the overwhelming guilt threatening to suffocate me. My mother's issues, while monumental, shouldn't eclipse Shay's needs. I've been so engrossed in my family's problems that I've neglected the woman who's been my cornerstone throughout.

Taking a deep breath, I decide it's time to remedy that. "Shay?" I scan the expanse of the penthouse for her. A faint sound of people talking from the balcony guides me to her, wrapped in a blanket listening to what sounds like a true crime podcast.

She doesn't turn around. "Hey."

I step out, letting the door slide shut behind me. Approaching her, I wrap my arms around her from behind and squeeze. "I miss you."

She leans back into me, resting her head against my chest. "Me too." She clicks off her device. "With everything happening, I've been trying to stay out of your way and not add to your stress."

"Talk to me." I move around to sit beside her.

Shay shifts sideways to face me, searching my eyes. "Austin, it's absolutely not about us. It's just...everything around us has been so intense. Your family's situation, the threats. You've been in such a bad mood for so long. I've been trying to figure out how to be there for you while grappling with my own feelings about the Zoey Pearson situation. She wants to meet with me later this week."

I feel a pang of guilt. "I totally forgot about all of that. I've been so caught up in my problems, and—"

"Shhh." She places a finger on my lips, silencing me. "Don't apologize. You're dealing with something major. It's okay to be consumed by it. I want to get back to prioritizing us as a couple. I really, really miss us. We aren't making love regularly and I want to be intimate with you. It's important to me."

I cup her face and try not to feel like a loser. Aside from the blowjob she gifted me a couple weeks ago, we haven't had sex in...? I haven't made her come in...?

Jesus.

I'm always so tired and distracted. "I'm so sorry for not meeting your needs. You can call a flirt alert too, you know."

"I haven't felt comfortable. I'm simply being honest with you, like you asked." She takes my hands in hers. "You're here now and I'm horny as hell. Before you give me all the orgasms, which I'm fully expecting, by the way—can you please give me an update of what's going?"

How I love this woman. So compassionate. Caring. I wish I were more like her.

"Let's make it quick because, as you know, when you tell me to give you orgasms my cock's immediately at full attention." I take her hand and place it on the bulge in my jeans. "I spoke to the lawyers today. They're confident we can quash Mitch's threats. And with Mom and the kids safe, I'm ready to put this behind us and focus on us again. Good?" I kiss her lips. "Right now, I only want to be buried inside your hot, wet pussy."

Shay shivers and squeezes my cock then rests her forehead against mine as she unbuckles my belt and unbuttons my jeans. "I think we need to make a rule. No longer than three days without a noteworthy fuck. These past weeks have felt like a lifetime."

Alrighty then.

"Fine. I promise, from here on, we're prioritizing us. Noteworthy fucks will abound. We come first—Jesus,

Shay." I nearly lose my shit when she pulls my cock out and strokes me from root to tip.

She looks up. Winks. "What did you say about coming first, Austin?"

"Oh, no. Not a chance. You're coming first. I'm going to lick you then fuck you out here on the balcony. Then we're going to order takeout, watch a bad movie in bed and fuck until dawn." I pull off her sweatshirt and cup her bare breasts, delighted that her nipples are hard as pebbles.

Shay yanks down her yoga pants. "Sounds perfect."

Half hour later, we've taken the edge off, so we head inside. The weight of the past weeks seems to have lifted after reconnecting. I make a mental note that, under no circumstances will I ever create a situation where Shay has to ask me for sex again. She's my priority from now on.

After the food arrives, we settle into the media room and the glow of the television casts a gentle light around us. Halfway through a particularly cheesy scene, Shay turns to me, a mischievous glint in her eye. "You know, if Mitch does spill to the tabloids, maybe we could sell our love story? 'Tech Tycoon Finds Love Amidst Family Drama and Corporate Threats'. Think it'll sell?"

"Only if they get Liam Hemsworth to play me." I laugh.

She rolls her eyes and playfully shoves me. "Sure, and I guess Anna De Armas will play me?"

"Sounds perfect." I cup her breasts. "Your tits are far better, though."

Our laughter fills the penthouse and things quickly turn heated. As our mouths mash together, I'm reminded of the strength of our bond. Shay straddles me and angles my cock inside her. This is going to be a quick, satiating fuck and I'm here for it.

I grip her hips and suck on her nipples as she rides me, the melodramatic dialogue from the rom-com serves as our background music. Reaching between us, I rub her clit and watch myself fuck up into her. She holds on to my shoulders and undulates back and forth, seeking the angle that will send her to nirvana.

Oh, I know what she needs. I press her lower back against me so her entire clitoral wall is stimulated against my pubic bone. She throws her arms around my neck and lets me take over. I keep her tight against me as I buck harder. It's not long before she squeezes my cock so tightly I shoot off into her as she finds her own release.

We're sweaty, exhausted, and satiated. It's a perfect evening until my phone starts buzzing incessantly.

"I'm so sorry," I groan, breaking our connection.

It's Miles. I barely miss the call but I'm not sad.

It's all kinds of wrong to take a call from my best friend when I'm naked and my dick is still wet from fucking his sister.

Shay tilts her head, concerned. "It's not like him to call this late, is everything okay?"

I unlock the phone and find a series of urgent messages from Miles.

Miles: Austin, urgent. Joar Jacoby will be in town in two days.

Miles: He's expressed a direct interest in acquiring Hungry Llama.

Miles: We need to prepare. He's sent over a list of things he'd like to discuss.

Miles: This could be the deal of a lifetime.

My heart races as I process the information. This is fucking huge. Jacoby is a big player in the media and technology space. If his interest in Hungry Llama is sincere, it could change everything. The financial freedom. Opportunities for the team. My future—everything.

Except—I've neglected Shay for weeks so the timing couldn't be worse.

Shay notices my extended silence. "Austin? What's going on?"

"Joar Jacoby. He's interested in acquiring Hungry Llama." I let out the breath that, apparently, I'd been holding.

Shay's eyes widen. "That's massive, Austin. Isn't he one of the top tech moguls out there?"

I run my hand through my hair. "Yeah. This is an opportunity we can't miss. But it also means my life is going to be incredibly hectic as we navigate the deal."

"More meetings? Late nights?" She visibly stiffens, and I can almost see the walls coming up.

I sigh, pulling her closer. "I'm afraid so. This could be our ticket to a secure future. I understand if you're frustrated after everything with my mom, I don't want to slip into that pattern again."

"Austin, I support you, I do." Shay takes a moment to collect her thoughts. "Sometimes things come in waves. This is a huge deal and we'll get through it."

I grip her hands, trying to convey the depth of my feelings. "Babe, I promise I'm not taking this lightly. This could be a once-in-a-lifetime opportunity, which means financial security for us and for our future family. I also know I've been absent a lot with my mom's shit and that's not fair to you."

She leans her forehead against mine. "It's tough because you're my favorite person. It feels like every time we get a moment to ourselves, something else comes up."

"If there was any way to reschedule or delay, I would. Jacoby's schedule is notorious for being set in stone." I slump back against the cushions. "Adulting sucks."

"Yeah. Having responsibility definitely has its drawbacks." Shay takes a deep breath, releasing it gradually. "You know what? We'll manage."

My relief is palpable. "We will. Once this is over, I promise we'll take some time off. The two of us. Alone. A vacation with no distractions."

"That sounds perfect." Shay gets up and motions for me to join her. "But for now, let's get some sleep. Tomorrow, we'll focus on the task at hand. You need to prep for Jacoby and I'm going to help."

Overwhelmed by her unwavering support, I grab her hand as we retire for the night. "I love you so much, babe. I never want to be without you."

Shay laughs. "I love you too."

As we get ready for bed, we chat about the acquisition process. Shay has so many great ideas and she's so insightful, having her be part of the team is invaluable.

I kiss her deeply. "I'm constantly amazed by you."

After all the shit with my mom, I can't believe someone like Shay stays by my side.

It's another reminder of how lucky I am to have her as my partner.

In every sense of the word.

Chapter Thirty-Four

A Few Days Later

The rhythmic sound of my heels on the polished floor of Hungry Llama headquarters is strangely soothing.

I can't bring myself to put on the kind of casual attire everyone else wears here, I love my tortuous designer shoes too much. My coworkers, for the most part, are great, but there's still that underlying feeling I don't belong.

I'd never say anything to Miles or Austin because they've gone out of their way to support me, but I can't stop thinking about The Rainier Foundation. Wonder if I'd be a better fit there.

At this point, I'll embrace anything that gives me a sense of calm. It's been fucking chaotic at work ever since Miles got the news Jacoby International was interested in the company. For the past few days, the entire executive team has been frantically pulling together the due diligence materials requested by Joar Jacoby himself.

If Miles and Austin pull this off, it's life-changing money for everyone who owns shares in the company. At the same time, Hungry Llama is doing spectacularly so I'm not quite sure why everyone feels like their future is hanging in the balance of whether this transaction goes through or not. It will be fine either way.

Oh well, I'm a team player.

After all, my brother is one of the founders and I'm desperately in love with the other, so...

As I turn the corner, I nearly bump into Miles, who's engaged in a deep discussion with one of our financial analysts. He looks up, nodding a greeting. "Shay! Good. Just the person I was hoping to see. We need those marketing reports for Jacoby."

"You'll have them by end of day," I assure him. "How are the talks going?"

Miles rubs the scruff of his neck, his "tell" when he's stressed. "It's a process. They're being super thorough. I *think* it's looking okay. We simply need to dot the i's and cross the t's."

My phone buzzes, interrupting us. It's a text from Zoey Pearson. My heart skips a beat. In the midst of the acquisition madness, Zoey reached out again, wanting to discuss the development director position at the Rainier Foundation. And even though I can't tell her about the acquisition, I'm interested.

"I have to run," I tell Miles. "Zoey Pearson wants to meet me."

His eyebrows raise in curiosity. "She's persistent, isn't she?"

"It feels fantastic to be pursued." I shrug. "Though I'm not sure why it's happening. There are so many qualified people out there."

Miles grips my shoulders. "Stop it, Shay. Don't put yourself down. I'd hate to lose you, but if this is an opportunity that you'd love, then I support you."

My brother rocks. He's wrong about my qualifications, but I love him for having my back.

In any case, it gives me a boost of confidence before I meet with Zoey.

———

Considering I have a ton of work to do, I'm grateful Zoey scheduled the meeting near the office. The quaint little cafe opened recently and I haven't had a chance to try it yet. Even though I don't drink due to my condition, the comforting aroma of freshly brewed coffee always feels cozy and welcoming. I spot Zoey in a corner, cradling her newborn. My heart melts at the sight.

"Zoey!" I bend down to peek at the gorgeous baby who's sound asleep. "She's absolutely beautiful."

Zoey beams, looking every bit the proud mother. "Thank you. This is Evangeline. Ty is over the moon to be a girl daddy. It's been a whirlwind, but she's worth every sleepless night."

"Two kids under two, my hat's off to you," I joke as we order our drinks, which turns out to be tea for the both of us.

Once we're settled, Zoey dives in. "Shay, I know we don't have much time today so I'll cut to the chase. The foundation needs someone like you. Especially with all the projects we have lined up. Have you given any thought to our discussion?"

I take a sip of my tea. "Honestly? I've thought about it a lot."

"Great." Zoey kisses her daughter's head and gives me a cheesy grin. "When can you start?"

I clear my throat. "I'm honored, you have to know that. I want to be upfront about what's going on. I'm needed at Hungry Llama for at least another month, possibly two. We're in the middle of a project that I'm a big part of."

"Oh?" Zoey tilts her head.

I hesitate. The NDA prevents me from giving away too much. "There's a lot going on behind the scenes at Hungry Llama and it's all very confidential. With respect to the marketing position, I'm not convinced I want a role that requires a ton of travel. Like you, there are reasons I'd like to stick close to home."

"Of course." Zoey nods, understanding. "Let's put that aside for a moment. Do you believe in our mission?"

I nod vigorously. "You have no idea. It gives me chills at how much good you're doing."

"Well then, let me give you some insight into the role of Development Director." Zoe places Evangeline in the carrier next to her and rifles through her bag. Hands me a job description. "You'd be overseeing our fundraising initiatives, building partnerships, and steering our branding and outreach—from our headquarters here in Seattle."

I take the paper from her and study it, genuinely intrigued. "This sounds amazing. And challenging. May I ask you something?"

"Sure, of course." Zoey breaks off a piece of her scone.

Biting my lip, I consider how to frame my question. "My resume isn't all that deep, and I know that. As flattered—and excited—as I am, why *me*?"

She stares at me, confused. Until she realizes I'm serious.

"Oh, Shay." Zoey reaches across the table and grips my fingers. "Look at what you've done for Hungry Llama in the past few months. The company profile has never been so prominent. If I'm not mistaken, the biggest game release yet. I'm not someone who offers people jobs without doing my research. You have the drive. The passion. The talent. Believe in yourself. I do. So does Ty."

I nearly burst into tears. My life's changed so much in the past year. If Miles hadn't hired me, I don't know where I'd be. Hungry Llama has been my whole world for the past few months. Aside from Austin, of course. Now, with the potential sale of the company, I'd like to control my own destiny.

It's such a hard road to navigate.

I mean, I'm not complaining. Not at all, but the idea I could have a fresh start has so much appeal. It would give me some autonomy and eliminate the shadow of nepotism I've been operating under. At The Rainier Foundation, I could truly pave my own way.

Zoey misreads my hesitation. "Take your time. We're in an enviable situation because Ty and I can fund the foundation indefinitely. The position isn't going anywhere if you have interest. At the same time, we're eager for it to stand on its own and be less of our passion project. We believe the foundation should be a nationwide force sooner rather than later, so if you're not interested, please let me know."

"Oh, I want the job," I speak my truth. "Let me talk to Austin and I'll give you a firm date when I can start by end of week."

Zoey claps her hands then fist pumps. "This is amazing. I'm so excited. I'll send the official offer letter to you tomorrow."

I stay for another half hour chatting about Evangeline and the joys and challenges of motherhood. The idea that Zoey and I will be working closely together on an initiative I believe in is so fucking exciting. By the time I leave the café, my mind is swirling with possibilities.

Back at the office, Austin is waiting for me. "How was the meeting with Zoey?"

Suddenly I feel sick to my stomach. He knew about my meeting. Knows about the potential of me working there.

But...I accepted the job without discussing it with him.

Wait—was I supposed to? God, I don't even know what the protocol is supposed to be with Austin.

Devon did whatever he wanted and never asked me for permission.

Although, he's also my boss? *Ugh*. I decide to tell him what happened. "She offered me a Development Director role. I accepted the job with the caveat that I need some time to wrap some things up here."

"Wait, so you *took* it? Without even talking to me? Your brother?" Austin's eyes search mine. I can't tell if he's hurt or mad.

"I did. I got caught up in the excitement," I admit. "I'm not leaving Hungry Llama until we work out a transition plan and obviously, I felt torn. Especially with everything going on. At the same time, the foundation's actually a better fit for me." I gesture to my suit and pumps. "I love working with you both so, so much, but I'm not passionate about gaming like you guys are."

Austin looks away. Squints as if processing what I've said. I know it must not be easy for him to hear, but we made a promise to be truthful and I've lived up to my end of the bargain.

He turns his gaze back to me. "I'll admit, I'm bummed we didn't talk it over, but I don't own you, baby. I want what's best for you and if you want this, I want it for you."

"Thanks, Austin." A lump forms in my throat. "The deciding factor was it doesn't require an abundance of travel. I'll be able to stay in Seattle."

"I'm proud of you." He pulls me into a hug.

I cling to Austin, grateful he's given me his support. At the same time, I saw how much it hurt him when he realized I took the job.

As my boss, I get it. He, together with my brother, gave me an opportunity when I was at my lowest. On a professional level, I'll honor it. Do whatever it takes to guarantee they're on solid ground.

On a personal front, though we're together, right now it still feels like we're merely roommates passing in the night who occasionally make time to fuck.

It may sound harsh, but I've been there done that with Devon. Until I have a true commitment, no man—including Austin—will have a say in my future ever again.

It's not like he asked me my opinion about selling Hungry Llama.

Right?

I love him with all my heart.

But, I wasn't about to turn down my dream job.

He's going to have to deal.

Chapter Thirty-Five

Austin

The Next Week

It's been another long, grueling day.

Shay and I finally get home around nine.

The stress of the past few weeks pulls at both of us. We're sluggish. Our laughter less frequent. The deal with Jacoby has made significant progress so there's a light at the end of the tunnel. We only need to get to the finish line.

"You could've gone home earlier." I shed my jacket and glance in her direction. I know I sound patronizing, which I hate.

She pauses, her fingers lingering on her diamond solitaire necklace—a birthday gift from me. "I'm a team player and had work to do."

Her softspoken words feel pointed, which doesn't help the fear and insecurity gnawing at me. The thought she might be moving away from me, both professionally and personally, is devastating. Every time I think about that engagement ring tucked away in my safe, I'm reminded that my hesitance might cost me everything.

"Shay." I reach out hesitantly to tuck her hair behind her ear. "You know I appreciate it, but overworking yourself can trigger an episode."

Her eyes flash with irritation. "I'm careful, Austin. I know my limits. You don't have to constantly remind me."

"It's not just that." I exhale, pinching the bridge of my nose. "It feels like we're back to where we were a couple of weeks ago. I don't like this gap that's forming."

She sits down on the couch, her expression pensive. "I don't either. As far as I can tell it started when I accepted the job at the foundation and you started the sale of the company."

"Yeah..." I suck in my lips. "That's when you started pulling away from me."

She sighs. Shakes her head. Beckons me to sit beside her, which I do. "Look, we're both tired. Coming off a rough few weeks. I'm looking forward to this transaction wrapping up so—"

"So you can start the new job," I interrupt, realizing how petulant I sound. It's ironic, I was pissed when Miles hired her. I said I'd support her decision and now I don't want her to go. I love having her with me every day.

"No, what I was going to say is I'll cut you some slack." Shay cocks her head, exasperated. "I'm giving you everything I have. I'm one hundred percent in this, Austin."

"Are you?" I nearly slap myself in the face when the words slip out. "I can't shake off this feeling that I'm losing you."

"Wow. You're serious?" She pops up and looks down on me with her hands on her hips.

I don't know what to say, so I say nothing.

"You're not losing me. Yes, things are *changing*." Shay's infuriated. Passionate. Her eyes are narrowed to slits. "Change shouldn't mean we drift *apart*. We *should* navigate changes together. But we have to *be together*."

"And you don't think we're together?" My heart is in my throat. My instincts are correct, she's pulling away.

"Austin..." Shay sits back down, her voice calmer. "Listen. After meeting Zoey's baby, Evangeline, something inside me shifted. I've been doing some thinking, a great deal of it."

I tense up, apprehensive. What does she mean by "shifted?"

She wrings her hands, nervously. "Seeing that little baby, that beautiful life…it makes me yearn for a family of our own someday. A home filled with laughter and memories. It made me realize how much I want that with you and I don't know if that's what you want with *me*. If it is, you aren't acting like it."

I'm taken aback by her raw honesty. The image she paints is, of course, one I've imagined many times in my private moments. Hearing her articulate it brings a newfound depth to the dream. Except for one thing.

"Shay, I…" My voice falters. I think of the engagement ring hidden away, a symbol of my intentions. "I dream of that future too. But with you diving into this new role and all the responsibilities it'll entail, I worry. How can we build our future, our family, if you'll be pulled in an entirely different direction?"

She jumps up and slaps her forehead. Marches to the kitchen. Points at me. "Whoa. Talk about déjà vu."

"What do you mean?" I'm on my feet next to her in a flash.

Tears fill her eyes. "You know what? I don't want to live together without any real commitment from you. I can't go through another relationship filled with uncertainty. I'm not willing to be in a relationship if your definition of 'being in it together'"—she punctuates her words with finger quotes—"means I'm supposed to give up all of my professional dreams to support yours. Right now, we're coasting, Austin. I'm not into ultimatums, but you're the one who's pulled away from me for the past few weeks. Don't you turn this around and say it's me that's not giving my all. I won't be in a relationship like that. *Ever. Again.*"

I swallow hard, my throat tight. A heavy silence settles between us. It's a lot to digest. She and I are both dealing with huge life decisions and the pressures they bring. As for what this means for us as a couple? This is uncharted territory for me.

"Well, your silence tells me a lot." Shay sniffs back the rest of her tears. "I'm going to take an Uber to my parents' house and stay there this weekend. That will give you some space to consider what I said and think about what you want out of this relationship."

I choke back a sob. "I don't want to break up, Shay. I love you."

"Austin, I love you too. We're not breaking up. But I deserve to know if we're working toward a *real* identical goal." She walks to the elevator and presses the button. Turns back to face me. "Whether it's tomorrow, next month, or a year from now, let me know if you see a future with me. If you don't—I need you to set me free."

She steps into the cab. The doors close.

I'm left in stunned silence.

What the fuck just happened?

Chapter Thirty-Six

The Next Morning

The sun begins to peek over the horizon.

I sit in the breakfast nook of my parents' home, a mug of herbal tea between my hands. The fragrant steam is a quiet reassurance as the world outside still slumbers.

Glancing down at my phone, which I've finally turned on, I see dozens of texts from Austin. He's worried about me. Which I get, but I did let him know when I arrived safely last night. I'm not in an emotional state to go back and forth with him right now.

We're adults. I'm not asking for a ring. I'm asking for some indication we have a *real* future together.

My mom shuffles in wearing her bathrobe and a concerned look. "You're up early." She places her hand on my shoulder.

"I couldn't sleep," I admit. "Too many thoughts."

She sees that I made a pot of coffee and pours herself a cup before sitting opposite me. "Want to talk about it?"

Before I can respond, I hear the sound of padding feet from the hallway. "Morning, sweetheart."

"Hey, Papa." I relax back against my seat. I've come to realize how lucky I am to have parents who adore me. They're not perfect, but I've never not felt loved. It's agonizing knowing that Austin had the complete opposite experience growing up.

His mom is trying to make up for lost time, but it'll never be the same.

I want Austin to know what it's like to be part of a loving family. Navigating life. Embracing each other's idiosyncrasies. Being there through triumph and tragedy. Providing unconditional support, even if you don't always agree.

It's what I envisioned for us.

Now I'm not convinced.

My dad pours himself a cup of coffee and takes a seat beside Mom. "I'm sorry you and Austin have hit a road bump. Your mother and I, well, we're worried about you."

I take a deep breath, searching for the appropriate words. "It's been tough. Austin's been pulled in every direction. In the midst of it all I met Zoey Pearson. How could I say no to a job that seems tailor made for me?"

"You must have had a big fight to end up here last night." Mom leans forward, her eyes searching mine.

"It's...complicated." I'm not a little girl anymore and I'm not going to share everything with my folks. Austin and I are not broken up. I need some advice, but I don't want to divulge anything that could diminish him in their eyes. "Austin's been grappling with family issues and the pressure of the acquisition. I'm trying to support him, but when I told him about the job, he took it as a sign that I was pulling away. Not only from the company, but from us as a couple."

Dad shakes his head. "He's a grown man, but he's inexperienced, Shay. You're his first serious relationship."

"Sure, I get that." I rip at a napkin. "But he said he'd support me if I wanted a career change and it doesn't seem like was being honest with me. After everything with Devon, I can't go down a path where the man I'm in love with's feelings take precedence over mine. We need to be equals."

Mom looks away pensively. "Huh."

"What?" I touch the top of her hand.

She shrugs. "Look, I think you should have talked to him before accepting the position. I understand that you were excited, but..."

"If you want to build trust you need to give it," my dad finishes.

"So it's my fault." I cross my arms over my chest protectively. Why am I always the one who has to bend? "I think that's bullshit."

My folks share a look, and my mom is the one to speak. "Shay, you can drop the defensiveness. It's no one's fault. We're having a conversation."

"I'm not *defensive*," I say without irony, considering I feel myself getting agitated. "I'm not going to let Austin lead me on the way Devon did. When am I going to be enough?"

My dad is aghast. "Is that truly how you feel? Shay, of course you're enough. Why would you say that?"

"I wanted to make my own decision." I deflate like a balloon. "I didn't want to answer to anyone."

Mom squints at me. "Do you see a future with Austin?"

I nod. Rip up more bits of napkin.

"Are you truly afraid he doesn't want one with you?" Mom sips her coffee.

I nod again. "I think he's undecided."

Mom and Dad share another glance, a silent understanding passes between them.

She hesitates for a moment, then says, "Speaking of Devon—he reached out to us again."

"He did?" My head snaps up. After I blew him off a few months ago, it didn't occur to me he was still bothering my parents.

Dad nods. "A couple weeks ago he called. Wants your number. He said letting you go was a huge mistake. Since then he's been remarkably...persistent."

"God." A sigh escapes my lips. The man hates to lose, that must be it. "Why now?"

"He claims he's changed. Said he took you for granted and didn't give you credit for all that you brought to the relationship. He *seems* genuine." Mom bites her lip. I can tell she's struggling not to tell me what to do.

I rub my temples. "I can't believe this. He's so messy. I'm not adding Devon back into the mix of my life. He's in my past."

Mom and Dad exchange glances. Silent words pass between them.

A few minutes later, Dad leans back and runs a hand through his silvery hair. "Who the hell knows anything. Maybe you should have told Austin about the job. Maybe you shouldn't have. Either way, I don't see it as a reason for Austin to doubt your commitment to him. That's the God's honest truth." He looks me dead in the eyes. "Remember, you're the one in the driver's seat. *You. Are. The. Prize.*" He points at me with each word. "We love Austin, he's a great guy. We can see how much he loves you. But if he's not willing to trust you and support your decisions, you need to think about what's best for you and consider your options."

"By options, you're not seriously suggesting I give Devon another chance?" I'm shocked. I know when I initially returned home, both my mom and dad were bummed about my breakup. They gave me some serious tough love. Over the past several months we seem to have figured all that stuff out.

Mom reaches across the table, taking my hands in hers. "It's not up to us. All we want is for you to be happy and fulfilled. You also need to own your choices and the triumphs and repercussions."

"The timing is so weird." I wrinkle my nose.

She shrugs. "Devon seems sincerely happy to know you're thriving. He told me he never *asked* you to give up your career to support him. Said you did that all on your own."

"Um..." All the air in my lungs freezes. This whole "butter up the parents" thing feels a little—shady, when he's actually undermining my recollection of events. I'll *bet* he misses me now that he doesn't have some poor sucker to make sure every one of his desires was fulfilled. "We never had a specific conversation about it, but it certainly was implied. Something kept me from trusting Devon enough to tell him about my epilepsy, which I think tells me everything I need to know about if he's the right man for me. I want to be in a relationship with someone who loves all of me. Not curated parts. That man is Austin."

"Hallelujah. Shay, I don't think you realize how amazing you are." Dad side hugs me. "From the time you were born people have been drawn to you. You make people feel comfortable. You're a hard worker. You're a beautiful girl—woman—inside and out. You don't need to ever dim your shine. Not for any man."

"Thanks, Papa." I fiddle with the salt shaker. "So we're clear, I'm not going back to Devon and it would be inappropriate for me to talk with him if he thinks he still has a shot. I'm with Austin." I bury my face in my hands. "I *want* things to work with him, I need to figure out where we stand."

Mom slides out of her seat and puts her coffee cup in the sink. "Shay, you're our daughter and we merely want what's best for you. But remember, relationships are about compromise. You have to be willing to work through the rough patches. There will be many over the course of a long relationship."

I nod, my mind racing. "I know. I'm going to take some time to think. In the meantime, could you do me a favor and stop talking with Devon? It's disrespectful to my relationship with Austin."

"That's fair." My mother squeezes my shoulder. "Whatever you decide we support you. Follow your heart. It'll lead you in the right direction. Now, I've got to get ready. Are you positive you'll be okay here by yourself? We won't be back until late tonight."

I hug her before she heads upstairs. "I'll be fine. I'm hoping to hash things out with Austin. I'll leave you a note if I go back home to the condo."

I take my cup of tea and stand at the back door to look out at the lawn overlooking the lake. The early morning light dapples the backyard, casting long, meandering shadows. For a moment, I let the peaceful scene outside soothe my frazzled nerves.

It's impossible, though. There's something else on my mind.

Something I haven't told anyone. It's too—petrifying.

I lean my forehead against the cool glass and try to organize my feelings into some semblance of order.

When did it happen? Three weeks ago? Four? My usual meticulousness about keeping a strict routine has been disrupted by Austin's family issues, the sale and now, my new job. It's no wonder I've lost track.

However, when I think about it, my heart starts to race. *What if?*

The mere thought sends a cascade of emotions through me. The possibility is not entirely unwelcome.

Of course, given the current state of things, the timing couldn't be more complicated.

Taking a deep breath, I decide that speculating won't get me anywhere. Compelled to take action, I push myself away from the window and I climb the stairs up to my old room. Every step seems to echo my frantic heartbeat.

I open the door to the ensuite bathroom and look in the mirror. Memories flood back. This was the identical room where, as a teenager, I would spend hours getting ready for dates or talking on the phone with friends. Glancing back at the shower, I'm nearly overcome with emotion.

Ironically, my reaction relates to a memory I can never push out of my mind. It's one that's stuck with me like a 3D movie. I'll never forget that fateful day when I slipped in the shower and hit my head on the porcelain tub. I don't know how long I was out, all I remember is, when I came to, I've never had a headache so painful.

And yet, I took five Tylenol and didn't tell a soul.

Hours later, at the pageant, I had a grand mal seizure. A couple of days later, I was diagnosed with epilepsy.

Recently, I confessed my recollection of what happened to my neurologist. I learned at this point, twelve years later, we'll never know for certain if my fall triggered my condition.

I know, though.

Oh well, it's time to get on with it.

Opening the paper shopping bag, I take out the pregnancy test I bought on the way over here last night. I read the instructions several times. Try to focus, despite my racing thoughts. Then, I follow each step meticulously, waiting for the stipulated time to pass.

Three minutes seem like an eternity.

I can't help but think about Austin. If the test is positive, how will he react? I don't want him to commit to me because of...

I want him to...

Wincing, I grip the counter when my heart seizes with uncertainty. He says he loves me, but how he reacted yesterday evening was—telling.

I remind myself not to get ahead of things. I'll deal with whatever comes next, but now it's crucial for me to know.

The timer on my phone goes off, breaking through my haze of thoughts.

Hesitating for a moment longer, I gather my courage.

And look down at the test.

Chapter Thirty-Seven

Austin

Two Days Later

I've never had a more brutal weekend in my life.

The heaviness in my chest is unbearable, and it feels like an anchor is pulling me under.

Every glance at my phone is a disappointment. Every second I don't hear from her is agony.

I've tried to get in touch with her for days, to no avail. Nothing. She's giving me nothing.

I'm hoping. Praying. Promising to sell my firstborn. *Anything* to talk to her.

I want to throw myself at her feet. Tell her how much I love her. Beg her to never leave.

Overdramatic much? Yes. Yes, I am.

Why wouldn't I be? All I had to do was tell her she's my forever.

I failed.

It doesn't matter that I have all this shit going on. Nothing should ever take precedence over Shay.

Not my mom. Not my siblings. Not even the stupid sale of my company.

How the fuck did I let Shay leave without expressing the depth of my commitment to her?

I'm *destroyed*.

Now it's Sunday morning. I'm sitting next to Miles in Hungry Llama's conference room along with our CFO and legal team. Joar Jacoby, his lawyer, Seth, and two other attorneys are across the table, which is filled with stacks of paper and legal briefs. Miles is clicking through a series of slides on a digital projector that displays the information we've been asked to pull together during the due diligence process.

My focus should be in this room, but it's everywhere but here.

"Okay, we're on slide fifty-two, profit and loss statements from the past twelve quarters." Miles subtly kicks my chair to alert me that my part of the presentation is beginning. "And now, Austin will take you through the financials."

I look up, force a tight smile. "Excuse me, gentlemen, I need a second."

Rising from the table, I step out onto the balcony and gulp fresh air.

It's unseasonably warm so the city is bustling with activity. Shoppers. Tourists. Diners. I look down at couples walking hand in hand to the symphony next door and all I can think of is Shay.

How my failure to pull the trigger has destroyed our beautiful love story.

She's still at her parents' house, not answering. Her engagement ring remains hidden in my safe. I should be mentally preparing for a tropical vacation with Shay right now. Somewhere exotic and warm where I'd find the perfect moment to ask her. Promise her forever.

Instead, she thinks I don't love her enough to commit.

Pulling out my phone, I scroll through my texts. My desperate attempts to reach out, each one met with silence.

I hear the door open. "Andrews, is everything okay?"

Fuck.

"Joar, my apologies. I know I'm being unprofessional, which isn't like me. There's a personal situation…"

Joar claps me on the back. "Woman problems?"

"Yeah." I shake my head, mortified. "It's fine. Give me a second, I'll be right in."

He crosses his arms over his chest. "Shay? She was here Friday? Did the marketing presentation?"

I nod. "I royally messed up." Embarrassingly, my voice cracks.

Joar leans back against the building. "Oh, I've *been* there. Tell you what, we're nearly done. If you finish the financials, Seth and I can finalize the offer. Then we let the lawyers hash the rest out. Reconvene Monday." He reaches for the door handle. "Then you can go make it up to her."

I'm not sure whether to be mortified or grateful, but it doesn't matter at this point, so I decide to get my ass in there and do my fucking job.

The room is filled with a buzz of energy as the representatives from Jacoby International process the financial information I shared. If they wanted Hungry Llama before, I'm confident they're going to make us a deal we can't refuse now.

Sinking back in my seat, I sigh with relief. I rallied and finished the most critical presentation of my life.

Miles fist pumps me, a huge smile spreads across his face. "We. Fucking. Did. It."

"Yeah. We did it." I'd like to be as happy as Miles is, but I'm not. When I was on my final slide, the reality of what we're doing hit me. Miles and I are selling the company we built. When Jacoby International takes over, life as we know it will change.

More than the stress of the acquisition, it's the distance between Shay and me that gnaws at my insides. Our most recent conversation replays on a loop in my mind—a chaotic mix of miscommunication, unspoken fears, and pent-up emotions.

"Wanna go out and celebrate?" Miles heads toward the door. "Or, do you have plans with my sister?"

He knows something's up. I'm glad he hasn't asked, though. We're past the point of my best friend involving himself in my relationship with his sister. Regardless of the outcome, we have to navigate our relationship on our own.

I shake my head. "No on both counts. I think I need to go home and crash."

"I get it. This is a big deal, dude." He steps toward me and we side hug. "Let's do something to commemorate—me and you. Soon."

Lightly pounding his back with my fist, I feel bad I'm blowing him off. If things were different, he and I would be going on a tear tonight. "Yeah, we will."

After I make my way back to my office, I flop on my sofa and turn on my phone.

Sit back up. I've missed a text from Shay.

Shay: Flirt Alert.

My phone vibrates, it's *her*.

"Shay?" I'm tentative when I answer because I'm not certain where her head is at.

"I won't keep you because I know you have a full day, but when you're done can you come pick me up?" Shay's energy is on ten thousand. "I'm at my parents' house."

"We're done." I resist the urge to ask about her well-being, though I'm worried. It's a trigger for her, though and we have a lot to work through without me adding to the tension.

She's silent for half a second. "Did you get my text?"

"Yeah."

I hear her take a deep breath. "I miss you. Let's talk?"

"*Yeah?*" Relief courses through me. The urge to rush to her side is overwhelming. "I'll leave now. Be there in a half hour."

On the way over, I try not to speed. Try to remain calm. Try not to feel road rage at every stupid fucking driver who's between me and my girl.

All that matters to me is fixing things with Shay.

When I pull up to her parents' house, I find the front door ajar. Pushing it open, I feel the familiar warmth of the home I've spent so much time in over the years. It feels comforting.

There's no sign of her in the living room. She's not in the kitchen. I check the back garden, nothing. I start to panic. What if she was having an episode? What if she has no idea she called me? Frantic, I bound up the stairs to where her room used to be.

I cautiously push the door open, unsure of what I'm going to find.

Shay sits waiting on the little loveseat by her window, her liquid blue eyes bore into mine. She wears sleep shorts and a white tank top. Her nipples are perfectly visible through the thin fabric. Her face is fresh, no makeup, and her hair is up in a top knot.

I can tell she's been crying, which breaks my heart. Yet, she's still radiant in her vulnerability.

"Shay." I take a deep breath. "I'm so, so sorry for everything."

"No, please don't apologize." She bites her lower lip. "Austin, I've been doing some thinking. We've both been caught up in our own baggage. I realize I'm pushing you to confirm your commitment to me, which is unfair. I'm not going to demand things of you before you're ready. We haven't been together long..."

"Stop it." I sit next to her on the couch. Our fingers entwine.

She slumps back against the cushions, her eyes squeeze shut.

I brush the tiny stray hairs out of her face. "All I've done is think about what happened and I completely understand, baby. Particularly after Devon. I had no idea you doubted my commitment to you. I'm so, so sorry. It kills me to think I've hurt you. My inability to communicate you're my future, *that's on me.*"

Her eyes blink open. Silence stretches between us, but it's not the cold, distancing void from the other night. This one is bursting with understanding, a chance to reset.

"As I told you that night, seeing Zoey with her baby, it stirred something in me." Shay rubs her flat belly. "I want that someday—a family, a life with you."

I cup her face and move closer. "I want that too."

"I've been scared, Austin." Her blue eyes seem to bore into my soul. "Scared that maybe you weren't on the same page."

The raw honesty in her confession leaves me reeling. "Shay, after I got my mom out of that situation, I immediately dove into the acquisition. I've been so caught up in securing our future, I lost sight of the present. Of us. All want is for my life to be wholly intertwined with yours. I've been so terrified of messing things up that I ended up doing just that."

"You're okay with my role at the foundation?" Shay's voice is so quiet. I hate that I've come across as unsupportive.

Fuck.

"Yes," I say with absolute conviction. "If it's what will make you feel as accomplished as I feel with Hungry Llama, then of course I want that for you. I want you to feel like a billion bucks, baby. I support you one thousand percent."

She lays her head on my shoulder. Places her hand on my thigh. "Thank you for saying that. From now on, let's try to communicate better. The potential of what we have is so exceptional. I don't want to let our pasts dictate our present."

"I know," I whisper, kissing the top of her head. I'm trying not to focus on the taut nipple trying to break free from her little tank top. "I've been thinking of a way to show you how committed I am. How much I want this. Can you trust me on this?"

Her eyes search mine. "Yeah, but what do you mean?"

My heart races, I don't want to come off as desperate. "After the deal goes through, I have plans, Shay. *Big* plans for us." I put my arm around her shoulder and pull her into my lap, her back to my front. Tilt my face down so our lips are touching. "Right now, all I want is for you to know how deeply I love you."

"God, I love you so much." A tear rolls down Shay's cheek. She angles her arm back to caress my face. "Austin, I've never felt like this. You have to understand that. I *need* you. So much."

Our lips meet in a passionate, yet reverential kiss.

A promise. An understanding. A symbol of trust.

Every layer we unravel, the bond she and I share deepens.

Proving that our love is the real thing.

A forever thing.

Chapter Thirty-Eight

A Few Minutes Later

There's nothing better than being in Austin's arms.

The warmth of his body and his clean, fresh scent feels like home. His arm bands my waist. His other hand holds my face as we kiss.

It's not long before our kisses grow heated and the hand resting on my stomach slides up to cup my breast. Austin's thumb works my nipple into a peak, then he pinches and pulls it a little, causing me to squirm against his cock, which is pressing against my back.

"I don't want to start something if your parents are going to come home." Austin groans and pulls away.

Gripping his jaw, I capture his lips again, murmuring, "They're gone for the day."

My revelation causes a frenzy. We're ravenous. He holds me tight against him as our mouths fuse and tongues slash together. Reclaiming our bond.

Austin trails the fingers of one hand down the front of my loose, sleep shorts. The other pulls the little strap of my tank top down, exposing my breast. He presses his palm against my pubic bone as he lightly circles my clit with his finger. Bends down to suck my nipple between his lips.

"God, Austin." I bend my knees and plant my feet on his thighs to give him better access. "Yes, keep going."

I loop my arms back around his neck and Austin shoves my shorts down a bit. Together we watch as his fingers slip back and forth between my slick folds. My thighs tense with each pass, each contact sends ripples of pleasure through my core. He dips his finger into my opening then leisurely trails it up to my clit, but doesn't touch it. He's mastered my pussy, knowing precisely how to bring me to the brink and then back off to build. And build. And build.

Austin drags my orgasm out for as long as he can. He sucks on my nipples until they pucker into tight bullets. Strokes every centimeter of my pussy until I'm lubricated and dripping. Then teases my clit until it's hard and pulsing. Every muscle in my legs and core quiver with anticipation of what pleasure he'll elicit.

As he continues his worshiping me, my knees splay open, though I manage to keep my feet anchored against Austin's outer thigh. He buries two fingers inside me and hooks them to rub my inner walls. "You're so beautiful." His cheek is pressed against mine as we watch him work me over. "Look at yourself. Do you know what it does to me when you cream all over my fingers?" He pulls them out and brings them to my mouth.

I suck, catching his eye. His cock jumps against my ass. "Jesus," he groans and presses them back inside me

"I'm so close, baby." I thrust against him shamelessly. "I need...ohhhh. Ohhhh."

"I've got you." Austin groans as his other hand snakes down to assist in his masterful pussy foreplay. "I'm gonna make you come so hard, Shay."

I can't tear my eyes away from his fingers pumping in and out of me while he rubs my juices all over my clit then circles and pinches it. Releases and presses his palm against my public bone, which stimulates my entire clitoral wall. My teeth are clenched as my head lolls back against his shoulder.

I'm coating him with my wetness as I arch and writhe. My own fingers now pinch my nipples as he goes faster, fastening his lips to the place under my ear that sends trembles all over my body. "Go over, baby," Austin purrs when he presses down against his fingers inside me, sneaking his thumb up to rub my little button. The combination of everything at once triggers an out-of-body, orgasmic religious experience.

"*Arghhhahhhhaaaaaaahhhh.*" My screams are garbled when I let go in a blinding, sparkling, glittery explosion.

I have no idea how long he keeps it going. I lose track of time and space. Reality and fantasy. Past, present, and future.

When I'm somewhat coherent again, I feel Austin kissing my face. Running his hands all over my body. "There she is," he purrs against my ear.

Twisting in his lap, I palm his stiff cock through his jeans. "I need you to fuck me, baby. Hard." My desires are basic. Instinctive. Within seconds I've freed him and use the precum dripping from his crown to lubricate his shaft so I can stroke him from root to tip.

Austin hooks my leg under his arm and takes over. He grips his cock and taps it against my clit before guiding it inside me until he's buried to the hilt. Fucks up into me. I bite down on my lip hard, because he's hitting the exact spot inside me that caused me to detonate moments ago. Within a couple of thrusts, I'm clenching around him and wailing when my third orgasm overtakes my body.

"Shay. Baby." Austin repositions me so I'm lying on my side and he's thrusting into me from behind as he holds my leg by my ankle. "I'm gonna come, baby. I can't stop now."

I hold on to the cushion for dear life, my walls rippling and clenching around Austin as he fucks me harder than ever. "Ohmygod, yess..."

"I. Fucking. Love. You." Austin's balls slap against my ass, adding to the sounds of our grunts, groans, and cries. I feel his cock thicken inside me and every muscle in his body clench when he lets go, wrenching another rolling tremor from my body.

We're spent. Completely out of breath, panting for air. There's nothing we can do but lie tangled together until our bodies recover.

Eventually we return to a state of consciousness. Petting. Whispering words of love and devotion. Relaxing into a dreamlike bubble of togetherness.

I trace Austin's eyebrows with my finger. "I love you. I trust you. I'm safe with you."

"*Shay*." Austin's eyes moisten. "I love *you*. I trust *you*. I'm safe with *you*."

Our lips meet to seal our vow with a kiss. "You're all I ever need, my love." I search his gold-flecked eyes. "I mean it."

"I know you do." He buries his face in my neck. "This is forever."

Now that we've hashed things out, the last place I want to be is in my parents' house. "Should we go back home?"

"I dunno." Austin props himself up on an elbow and tweaks my nipple. "I doubt Goran and Annika will mind how loud we are when we fuck. Maybe we should stay the night here."

"Austin!" I swat him.

He sits up and tucks himself back into his jeans. "Fine, let's get outta here before they get home."

"I'll be back." I adjust my skewed sleep clothes and head to the bathroom. I grab a washcloth to clean up but when I turn on the water I notice the little stick on the counter.

Shit.

I pick it up and find Austin staring out the window.

"Austin?" I'm nervous, but also excited.

He turns around to see me holding out the stick to him. "Shay?"

"There's something I forgot to mention..."

Chapter Thirty-Nine

Two Months Later

The glare from the overhead lights is blinding as the camera focuses on us. Miles and I are seated side by side dressed in jeans and Hungry Llama hoodies, ready for the final interview of the two-day press tour about the acquisition, which finally went pubic earlier this week.

The muted background hum in the *BizTV* studio fades into silence. Tasha Adams, the sharply dressed host of *Business Rockstars* turns toward us with a practiced smile. "Good evening. Tonight our guests are Austin Andrews and Miles Stojanović. Your story has been making headlines around the world. Hungry Llama's sale to Jacoby International is being touted as the biggest deal in the gaming industry. How does it feel?"

I clear my throat. "It's been a whirlwind, Tasha. We started Hungry Llama as freshmen at University of Washington. To see it grow and gain the attention of a global giant like Jacoby International...it's surreal."

"It's a testament to our team's hard work and dedication." Miles nods at me. "We've built something special, and while the acquisition is a significant milestone, we're excited about what's next."

Tasha's eyes flicker with curiosity. "You've both agreed to stay on during the transition. Why make that decision? Surely, after such a successful sale, you could've taken your earnings and retired to a beach somewhere."

"True." I chuckle. "But Hungry Llama is our brainchild. We've been entrusted to ensure that its values and spirit remains intact, even as Jacoby International takes the helm. Our commitment to our team and our users doesn't end with a sale."

Miles adds, "We're still very much in the thick of it. But Austin and I, along with Jacoby's leadership, are committed to smooth sailing."

The rest of the interview touches upon our journey, the highs and lows and our hopes for Hungry Llama's future. As we wrap up, Tasha delves into our private lives. "Away from the boardroom, how has this transition impacted your personal lives?"

I glance at Miles, who simply smiles and gives nothing away. "It's been a ride. And we're grateful for the supportive folks we have in our corner."

When the interview is over, we take off the microphones, extend pleasantries to Tasha and the crew, head down the elevator to the parking garage.

"Well, that's that." I extend my fist out toward him.

He taps his fist against mine. "I'd be sadder if I didn't have two hundred million dollars clear in my bank account."

"True that." I laugh. "With another two hundred mill coming in a year."

We walk to our cars in silence. He and I have made our peace with selling Hungry Llama. We're proud of the company we built. Proud of the opportunity it's provided to so many. Jacoby is keeping the entire team. Miles and I will continue to participate at the board level. All in all, not too shabby for a couple of twenty-nine-year-old gaming geeks.

"See you in a bit. I'm looking forward to dinner." Miles waves as he gets into his car.

I watch him drive off, get in my own car and text Shay: "I'll pick you up out front in 5."

Inside the private dining room at Canlis, ambient light sets a gentle glow upon the mahogany table with seating for ten. Shay and I are a few minutes early.

As we settle into our seats, her sparkling blue eyes find mine. "I can't believe we're here celebrating after the past few months. A little surreal, isn't it? We got through it all."

"It sometimes feels like a dream." My fingers graze hers. "We had a few rough moments, but we stuck together. I love you. So much."

"I love you too, Austin." She strokes the side of my face.

I hand her a flute with a splash of champagne. "Before everyone arrives, a toast to us. To our future."

"Yes, to us." We clink glasses and she takes a sip and puts the glass down. "It's delicious. I know my doctor cleared me to have a drink now and then, but I think that was enough. Besides, if I'd been pregnant, I wouldn't be able to enjoy even a taste of this exquisite champs."

"You'd have a cute little baby bump instead." I stroke her flat stomach. "Be warned, I'm determined to knock you up sooner rather than later."

"Don't feel pressure because my neurologist thinks it's better for me to get pregnant before I'm thirty-five. We have time." Shay says this to me, though I know she's reassuring herself. Pregnancy scare aside, both of us want to be married before she gets pregnant.

Little does she know...

Our private discussion is interrupted as the doors swing open to admit Joar Jacoby with his wife, actress Clover Callahan. Ty and Zoey Rainier follow. They're with Connor McGloughlin, Ty's bandmate, and his wife, actress Ronni Miller. Clover stars in Ronni's latest television show.

When Miles joins us a few minutes later, his eyes nearly bug out at all the star power. "Holy shit, I thought I was in Hollywood for a minute."

Everyone laughs at his self-depreciating humor. He's become quite the celebrity over the past month when *Shark Tank* tapped him to be a new shark this season.

Shay, Ty, and Zoey gathered us for the dinner tonight because of the Rainier Foundation endowments. In Shay's initial month as Development Director, she shored up funding to launch educational programming in film, media, gaming, and programming by obtaining financial commitments from Joar, Ronni and, of course, me and Miles.

With the educational initiatives fully paid for, Shay has literally quadrupled the reach of Ty and Zoey's foundation. Children in underserved communities all over the country will now have access to top-notch education in the arts.

Once everyone is seated and has a glass of champagne, Shay stands. She's stunning in a simple black fitted dress. Her hair's pulled back into a loose bun. "Congratulations to us all. We're making history. Children who have creative aptitude will not be passed over. I can't wait for each and every one of you to see the impact you're having on future generations."

Ty stands, every inch of him oozes with stage presence. I've never seen someone so softspoken be able to command an audience of any size. "Shay, Zoey and I knew we were on the right path pursuing you. I'd apologize to Hungry Llama for stealing you away, but there's no need. We're all in this together."

Zoey clinks her glass with the rest of us, but doesn't take a sip.

"Z, don't tell me." Ronni points at her laughing. "Again?"

She blushes and nestles against Ty, who beams like a spotlight. "He threatened to keep me barefoot and pregnant, and he's a man of his word."

"We're due next summer." Ty pats Zoey's nonexistent belly. "We'll stop when we have a baseball team."

"Jaysus." Connor shakes his head.

Ronni grips his forearm. "We're done, babe. Done. Done. *Done*."

Clover and Joar exchange a look and a smile.

"Should we tell them?" Joar asks her.

She throws her hands up in exasperation. "Uh, for a guy who is so astute in business, you're not particularly great at keeping secrets. Yes. We're pregnant again too."

"I'm in dangerous company." Miles gulps down the rest of his champagne. "As the sole single person here, I hope whatever fertility fairy dust that seems to touch all y'all doesn't touch me."

We all laugh but I know there's a grain of envy in Miles's comment. For nearly two decades he and I have been a duo. He's all but come out and said it: with the sale of our company he's worried our sole connection will be through Shay. He's wrong, of course, but if the situation were reversed, I'd definitely feel similarly.

The atmosphere shifts when the appetizer is served—an exquisite Dungeness crab salad with citrus dressing. Ty, a food aficionado, moans in appreciation. "This is fucking awesome. I love the fennel." He pats his rock-hard abs. "I haven't eaten all day."

Miles twirls his fork, still in awe of the lead singer of Less Than Zero. "Are there any tours on the horizon?"

Ty grins. "Maybe. But we're focusing on life too, not just the music, right, Connor?"

"Aye." The big burly bass player kisses his wife's head and goes back to eating.

The dishes keep coming. A seared halibut with apple-cider glaze arrives, followed by a luscious duck confit paired with wine-soaked cherries.

Ronni, ever the businesswoman, muses, "The key," she gestures to Miles and me, "is balance. Work, while fulfilling, should not be all-consuming."

"*Hey*..." Miles raises an eyebrow, playfully defensive. "You make it sound as if Austin and I are workaholics."

"Do you know yourselves?" Shay laughs. "You both are! But I adore you regardless."

I play it cool. "Well, now that the deal is done and the endowments are finalized, I've got plans for Shay and I to sneak off. A beach perhaps..."

Zoey exhales dramatically, "Shay, has he been holding out on you?"

Shay giggles. "Austin's full of surprises. I've been dreaming of the sun; this summer hasn't been the warmest."

Joar's voice turns soft, as he takes Clover's hand. "Experiencing the world offers great perspective."

"Excuse me?" She bugs her eyes out at him. "Who did you steal that line from?"

He laughs. "You, sweetness. Always you."

Dinner evolves into a delightful mix of jesting and profound travel stories and more delicious food. A beef tenderloin with a blackberry reduction is followed by a discussion on life's unpredictability. When dessert—a velvety chocolate mousse with fresh berries—arrives, the conversation turns personal.

"So, Austin, any plans post-acquisition?" Miles asks, with a twinkle in his eye.

I could kill him. He's the one person who's privy to my grand scheme.

Before I can reply, Shay interjects, "Oh, let him breathe, Miles! The man's earned a break."

"I think, for now, it's about cherishing the present." I smile and hold up my wine glass. "This moment, with all of you, means the world. To dear friends, both old and new."

We all clink glasses again and I'm overcome with how cool my life is. It wasn't long ago that Hungry Llama was my focus every hour and every minute of the day. I was a shell of a man. Now, I have an abundance of love, friendship, and hope. I'm grateful.

Our evening winds down, filled with laughter and promises of future gatherings.

Outside, as we wait for the valet in night air which is beginning to turn crisp, Shay snuggles close. "Tonight was perfect. I had so much fun."

I wrap my arm around her. "Every moment I have with you is perfect."

Now, it's up to me to create the perfect moment for her.

Chapter Forty

Three Weeks Later

Golden hues dance on the water, the distant sound of tropical birds serve as a gentle reminder that we're far from home, where it's rainy and wet.

Islas Secas is a whisper of perfection, a slice of paradise. From our private casita nestled between lush vegetation and the azure sea, the world seems to fade away. In fact, we're so secluded, it feels like we have the entire island to ourselves—no staff pops in unexpectedly, we don't bump into guests during our strolls. Just Austin and me, soaking in the sun, the sea, and the luxury of complete privacy.

The ten days we've spent here have been full of rest, relaxation, lots of sex and, well, an abundance of noteworthy sex.

"I never even imagined anything like this." I fondle a seashell I found on our early morning walk.

The beach stretches out before me, untouched and inviting. The scent of coconut oil and saltwater wafts in the gentle breeze. Austin is beside me, an impish grin playing on his lips. I'd chalk it up to the epic blowjob I gave him an hour ago, but from the moment we stepped foot on this tropical paradise, that grin hasn't left his face.

It's contagious, but it's also suspicious.

He leans back on the lounge chair, his sunglasses reflecting the shimmer of the water. "Not in my wildest dreams. It's like we're Adam and Eve, and this is our Eden."

"Except with better accommodations and all of the forbidden fruit." I cup my naked breasts and jiggle them.

"Ah." A teasing smirk plays on his lips. "My favorite."

I elbow him playfully. "You're looking far too pleased with yourself. What are you plotting?"

"Who, me?" He feigns innocence, raising an eyebrow. "Just enjoying the view."

"Nice try. I think you have something else on your mind." I sulk back in my own chair.

Austin reaches inside his board shorts and strokes his cock. "Is it that obvious?"

"*Oooohh*." I lean over to his ear, my voice dropping to a conspiratorial whisper. "Are you going to fuck me right here?"

Austin chuckles, a playful glint in his eye. "You might be one lucky girl."

Our laughter dances in the air, joining the songs of distant birds. I dip my toes into our private plunge pool, appreciating the contrast between the cool water and the hot, tropical sun. Don't get me wrong, I'm always down for making love with Austin, it's just that we're here. Alone. It's the perfect time for him to propose.

He's been dropping hints for the past few weeks. Then he planned this romantic getaway. I was convinced it would happen before we leave tomorrow. Now I'm not so sure.

Maybe I should take matters into my own hands.

"It's incredible how secluded this place is." I trace my finger on his bicep.

He nods. "Yeah. It's been liberating. When we got here, I thought it might feel too isolated, but it's made everything more...intimate. Just us and nature."

"It's so rare for you and I to have a stretch of alone time like this together," I muse, "to find a place where we're truly away from it all. No work calls, no meeting reminders. Just you and me. Reminds me of our ski patrol cabin."

Austin reaches out, pulling me closer. "It's been magical. I'll always cherish these moments with you."

"We can do anything, and no one will know." I trail my fingers down to the waistband of his board shorts.

"Oh yeah? And what, Miss Shay, do you propose we do with our freedom?" Austin raises an eyebrow playfully.

I withdraw my hand and roll my eyes. "Well, let's see. We've gone skinny dipping every day and fucked in every location I can think of. I wonder if we can ask a staff member to get us a marriage license..."

"A marriage license?" He pouts dramatically for comedic effect. "And here I was hoping for a treasure hunt of your beautiful body."

A soft smile tugs at my lips to mask my disappointment. "You and your schemes."

"You know how I like to draw your orgasms out? Bring you to the brink and then back off. When I eventually let you go over, it's better than it could ever have been?" He tips my face up with his finger to look at him. "Trust me."

The look in his eyes tells me *everything*. It settles me. "I do."

"I'm not Devon." He tilts his head.

I can't help but wince. "Not even close, babe. I'm sorry I ever compared our situation to that one."

"We're *forever*, Shay." He pulls down his shorts. His enormous cock slaps against his belly. "And now, I'm calling a flirt alert."

"You've called about a million over the past week." I grip him and guide his shaft to my lips. "You might be running out."

He laughs as he presses himself into my mouth. "Never. There'll never be too many flirt alerts."

<hr>

The gentle sound of the sea and the delicate chirping of the nocturnal island creatures create a lullaby that has coaxed Austin into a deep sleep. I lie next to him, my body tucked comfortably into his embrace. With every rise and fall of his chest, warmth and contentment wash over me.

A year ago, if someone had told me this is where I'd be, I would've scoffed in disbelief.

I remember the sting of betrayal and the heartbreak I felt when Devon walked out of my life. What I had once thought was a fairy tale had crumbled into a nightmare—such a painful lesson for me. I wasn't myself in that relationship. I'd never been honest with him about my epilepsy and put his career and ambitions above my own.

A part of me thought I'd never recover, that my life was ruined. Looking back now, I can't help but feel grateful for Devon letting me go.

It led me to Austin. It made room in my life for a love that's genuine and nurturing. Austin knows me. Loves me. Understands the core of who I am.

I think of Austin's recent breakthrough with his mother and his younger siblings. Their fractured relationship has always weighed on him, but he's been taking steps, mending what was broken. His resilience and commitment to family inspire me. Here's a man, with all his vulnerability and strengths, who's committed to rebuilding, to understanding, and to loving fiercely.

I'm the luckiest girl in the world.

My fingers trace circles on the back of his hand, my mind drifting to my own journey. The challenges I faced with my epilepsy sometimes seemed insurmountable. With me taking control of my own health, I've reclaimed parts of my life I feared I'd lost forever.

Now, with my role at The Rainier Foundation, I'm helping the organization make real, tangible differences. The passion and purpose it has ignited in me are unlike anything I've ever experienced in my career. It's fulfilling in a way I hadn't anticipated.

A contented sigh escapes my lips as I think of Austin. He's my future.

The sale of Hungry Llama has changed his destiny. It's not just about the money, but the opportunities it provides. Generational wealth, a term I'd heard but never thought would apply to Austin at such a young age, is now a reality. Through his hard work, determination and a touch of serendipity, he has unlimited freedom to pursue passions and to safeguard the future of our family.

The gentle rustling of the canopy above our cabana brings me back to the present. Here we are, surrounded by nature's opulence, taking a break from the world. This trip, this moment, is a culmination of everything we've been through and everything we've become.

Austin murmurs something in his sleep, pulling me closer. I lean in, pressing a soft kiss on his forehead. The love I feel for him is overwhelming, intense, and all-consuming.

'You're a million star flirt alert," I whisper, more to myself than him, thinking of our struggles, victories, and the beautiful uncertainty of what lies ahead.

As I close my eyes, the rhythmic sound of the ocean lulls me into deep relaxation.

Gratitude fills every fiber of my being.

Life has a funny way of leading us to where we're meant to be, and right now, in this moment...

I'm in exactly the right place.

Austin

Epilogue

The rain from Seattle has given way to a driving snow storm as we drive toward Crystal Mountain.

With each passing mile, I get nervous. Beside me, Shay's eyes are fixed on the notes for her supposed meeting with the resort executives. Little does she know, the entire premise is a ruse—a meticulously crafted plan with Zoey to give us this moment.

"I still think it's odd Zoey wanted to meet here of all places." Shay wrinkles her nose. "But then again, I've gone on and on about the Hungry Llama retreat. If having an event at the resort helps the foundation, I'm all in."

"Oh, I've got a phenomenal feeling about this. I'm just glad to tag along." The corner of my mouth twitches upward, hopefully betraying nothing of the surprise ahead.

We arrive at the resort, and its familiar visage pulls me back to when fate threw us together in the most unlikely of scenarios. We went from enemies to lovers within hours. Our accidental overnight stay in that dank ski patrol hut turned into the backdrop of our epic love story. My memory of making love to Shay all night is still vivid, punctuated by our laughter echoing in the frosty night and the warmth of our huddled bodies amidst snow-laden pines.

Tonight is going to be fucking epic.

"We're running late. They're most likely already up at the peak. We should head straight to the gondola." Shay's voice pulls me back to the present, her professionalism always at the forefront.

We walk the short path to the gondola hand in hand. Unlike last time, both of us are prepared for the cold. I wear fleece-lined jeans, snow boots, and a thick ski jacket, and I didn't forget my gloves and hat. Shay is, of course, as stylish as they come in black snow pants and a bright-pink puffer coat, pink hat, black gloves, and scarf.

"Where is everyone?" Shay looks around. "This is weird."

I shrug. "Dunno."

Unbeknownst to Shay, I rented the entire resort out for her surprise.

I asked for her trust and she gave it to me. Now she gets her reward.

The hum of the gondola fills the air, but it's the backdrop of Crystal Mountain and the silhouette of Mt. Rainier that steals the scene. Shay and I sit in silence. The ascent is breathtaking as the world unfolds below us. Pine trees stand tall like an army of guardians, and the white caps of the distant mountains play peek-a-boo through the drifting clouds.

As majestic as the view is, Shay's sparkling eyes are what captivate me.

They have from the day I met her.

She chuckles softly. "Remember our first trip up this gondola? We may not have ridden up together, but think about how clueless we were about what awaited."

"A night of confessions, a deserted hut, and the most intense romantic night of my life." I kiss her softly. "It has been the best twist of fate ever."

Our laughter fills the space, merging with the gondola's rhythmic sway. The past and present blend seamlessly, making the journey as memorable as the destination.

At the top, Shay and I disembark from the gondola, our breaths visible in the cold mountain air. As the doors behind us close, the panorama of the resort comes to life in a magical way. It's dusk, and the entire mountain top is blanketed in the soft embrace of twilight.

The resort has undergone a planned transformation, rendering it almost ethereal. Strategically placed lighting casts a warm glow on the snow, making it shimmer like a field of diamonds under the night sky.

"What's this?" Shay murmurs in awe, her eyes wide as they trace the lighted trail snaking up to the little ski patrol hut. The path, illuminated with soft blue and white lights, looks like a river of stars flowing from the hut to where we stand below it.

"It's for us." I take her hand and we start up the short trail.

Alongside the hut, lanterns hang from tree branches, their faux-flames dance gently in the wind. Every few meters, there are intricate ice sculptures, catching and reflecting the lights in a kaleidoscope of colors. The ambient soft music from hidden speakers completes the enchanting atmosphere.

Shay gasps. "This is straight out of a fairytale, Austin."

I wrap an arm around her. "I want tonight to be a dream, a reflection of what you've brought into my life."

Realization dawns and she buries her face into my chest. "It's beautiful. So beautiful."

As we stand at the door of the hut and look down, the world beneath is awash in fairy lights and starlit trails as the snow falls softly all around us.

It's perfect.

When we turn around, Shay's mouth drops open. "Wait, this isn't...our hut. Is it?"

The once rundown shelter now stands transformed—elegant wooden exteriors, clear glass windows reflecting the amber glow from within, and the faint scent of burning wood wafting toward us.

"It is." I gently pull her closer and guide her inside. The interior is a romantic haven: soft rugs, a roaring fireplace, plush velvet couches, and a table set for two beneath more twinkling fairy lights. The walls are adorned with pictures—dozens of candid shots from our time together, even a few from high school.

Shay turns to face me, her eyes shimmering, a thousand words pass between us in a heartbeat. "Austin, what is all this?"

"This is our place, Shay. Our beginning," My voice is thick with raw emotion. "I wanted to create another beginning, right here where it all started."

Tears well up in her eyes as she looks around. "You're so sneaky, making me believe this was all about work. You did all this...for me?"

I step closer. "Every detail, every light, every note of music out there is all for you. From the moment I met you back when we were teenagers, I knew my life had changed. And today, I want to create a memory that'll last us a lifetime."

Her eyes shimmer, and I can tell she's trying to hold back a floodgate of emotion. "Austin, I never imagined..."

Before she can finish her sentence, I gently kneel before her, taking a deep breath as I pull out the black box from my pocket and open it. The ring, a stunning seven-carat diamond solitaire, captures the firelight, reflecting it in a spectrum of dazzling colors.

"Shay, I've had this ring for six months, waiting for the perfect moment. In that time, I've come to realize that every moment with you is perfect. Tonight, surrounded by the magic of this mountain where we realized how we felt about each other, I want to ask you the most important question of my life." I pause, taking a deep breath to steady myself. "Shay, will you marry me?"

The silence is palpable. I see a myriad of emotions dance in her eyes—surprise, joy...*love*.

A tear eventually escapes and trickles down her cheek. She nods vigorously. "Yes, Austin. A thousand times yes."

I slip the ring onto her finger. It fits perfectly, as if it was always meant to be there. Tugging her into a tight embrace, our heartbeats synchronize and, for a moment, it feels like time stands still.

"This is the best surprise of my life," she murmurs into my chest, squeezing me tightly. "We're engaged. I'm so fucking happy. I can't wait to marry you."

Holding her close, I whisper against her ear, "Well, you've been the best surprise of my life. Every single day. I can't wait for you to be my wife."

For the rest of the night, in the cozy cabin atop Crystal Mountain, with stars as our witnesses, Shay and I seal our future.

A lifetime of flirt alerts. With a promise of forever.

Want more of Shay & Austin Bonus Scene

Look for Kaylene's next stand alone novel The Tryst List to be released Spring of 2024.

Want to learn more about Ty & Zoey and the rest of Less Than Zero, read my Romance Series starting with Endless

For special offers, promotions, news about LTZ and all of my upcoming releases and all sorts of behind the scenes stuff, please sign up for my newsletter.

Behind the Scenes

After every story, I like to delve into the behind the scenes reasons of how it came to be.

The Flirt Alert is the second "Spicy Standalone" in my trio and follows the love story between Austin Andrews, founder and CEO of Hungry Llama games and Shay Stojanović, his co-founder and best friend's Miles's sister.

Though he's wildly attracted to her, Austin can't stand Shay or anything she stands for and is horrified to learn that Miles has offered her a coveted role at their company. With this set up, my goal was to explore the event which soured Austin on Shay and how that has impacted both of their lives.

This is where things get a little personal for me. One of my close family members developed epilepsy in much the same way that Shay did. It was a profound moment that really reshaped our interactions as a unit going forward.

I experienced first-hand the behaviors some of the medicine triggered as well as the aftermath. As someone from the outside looking in, it was very frustrating when events were not recalled. Horrible insults and hurtful behavior wasn't really within their control. Not to mention the bone-chilling fear when there would be some sort of seizure incident.

Like Shay's family, my family clammed up. Wouldn't talk about it. Address it. Discuss anything having to do with it. As someone who was directly affected by the impact, it was stifling. Scary. I hated the stigma epilepsy carried, and in many ways understood why such great efforts were made to cover it up and hide it.

Bury our heads in the sand.

The thing is, times have changed so much and this, for me, was an opportunity to learn a lot more about epilepsy and the different "flavors." I did countless hours of research, not only to learn about the variables on the medical side, but also reading hundreds of stories about people who live with the varying degrees of the condition on a daily basis.

I'd like to think that I'm more empathetic now, rather than resentful. For so many years, the amount of what I have perceived as preferential treatment has been drastic. Unacceptable behavior excused and explained away – time after time after time, often to the detriment of everyone around.

I wanted to reimagine what it would be like if my heroine actually took charge. Assumed responsibility. Wasn't ashamed of a condition she has no control over. In many ways, writing about Shay has been so cathartic and healing. Being able to give Shay a normal life with her own HEA was so fulfilling.

Before I go, let's talk Austin. You first met Austin in Endless Encore, when he met with Ty & Zoey about the Rainier Foundation. Purposely, I made sure to keep Austin's age out of the book because I knew he would be a young CEO. In my "other life" I've had the great fortune to work with some of the most brilliant young minds in tech, gaming, music and media.

In many ways, Miles and Austin are a tribute to two wonderful game company founders who made an amazing game nearly fifteen years ago and I've been with them on their journey all of this time. This is a game probably most of you have played, or at least your kids or grandkids have played. I love the idea of a young entrepreneur hitting it out of the ballpark, and that is exactly what Austin and Miles do.

I've also been around so many tech "geeks" over the years, I can honestly say that imbibing the personalities (a conglomeration) into Austin and Miles was such a joy. I hope you feel the authenticity through the pages.

Finally, what would be a book without a guest appearance or two. I hope you enjoy the cameos, I know when I'm reading books by other authors, it's one of my favorite things so expect more and more of this.

Next up, The Tryst List, featuring Jordan Deveraux, the stunning tattoo artist who is seeking to break free from bad relationship patterns. Enter architect, Peter Vander, an unconventional tattooed billionaire who gives off serious Jax Teller vibes. She's just not into him, but Peter isn't a guy who backs down from a challenge. Little does he know that Jordan is going to test him beyond anything he could ever imagine...

March 14, 2024...The Tryst List.

Until next time!
Love,

Dedication

To my family.

Acknowledgments

Cover/Graphic Designer/Finder of HOTTIES: Regina Wamba

Editor: Grace Bradley Editing, LLC

Proofreading: Letitia Delan

Formatting: Willow Yanarella

PR: Valentine PR

Publicity: Next Step PR, Xpresso Tours

Website Maven: Sherri Kiarsis, Sublime Creations

My Right Hand: Willow Yanarella

YAY to KAYLENE'S KREW!!!

Thank you to all of my ARC readers, bloggers, influencers and readers - you are amazing and I adore you.

Thank you thank you thank you for helping spread the word—I'm overwhelmed by your love, support, kindness, etc.

Thank you for making my dream come true!

About the Author

Kaylene Winter is an Amazon best-selling author of steamy, contemporary romance.

Each character-driven novel is filled with snappy dialogue, pop-culture references and enough steam to make you fan yourself. Kaylene weaves authenticity, emotion and angst into a turbulent rollercoaster ride of love, passion and soul-searing romance always ending with a delicious HEA.

Kaylene lives in Seattle with her amazing Irish husband and gorgeous Siberian Husky. She loves creating art of all kinds.

Other Titles